BLACKOUT

BLACKOUT

∞

TED HODGE

Copyright © 2016 by Ted Hodge.

ISBN:	Softcover	978-1-5245-1250-7
	eBook	978-1-5245-1249-1

All rights reserved. No part of this book may be reproduced or transmitted in any form or by any means, electronic or mechanical, including photocopying, recording, or by any information storage and retrieval system, without permission in writing from the copyright owner.

This is a work of fiction. Names, characters, places and incidents either are the product of the author's imagination or are used fictitiously, and any resemblance to any actual persons, living or dead, events, or locales is entirely coincidental.

Any people depicted in stock imagery provided by Thinkstock are models, and such images are being used for illustrative purposes only.
Certain stock imagery © Thinkstock.

Print information available on the last page.

Rev. date: 06/24/2016

To order additional copies of this book, contact:
Xlibris
1-888-795-4274
www.Xlibris.com
Orders@Xlibris.com
741577

1

APRIL 27TH 1986; Father and son of the secret dying sector were in the combine of disguises. The wisest of a set offered five related small town offspring singularities, they are the members of an introspective family and members of the secular sectioned for elimination dawns, a conspiracy plot governmental, inter information, actions in from a lie and the dawn of a shit hit fan waited until the days when the youngest member of this five jibe of water fires desired for a go. Spent from a proper childhood to the perceptive mind was the youngster of this father and son. The father was the transporting tool for youngness in plotting for the defenses of sectioned ill knowledge. The youngness of the stool was no pigeon or victim to be scrutinized, subjected to interrogation, nor was this youngness singularity able to be contained by laws of labeling created by plot hoods who were deceived by the mystery existence. No containment institutional, no pertinence trap plot trappings amended constitutional, no walls with metal bars to escape from other than the using of a trapping law trick conspired as a weapon against. This singularity boy is a son to the transporter watching the red light in occupied. It made his apparent weakness a stronghold. He in this art of a die roll had learned to use the weapons against him to his advantage altogether. Weathered from death lying and the unwinding of a digital time bomb. Grids grind and the explosion would never happen. This youngness singular mover in prime was the outbound overachiever non academic. He was outbound in secret entrance and the counting down in digits of digital was in reality not a bomb set. It was winding into dimness then into lessons learned by learners of past and the result was darkness. Singularity boy of twelve years young as a frontal mover maintained as his mates deceptive and trustworthy had called his name for favors. He moved away into posts sectioned of the sector. Xavier was his termed calling of identification however as you might imagine he went by some aliases, a necessity gaining labeling saving fact for him in his situations resulted from a witnessing. Unfounded so he might have viewed himself in terms of the set sectors that were now terminal for unification. Downplayed was the smarts of the guardian named who was the contraband victim of a plot against Xavier his offspring. The other of this guardian father was the warning of times ahead. She was a hidden girl who had fallen off of the wagon, her name was Sarah she had an ill mind and paranoia had deceived her realism as her hatred was born from the falsities of ages past. Sarah was the teller of times tales in propaganda, a girl with clairvoyant sights biblical from her readings. Codes of digitized actions robbed the modern Floyd hood thefts, the independence was not sound for the family and so it was that Xavier must return favor and defend his sister who was simply lost in sectioned lies. Sarah was sent away by authorities money grubbing and police, and the guardian father downplay sat in cavernous vision in blackness staring into a screen with the origin formed with smoking gun in hand. Xavier in prime was in a social scene typical of an American youth in pre-teen years and fears mustered had aided him. He sets no prey of those to be eradicated in the dim light of new dawning. Xavier set sights to an offset mind and he went the way of educational figures. He learned the political, he broth brewed his output onset of liberal arts, he stigmatized theories of the guardian sensational, most of all he did not obey the father and in time Xavier was to witness a happening on a shared screen paid for with the heart feels of a future friend. Nevertheless this smart young man followed the side steps of a guardianship, he had not realized that a message that was to come was not just a friend but it was himself in the form of an alias. Singled out by the signals of cable television and the satellites newly construed by intrusions put into effect by computer technicians, their company paper workers, and elites of economic power were firmly holding out. From singularity boy Xavier was the mindset compliant for defiance if necessary. He was more interested in girls than his school work. Xavier was considered by his teachers to be a smart aleck ill profound and this was an opposite term of a two word adjective explained. Those who had tried to teach him were opposed to his success although some of his other education mentors saw him from a different perspective. An underachiever academically Xavier was but an overachiever on the outside he was already and in futures' time Xavier was to achieve the self fulfillment only few could ever dream of. Agendas of the days for Xavier had been filling with athletic pursuits since the six years had passed by since the re-lit moment of his first experienced blackout. Singularity

Xavier was a regular at the local boys club. He spent his days riding his BMX bike through city streets and sometimes the trails of the woods where his cousins had lived. Little league baseball and his imaginings of playing for the red sox distracted his future destiny that was to happen in imminence and shooting baskets at the boys club was regular practice for him. Xavier's affinity for a social scene drew him to kid venues like arcades, traveling carnivals, and most commonly the local roller skating rink over in the next town. Xavier was a regular on weekend nights on both Fridays and Saturdays seven to midnight and sometimes when he had some pocket money from his paper route his mother who he only saw semi occasionally since the divorce that plagued the family would take him there for a Sunday afternoon roller rink session. Xavier often went to the rink with his sister Sarah who was seven years elder to him. Sarah had grown into her last year as a teenager whereas her talent in observation prolific had begun to diminish. This diminishing of such observances of worldly prolific past writings for her mind took a toll on her leading her to the benefit of a higher social standing yet this was a severe subtraction to the somebody that she never knew she was. The girl was pained from family strains and the plot on her younger brother had misguided him, he used her wisdom in her name and it would send the lettered code to the future alias of Xavier individually in future wearing disguises. Digitally this was of no lie! It was the communication reel of future Xavier. The guardian instilled kept eyes intently on the red light for a guarding. The workers in the technological institute had joined the union of the red light guarder and they with this guardian father to Xavier had worked hard in the cold rooms for satellite workings and on placements of the branches on the grids, the motherboards of the processes, and on the chips of actions for an interface. On this Saturday night of the 26th midnight had passed into the early hours of the 27[th.] Xavier was being driven home by his father guardian from a night at the rink. It was well past midnight and father had just dropped off two of Xavier's friends. They stopped for a usual weekly tradition, a coffee for father and Xavier had his usual fill of two chocolate milks and a chocolate chocolate chip cookie that Xavier made sure was heated for one minute in the doughnut shop microwave. Father was with his new girlfriend earlier that day he told Xavier that he was tired of the blondes he was seeing all the time and that he was going to work on a new one, a blonde. Father congratulated Xavier on the usual subjects over this coffee and chocolate consumption of a talkative guardian with offspring. Father gave a pleasant mentioning to a home run Xavier hit in one of the first games of Xavier's little league season as a catcher for the Tigers. Father also was proud of Xavier for his outgoing pursuits and he took esteem in the fact that his son was a youth who had always kept busy with things such as baseball and the boys club. Xavier with father left the small eatery and father drove the two of them back home, it was about ten minutes to one in the morning. These two were weekend night owls who had some kind of uncanny ability to stay up late on these nights, sleep late into the next day and still father would head off to his technician job in the morning and Xavier was still able to head off to school on Mondays whereas his grandfather the sports fanatic would give him a ride and the two of them in grogginess made small talk on the happenings of up coming sporting events. Father pulled the old family car up to the front of the house and they entered their home in an awakening stated consciousness. Xavier with father guard went into their living den where Xavier's sister was sitting still sipping a soda pop and watching late night television. Sarah was distracted and was not paying much attention on this night of which she had opted not to join her younger brother at the skating rink. Father was still hungry and he had prepared himself a snack that Sarah and Xavier had laughed about sometimes behind his back. On this night of a snack fix for father he had prepared a classic delicacy called potato chips and milk, the funny thing was that on other nights his snack fix was two peanut butter sandwiches and a cola "reverse the beverages and maybe that might make some sense" is what Sarah said to Xavier one time and the two laughed about fathers strange appetite of a bad beverage non matching snack mix up. Father guardian grabbed the channel changer away from Sarah seeing that the credits were rolling at the ending of the Friday late night satire she was watching before these two arrived at home. Outside blue neon flashes passionate killings grew in luminescent view of blue on and through the black laminate of the reflection shadow windows inside the sitting den it was. Sarah opted for bedtime and father sat watching television with Xavier as father flicked through channels. Father stopped at a movie station and these two members of singularity wholes and relatives just watched with no anticipation, no warning, no development of a drifting away, and no effect from the shining of the blue lights. Mild conversation had ensued and had not even achieved petty small talk when something strange happened and the two of this five member singled out secular related stared into a changed television screen. Flashing sounded static flickered in black lined intrusions and a clear yet interrupted frequency colored bar screen that must had been superimposed by satellite works showed clear enough for strong legibility on this television screen. In seconds timed it gained a solid clarity of perfection. On this bar screen was a message that read in 80's style cable computer bold . . . . GOODEVENING NATIONAL CABLE FROM MAJOR NIGHTCRAM $11.95 A MONTH NO WAY! [OTHER CABLE STATIONS BEWARE!]. The late night movie that guardian father and Xavier had begun to watch was just past opening credits. The satellite cable television interruption stayed on screen in its color bar display for nearly five minutes. Sarah had gone to bed already and so it was that a paranoid conversation ensued between the father with his milk and chips and Xavier the son with no food and he esteemed in wild eyed surprise, amazement, curiosity, and attention to detail from the feelings caused and the questions he now wanted to ask father regarding such a rare mishap for the cable company and victory for a mystery hack trade jack of a supposed guessing. Father guardian, jaw dropping of inches of two and lessened by the physics of his fungus tongue eyeballs. Avoire savior Xavier eyes of two shifted left in bare similar to two greased perfectionist symmetrical pinball spheres. His stare glance dominated father's observation in red lighted observation dignifying the sounds of the near five minute static and the silence outside that drew in the colored prime in form of a combination unit. Xavier breathes an inward gasp and asked his guardian whom he liked to call dad "what the heck happened?" Father stared back at the screen colored and barred and played star in a roll of son in father and son surety of the blank mind. A mind blanked yet filled unfathomable with the mystery elements of negativity anti formulas. Father sipped some milk and stared at the screen and before biting into another of his chips he played poker stratego with his son. This poker stare strategy was a method of fooling his son that still worked charm enough for an effect at Xavier's age of twelve. In star strategy he offered a chip to Xavier intending to desperately distract attention from either a conversation that would diminish father guardians pride in intelligence or his top secret methodical doings of his technical occupation. Xavier accepted the chip and gave father a look of "you're fucked!" he ate the potato delicacy and awaited analysis. Crunches doubled a swallow in pleasure of coolness social and Xavier asked "What happened?" The guardian then stared in virtual normalcy and began to speak to his son offspring Xavier in a shorthand moment "Uh um . . . . I think, well, somehow someone did something major that can't be done these days as far I know." "What do you mean?" "Well Xavier I work in my field but I'm limited as far as what I can know but it appears this guy has intercepted a signal from space and he doesn't like the cable company, I tell you for certain the high ups of the government are going to do whatever they can to obtain this guy so that they can find out how he did this, he might be driving in a truck so that they can't detect his signals." Xavier became puzzled and his face strained "Do you think they'll catch him?" Father answers "It depends on how he did whatever he did." Father laughs and the two calmed down right away "He's probably some genus nut with long hair driving around figuring out another move." Xavier impressed with father just commented with a dumbfounded questioning "wow?" A moment later the black of the windows of the living den began to shine with blue lights that streamed blinking flashes at and through them. Nerves over took the pair as Sarah was in her bedroom already fast and sound asleep. The color bar and message disappeared off of the screen and the movie set for this cable station that night continued from where it would have as if it never stopped playing. Night was morning it was about ten past one. The father son pair talked for a while about matters of Xavier's remaining school year and that father was to chaperone a field trip at the end of the school year. The blue light of the police had driven away from a setting and these two of curiosity would not retire due to their excitement from the occurrence. Hours later they both went to bed and the following day peculiarly seemed normal and average other than a news reel. On the 27th Xavier was with his grandparents and his guardian as well when after a commercial break the hack job was reported to the public. The reel played on the all news station channel that the family had preferred for years. The reel reported this occurrence in some detail however the mood of the anchor woman was dull and boringly and professionally tactful more so than on other reports she usually would give. The family of five sectioned as four during late breakfast with tarts, waffles and iced tea. Sarah was absent from breakfast this day yet despite daughter, grand daughter, and sisters absence the family made commentary among one another and Xavier was off to the boys club for the day.

2

SUNDAY PASSED BY in immediate play of a sleeping and awakening. Monday morning had come in dreaded typicality and a sick faking for school avoidance was not in the cards for Xavier on this day. Xavier readied himself for his ride to school from his grandfather and he was looking forward to his little league baseball game that was scheduled for play on Wednesday. He put on his usual Monday clothes a pair of whitened bleach corduroys and a tropical Florida pinkish orange hazed t-shirt that father gave him as a gift on an Orlando vacation earlier in the school year back in November of 1985. Grandfather who was the casual man of the sectioned sector beckoned leaving time to Xavier and the two were off for Xavier's school day. Xavier scraped some frost from the windows of grandfather's car. The two of them felt the frustration of New England weather and the fact that it had been cold enough for an overnight frosting just days before May commenced was mildly strange however not quite freakish as was the weather up north in New Hampshire. Despite this frosting the season of spring had nevertheless sprung and this was likely one of the last if not the very last frosting of this season. Grandfather drove Xavier to the school destination and it was another day of common. Normalcy it was on a Monday morning uptown where Xavier attended junior high school. At arrival Xavier had realized he was a few minutes late for homeroom and by the time he had arrived at his school with grandfather rain drops began to lightly pour down. Puddles of a splashing to avoid as Xavier carefully walked around them, a school chum of Xavier's liking with others stared out of Xavier's homeroom window looking down at him. A slew of kids maybe 10 of them in estimation were behaving erratically with a common trait mischief persona of an 80's kid. Xavier's chum friend made a gross sound of a spit hocka gathering. He spit down and yelled Xavier's name in anticipation for another day of bad conduct and possibility of suspension room for a period. Xavier knew in his case anyway that another day of detention was inevitable. Xavier was a bad boy to some when considered feebly and although others saw him differently the true fact of the matter was that he was the glutton for punishment and his classmates had ended up awarding him the entitlement of class clown. Friend hit spit hit the paving of the school sidewalk in form of a loueyhocka but to Xavier's surprise when he turned around in embarrassment to see a look of disapproval on grandfather's face grandfather in contrary of expected notion smiled in childhood reminiscence, he was thinking back to the 1930's hopping of trains and having cut class for the entire third grade, a mistake he knew it wasn't grandfather had thought in clarity especially for the man he grew into with an intelligence quotient of 145 and an adequate ambition in a better time of living. Xavier arrived at homeroom after climbing the wide stairway to this meaningless class. He sat in his usual seat avoided some spitballs from behind, eyed the bully and was ready to avoid this past and future friend, eyed a few stock options of his favorite gender while feeling the gum stains three dimensional under his desk, he was looking for a cheat sheet he had stuck underneath a wad of a chewing he had the day prior. Little did he realize in his lacking ingenuity that his doctoring doctrine for science class would not stick foolproof style. Xavier instigated a day ahead, he dreaded gym class and the English before gym was never of a satisfactory subject matter. After gym English was scheduled again in the form of grammar teaching intro-scoped repetitive throughout the rest of a school career. Sentence examinations and devoured in wasted times this basic subject and predicate sentence dissection bullshit of which it was. Science class was fun and cool but Xavier knew that he needed to behave in this class because other than his history class it was troublesome for him in terms of detentions and possible suspension. Geography class was good for Xavier due to its aiding of his history gatherings of acknowledgments. Math was his weak subject because he knew the importance of reading therefore he underestimated the brain development of steps in future algebra, things like orders of operations etc. Computer class taught him about a fairly new advancement from the first computer language called (ALGOL) which was the starting computer language that was structured and inherent of algorithm procedure progressions. Xavier in rhythm algorithm mystified from others is offered a television dish reflection prism that was dealt with a handing of classes on a schedule. The BASIC language stemmed from ALGOL and the day was rode like the bicycle wheels large by Xavier and the teacher sentenced him to another detention. It was the end of the school day and ever since Xavier had started compiling multiple detentions his detentions had backed up for weeks to come. Xavier had told his grandfather beforehand that he was scheduled for a last period class so that grandfather wouldn't be aware and tell the guardian of this scholastic defiance problem that Xavier had been developing. Besides this point grandfather himself wanted to make sure that Xavier was not under grounding punishment so that he and Xavier could watch Sunday football together with grandmother who was more concerned with her lone shark betting cards with over and under point spreads rather than having to deal with the conduct problems of another offspring. Guardian father was plenty trouble enough for that matter and it was his responsibility and not hers to inherit. Xavier knew grandfather would arrive in less than an hour. Xavier dragged his school bag down the hallway past the school library and into the cafeteria where he was to serve Monday afternoon detention. Xavier took a seat in the front row of the detention hall, a decision of opposite to the common choice of such a type of mischievous character youth as Xavier was. Xavier leaned back in his chair of choice in front of the detention hall's teacher pick of the round for the day. Mister Rojas began his duty of roll call detention attendance; "Gerald Squire" "here" "Thomas Messenger" "here" "Amanda Currington" "I'm here too asshole" "And that will be another three days for you young madam of a person I don't like anymore." Mister Rojas speaks intuitively back to the punk girl's way and brushes aside this insult and continues while thinking over a sending of her or another of the wise to the indoor suspension room of next week. "Barry Luzzin" "YEESSS MAASTTUUHH!" the Luzzin boy yelled in deep toned voice stalking of the education enemy alike that of a mongering bearlike wolverine. Mister Rojas rolls eyes and stared forward, he voiced the following of a repertoire. "Okay I'll take that one into account Luzzin" Mister Rojas waves left hand to the wind smacking feeble words of no importance to him aside. "Huuhumm alright let's continue; "Franklin Flannigan" "here" "Doreen Mclorey" "present" "Xavier Tareynton" "here" secular selection Xavier answers the call while placing the front legs of his chair back onto the foundation of the school floor and Mister Rojas continues on with detention roll call; "Wendy Smith" "here" "Joseph Zimmer" "I donno" "Joseph you're here right?" "Why?" "I'll take that as a yes" Mister Rojas smirks for a moment and looks to an unidentifiable direction and Zimmerman the man comments one more pellet fire "OkaBi!" and he fakes a run threat the exit of the cafeteria but steps slowly back to his seat and drops into it relaxing. "Huuhumn" and a cleared throat for the teacher "Beth Magee" "here" "Tabitha Caresser" "here" a few laughs could be heard from the back of the detention hall from the peculiar and funny named entitlement of this girl and Mister Rojas once again continued with roll call.

"Hhuuurrm" and it was clear again. "David Lunen" "here" "Richard Mooney" "Here" "Xevon Tareynton" Xavier in nervous manner like a stool pigeon jailbird scapegoat raises a hand and beckons again for the second time in detention roll call "here." Mister Rojas looked to Xavier in confused stated exampled and in a sampling of a question of the oblivious the obvious question was of the way "I thought your name was Xavier what did you drop a few letters or something?" "No" teacher Interrupts "Xevon? What kind of nonsense is this?" "Oh I used my middle name because my computer lab teacher told me that my study hall teacher was going to suspend me if he found out who I was." "Your first and middle initials are XX?" "Yes, I'm dirty double X and a T for triplets you know, my lab teacher is a hottie." "Your computer lab teacher?" "Yes, my study hall teacher gave me class detention not to be served here so I have been getting a computer lab pass for the last month and a half to avoid study hall and he'd suspend me if I didn't hide from him." "If you didn't hide from him?" "Yes, I have been hiding from study hall for reasons that I wanted to learn some computer stuff too you know?" "Computer stuff?" "Yes, Algorithms, Basic language text, floppy disc control, and some minor programming and drawing sailboats and cars and some things like that, they kind of look like old Atari 2600 graphics with one color.""Atari?" "Yes, Atari, I like donkey kong, centurion, broaden your horizons, links to the secret unknown internet, sinister ministers, Adventure, and missile command." "Missile command? "Yes, Missile command, I like the sound at the end especially when you have five squadrons left and there's that countdown you know it ends fast chuchuchuchuchuchuchuchuchupchupchupchup." "Alright Xavier just remember to use the right name next time okay?" "Yes, but do I get credit for serving two detentions instead of one because my name counts twice?" The detention hall broke into some lightened sounds of humorous youths in hoping as others snored, doodled, made gossip or passed a note to an opposite gender member. Detention was on with its duty of the liking and the 50 minute period passed slowly but ended in time for another boring rain soaking Monday afternoon.

3

XAVIER WALKED OUTSIDE into some light rain that had since died down from earlier in the day. On the way outside his school Friend Luzzin who was always called by his last name rather than his first one was on an instigation prowl seeking. Luzzin was with Zimmerman the man and in bumbles of can they passed by Xavier who on this day of a possible hanging out he was of no can do. Xavier darted on his way out of the school front doors. Zimmerman was carrying his school bag with something inside that didn't look like the books issued by the school faculty for certain. They gave Xavier a looking of an adamant solitude maybe for reasons of a planned rendezvous made by Zimmerman the man for a meeting of the three at the local skating rink on the next weekend, the three would sing for the true definition of the sectors word. Zimmerman the man and Luzzin were off for a pregame rendezvous and they sneaked out of the back door of the school into the woods for an expanding of their brains. Xavier was standing at the front side of the school awaiting his grandfather as he reflected in wonderment of what would be the outcome of his little league game that was two days away. He heard a beckoning silence telling him that there was a presence nearby. This presence was to surprise him in formation of a shaded feel in rain drops. Déjà vu familiarity shadow downs of yellow carbonation out in the woods made clear. The day light rain spotted a female of flirtation in front of Xavier's line of sight he gasped in pleasured serene looking at this girl and trembled inside when realizing grandfather was to arrive in moments timed. Two eyes oval stared into eyes of a wise guy boy of a new aged seeking. The non tear was the defiant ring to the rain that befell on the heads of the two with the eyes counting to four. Déjà vu girl looked aged and beautiful and not only was she of such stature but she was an upper class girl. Déjà vu girl in vein naivety of this time of Xavier's short lived span of this lifetime had glimpsed into eyes of unwise on this present day. His maturity was lacking even for that of a seventh grader. His future was ominous and pelted by the pebbles of objection was his bare body of a soul. This obscured explanation of Xavier sets the implored déjà vu of this female youth in predominance. Odious was the true word for such an explanation and this saddened feeling was only felt from eyes above. The glory for the two in this case was not to be of manifest destiny but to the rather it was in the form of a cute fabled outcome of two eyes staring into another pair of two eyes. Satires of the tired mind had healed them in their years of stressful grade school and when they viewed themselves as the fools of the world it was the news of their world in common knowledge and humors healing that would be restitution in the coming years and decades. Four eyes as one they look on in brawn of the rested young minds and the lighted days of boys spark hope to the darkened bulbs of a mind game comic strip caption frame for the females called by the name of the downward term. Grandfather was on his way and the rain was misting at his car windows. As he rounded the way roundabout toward the school for a picking up of his grandson he sighted the clearing of a gathering. Grandfather peered in such a direction only to remain in mystery, the kids termed as rats with denim on had to run inside of a pizza joint in searching for non failed vision on the veils of their clothing. Grandfather was wearing his gray winter hat of an older time and the winds of mystic blowing caused a series of hand fixings. In petty reasoned determination of a minor frill of no important matter he tightly fastened his hat on head. With hand on heart and nobility on his mind he became irate because of the new invention of power windows, a commodity of which his old beat up Cadillac in rusted red and black did not have. Grandfather rolled up his driver side window manually as the mist had sanitized the left half of his face. Paced he was of patience way and not only that but he had to escape from the wife on this afternoon for reasons of nonexistent phrases political within the sector of which he was only a member by the word of which defined it. Down the way of the school yard by a new ballpark for the softball girls of the town grandfather daydreamed hearing the sounds of music in the form of a spy show television program jingle. Grandfather was now police, FBI, CIA, SECRET SERVICE, Ambassador of France, the president of the IRA and the cunning baffler inside the Gotham mobile mover of the superhero counterpart mover in prime and x marked the spot. X was spotted in the distant mist and if he saw the girl grandmother might have made a hit list blacklist. Xavier was the X spotted and with ground engine velocity Xavier and déjà vu girl became larger with a moving closer of the black mobile. Eyes oval had blinked slowly and eyes widened in side frames of the portraits of angels. Head detective for the boss wife was the sent ambassador of a granting. Shunted, shunned, procured accordingly, and set to the basics of a married life they might be but dad of the grand gender with his slender frame had exited his now parked black car and although he slammed the door to his side of an exiting nothing was heard by the two flirting kids. In mission of a minor style he saw something major. Grandfather was only a private to the wife of no patience weighing. Under scorn and in prevention of the new born tragedy of possible the hat had given him away. Heads counted was two and it was the flirtatious two in a stare of no scarcity. Xavier inwardly gasps and he was caught blue handed by grandfather detective but the eyes that were on him remained still in solidity of a perching peering. Grandfather detected the grandson of the good sectioned place and he took his boy away for safety of a lot. Xavier says goodbye to the déjà vu girl and inside she swarmed a placement pacing timing for a walking home. Xavier got into the black Cadillac passenger seat and the two drove home talking trash and they were looking forward to the weekend for another Sunday of American style football grid iron classic, cowboys and Indians rivalry game was on for Sunday.

4

6 YEARS EARLIER; THE sector family jibe had arrived at their new home one year prior to this six year back in time incursion. In their new yellow house when it had rained the family in togetherness of a better time for the sectioned of the original demographic sang humorously the words of the house in the form of a song. Preparations for emergencies were not priority for father guardian. From the move that they made this family of four with one not included in this sector sectioned were not of ill preparation. It was the summer of 1980. The family had from their leader combined into the unit leader. A foursome minus one in code with a son interrogated by suspended animation and a sensationalist evil lying was demonstrated as an omen. The mother was the absence from within a scoped regularity possessive of the new virtue. Defied was the son unannounced for inclusions not quite neglected by the father whom was the predecessor. The preceding teachings secular sectioned of this terminal termed word set example were from father guardian to Sarah the daughter and mirrored in time was the interested mind of Xavier. Fear in teachings preached of a word in techno color had frightened Xavier at the age of six during this summer season of his fearing and lured deception. It was that wars intended to defeat him. A claiming of accusations he must take in self identification and by the will of the goods. It was the chilling sight of the gods as one that set the ill-forsaken path for the son of the guardian. Ill forsaken assumed for a rover and the mother in shame made living examples of a four way basket case. The family lived life of the uncommon. The parental situation was fine living at the time of this past present. The family of the

sector willed the ways for self wellness although the underlying fact was that this family was in future to experience tragedy. The tragedy of the sector family was a premature divorce introversion outbound deception, the extroversion of Xavier as the outgoing one was to explore the fire light and from the chemistry of his make up his bloodline he had to work as the distinguished elimination extinguisher. Late one night the jibe was up watching techno color television screenplay. Swells made Xavier swallow for the feared warnings of an ending. He was bonded and attached to a nursing mother. He liked to play games of trickery with his sister. The father guardian was not successful in guarding for the mysteries of the night imposed on the colored television screen. Swelling wells of prognosis predictable, undone truths boned in damnation non typical. Hospitality evil sending waves of information from the satellites of the time and the illusionists knew for certain what they did not know. Some impostor stop recognized incredible for a day time but this night time of the mixing color bars of an old code informed. Deformity illusion to the sector and impostors replaced as units whereas the worded messages of the screen sent Xavier into fears of a world that might be ending. 1999, 1997 prophecies the talking matter gossip of the future and a sensationalist uprising appraisal. Fear wrapped in rapping rapidity of his skull frame as Xavier wore the fear garments around his being for a night. He sighted the face of a dogma, he heard the voices of the deceived, he feared messaged of a conceiving. Father guardian slept with the manner of alive chainsaws, he snored. Mother neglected form false will to the sector of the sector she only worked for. The sector was under attack from a plotting scheme. Return to the gentle mind Xavier would do in stamina. He acted as a gun silencer for a shot in darkness the entire night through. Upon awakening Xavier was unable to breathe. He had had a dream of being caught in a whirlpool and had been victimized by a nemesis of himself in the form of the superhero he dreamed to be at this age. He lied down in early morning sunshine on his bed with the sun shining in from the open window. Natures' air breathed breaths into his room with a closed screen in back of him. In sickness he felt swarming vultures that looked the eagle and he was a bitten worm of a slaving tongue. Xavier gasped and he took a grasping of a motive true, amazing this was and is for this young boy aged only at six years of age. He dodged the bullet, he fell downward in a parallelogram disappearing and avoiding the swing of the pendulum. He sailed high and low in slower sloth. From happiness inside his moving about commanded him in the directive. In one direction of no sorrows and in futures timers not a dime to borrow or a smoke to bum, welcomed he was to the night time six tears before superimposed improved. The sixth tear fell in a saving on his left facial gland and he is welcomed to the time of yesteryear. Those from whereabouts were counting the continuing heads suffocated. They were on the other side of an existence. The existence was termed primitive by secular controllers. The developer had our good ones as collateral. The counting was summed at the number between negativity and positive. Equalized to a whole was the section. Protection mode took truth in the form of victimization and future transport. Liberal law took the good minds of these placements Asiatic for the karma of the sector of this one of five and his suffering of relations. Negotiations became subconscious telepathy and diplomatic diplomacy of Cambodia in between the number system, Korea dreams, and the Philippines. The stars in red had powers of no mercy but old glory felt its beginning and the sickle gold personas ran in industry hiding for the new born. One won an awesome outcome and the messiahs toning appealed to the sector one. Arts became his marriage and by horse and carriage the singular section boy named Xavier saw the stars of Xenon sky. This carriage carried the will of a megaton dead it was the chariot of the sun. The time was coming! The theory of development was still ill defined. The combines and advents were sighted in reflections. The camps were stamped on envelopes and sent to the singular unit of the five jibe in form of a crest United Amerigo vest Kampuchan on black dark night sights. The recording was sent to the true taker of the blame game. He was at risk. A kiss of life for his futures dying causes made the developing theory of good equaling the word of the old sector. The higher ups replaced them with currency rule republic compost kings. The beam shot to the farm of a shear and the manure shined in new growth. The growth was named as gowth and a gown healed the timing timidity of the low crown. Down was the result and in consultation good was liberalized and the sector survives independent as this unit singled. Downplay in frayed cut noose holds of the hangings for the real star. The crosses were changed and the crucifix had grown wings as it laid in craft and demonism. Understanding was anew and attempt number three of a fire spherical drop was to be undeniable in it all rising. The sold souls aimed at Seoul were living and dying and only space information from outside aloud were permitting the baby of the nothing no denials and crying. Sectors active completed a first phase and the mazes ill were to be downed by the developer. True collection in the diamond basket of no bullshit! The days of death were sacrifice for the born. Torn healers from wooden stemming bled the revolver roses on the thorns of the upward rolling eyeballs. Silence wins the day. It was Saturday and Xavier in typical routine walked out into the den living room hall of his family's yellow home. Xavier knew it was the weekend. As he heard he saw the sounds and sights of animated suspended. The Road runner and a coyote across in techno color screen and the words of the jingle said for this day of sectioned Xavier and the others "let's get on with the show this is it" and silence for the hunter of the rabbit, this is a flashback for the rats star. Father snored, Sarah hacked with some effort on her acoustic, mother was off for her weekend part time job and Xavier went out after the Saturday morning cartoons got on his hot rod big wheel and chased the fairy tinker bell demon. Yes it was another of the other gender, a kindergarten possum girl named for the city of sin. Lynn city sin begin a win/ din pity kin bonds twins/Kinta Santa gift Atlanta/broth in Goshen takes in Gotham/mothers, fathers, sisters, brothers/zero Nazi Rwanda Darfur/a Syria Assyiran pogrom choice/colossal apostle proposed philosophy/a rustle tussle Indo prophecy/Audicy oddyessy modesty travesty/ majesty tragic sea red meat tea/snare drum did come outdone outcome/end it send it hack defiance genocide/stack them whacked them the 5 do stay alive/liberal simple dimple pimple/demo memo public cripple/republic dawn wick drawn chart gamble/sampled exampled exam pulled the trample/New York Boston Hong Kong Beijing/trading aging Viet Kong of wings/guerilla warfare and welfare memo bring/Beatles Elvis talent youth and swingers/old time new time robbing is a hood/Floyd had avoided and new knows understood/numbers in summits the baring deal of man/women mayhem sector eats from cans/down under in thunder and lightning hit some land/ . . . . Xavier met with his buddies at large and they raced with tricycles, big wheels, and one toy fire engine wagon, exit stage left and sighted was a dragon. Five were in line on the Liley sidewalk barely wide enough so two were on the roadside. It was race time USA and the avenue and sidewalk was the track. Xavier to the left inside was revered the plastic handlebars of the hot rod big wheel he rode back in the days. Silver streak and black streamers from the edges of these handle bars committed to excellence like the team with its silver and black and pedal system powered by the legs and feet of the Xenon Xavier star systematic. To Xavier's right was another his name was Gus he was a fine spirit. Gus had sighted a nova at young age and he told Xavier that the nova was of a social classification, it was a car. On this day however Gus whom was aged at six years old the same age as Xavier was not pushing metal to the floor of this classic machine but instead he was gripping the grind of a huffy tricycle. Gus eyed Xavier to his left and let him know that he was to be left in the dust. The hand was dealt just like their first day of kindergarten and the hand of a trick were intended to leave burn holes in the ace drivers to his sides. There was enough room on the side walk for another it was Raymond and Ray for short. Xavier wanted badly to at least defeat Ray on this day for avenging the time he stole his hot rod. Ray was rearing a classic yellow and blue big wheel that his father had bought him after he knew he had stolen Xavier's hot rod some time back. Spoiled some might see this boy in assumed notion but this Ray saw the nova on other days. Although he knew his competition was determined he planned to streak in light speed down this walk walkway. Two were on the road beside the three underdogs that it would be presumed. This was the fire wagon pedal machine of Justin and his older brother was his pit stop coach. Justin was favored over the others despite the speed of a ray, the power of a hot rod, and the powering wheels of Gus' three wheeler spokes with wheels surrounding. The last and furthest to the right on the right side of Justin was the teenager and he was of course the favorite by a landslide. He was of a name left to be anonymous and the predominance he had in this race preparation was overtly evident. The unknown rider of 13 had a stronghold gripping on his early version mushroom handlebars and he played the bully of this race. Unknown rider bore a classic BMX racing bike and a coasting might be enough for his seemingly imminent and certain victory. Justin's coach held an invisible checkered flag in the form of a hand. He was bias for his younger brother so he had to be neutral in his calling off of the start of the race. He held his hand up in the air military style for a kid and in race quotation of the calling he barked out the words "ready set go!" Four kid vehicle contraptions began their pedaling proceeds for a winning. Justin was immediate disappointment it appeared that the red of his fire engine overrated his chances. He was off to a slow start and his chain inside his fire wagon was too rusty and had required and oiling job. Ray was quickly ahead like the speed adjective of his name entitlement described him. Gus was the turtle among these hares and he paced in wisdom way of a six year old. Xavier's hot rod as attractive a toy as it was required a valiant effort of a pedaling. He made way ahead of Gus of a pacing, lurked behind Ray with a chance of an upset come from behind win, and he maintained his determination as pain dominated his weak six years of age calves and leg biceps. The unknown rider of 13 years was nowhere to be seen so Xavier felt bad and he stopped to see where he was thus losing the race by submission easily. Xavier spotted the unknown rider behind. He was sucking on a grape freeze pop and laughing at these racers at what appeared to this opinionated young teenager as a pointless effort. Two were down, one by accidental submission and the other simply wanted an ice cream snack fix. The other three were still full steam ahead. Justin was a definite loser and his brother often convinced him of the same. Justin was a friend to Xavier and their friendship was of fondness for in futures time as was in the past they were to race again but this time this winning boy of Justin had to quote Boston's home team and say "there's always next year." The unknown rider was out of air from his humorous sighting and after a series of inhalation gasps he drank down the remainder beverage result of his ice cream delicacy. Xavier sat in still life, Justin's legs ran out of fuel, Ray was nearing the finish line and Gus in the wisdom pace realized too late that it was not a marathon but that it was a sprinting race and so his strategy had failed him. Ray crosses the finish line which by coincidence was located in front of his grassy front yard. His father was heard ranting and raving, Ray's dad reamed Raymond downplaying his hands in air victory gesture sending him into momentary morbid. Ray's father saw that he won the race and he had thought that little Raymond had stolen that day. He picked his boy up in good nature and brought him into family abode for a feast in typicality way of the times of the days. Tally is taken, unknown rider credited with an incomplete, Xavier in last place sat confused, bewildered and stone faced despite. Xavier was an astounding five yards behind the pacer of Gus whom was credited with third place. Justin had beaten Gus in this case of a racing but his efforts disregarded leaving him in second place. Ray was already inside eating his lunch, he told his family of his first place finishing. Xavier moved in prime throughout the remaining day although he had not yet met the summit setting for a merit worthiness of entitlement as so. He met with friends and played some kickball. He escaped some bullies and found his stolen football. He avoided characters and he went to a gathering and signed up for baseball. He walked home and threw a rock at guys playing basketball. He met with mom and shopped at the local mini mall. At night he watched the Celtics and wished to grow tall. He dealt with father and it was like talking to the wall. He rimed some words. He left his nerds. He made proportions of the calling of past days. He fell asleep and slept in silence. In dream world Karma he outdid violence. Little did little Xavier realize however that in due time from a meriting of his being past, present, and future as sending back from a coming wellness and a bridge of a new coming day he would experience a blackout.

5

FRIDAY MAY 3RD 1986;–Unrelated–
The family escaped the compost of an angry hill. The damnation of the breathers felt the pains of walkers past the fields of green. The dawn light singled boy sectioned in the city sparked the raptures word in caption. The girls in the park learned love not passion. The activists of the downward land ran up a hill to the bunker. The compromise on central land in east mimicked a symbol. Two monuments of false marches came unto the people. The one up north was climbed atop and pissed down the steeple. A pair went west. The expedition rated cons. In the future time went back. Genghis khan on the other side toured and got some people. The population rats of density lands grew hands like the clocks of towers. Some salvation bred when they walked skulls for hours. Related was the one world scoping. Jonah died and born a girl was hoping. Xavier in wool of lambs walked down roads of mammoth. With tooth and nail the leader had met Hitler. An untold lie of denials truth was a mistress. A young boy running hides he arose from poverty. The leader saw wrong but he had not yet hit puberty. The jibe figure numeral five gets the message of post meridian offer vitality spelling out the initials VOMP.PM of the mourning sounded the fire drill. The ham and veal made some sand on moonlit creeping. Back in the logical world of the obvious reality and not the oblivious figurative universes for a genus mind Xavier was up at 6 AM getting prepared for another school day when he heard his grandfather call his name from the downstairs where he and grandmother lived. Xavier heard the call of grandfather and he reacted with a rushing. He downed his juice and threw on his favorite football jersey. Xavier met grandfather at the

driveway and they rode to school. Homeroom was the usual joke of which it was whereas the day plans of Xavier's instigation in school crimes sometimes were of his finding. On this day of a past rainy time of the grand parental spy investigation Xavier's first worry was to make sure he was able to cut study hall and attend his computer lab class. This time his avoidance in a sneaking for his library lab pass led him right into the claws of the hall monitor disciplinarian. Xavier reacted fast to the period bell sounding. Outward down the hallway he slipped passed the doorway where his livid study hall teacher was sitting while reading a newspaper. Xavier performed a quarterback sneak accessing Tabitha Caresser as a blocking center. Luzzin played offensive tackle but he distracted the defense instead. The school principal was strolling merrily down the way of the halls nearby so Luzzin led him into the boy's room with a luring of smoke mentioning. Tabitha was unaware of perverted eyes that were scoping her from inches behind. She was a habitual caressing possessed by doomsday machines, the tomfoolery of winos with no hair, and her seriousness of a sorting gave her the reputation of the easy. Tabitha takes a left into her period classroom and low and behold Hall Monitor Franklin the frank of the tank was standing. This Franklin character was some kind of special privilege kid, likely a member of an evil plan for disguising intentions for this towns' over taking of the world and he was one of those assholes who would say things like "If you can't speak the language get the frig out" or "we should just blow the fuckers right of the face of the map" or "its not your girlfriend its my girl friend" or any words of bias uncalled for. Xavier became boggle eyed and in desperation grievances out of his disliking for conversation with this boy he looked around for an escaping classroom door. To Xavier's dismay on the right of Franklin's chest was the hall monitor badge with his name written right on it just like those old bumper stickers matching with the future negative nostalgia of this situation for Xavier "shit happens." Zimmerman the man ran bye and made a quick scag on Xavier for his loss to the little league Braves which was the team Zimmerman was the pitcher for. Zimmerman the man commented in egotism "nice performance Xanadu 28 to 4 isn't that the total of your IQ on the mound." Xavier admitted another defeat after the game of two days ago that sent his team on the quest for another little league draft pick and he took another detention slip from the special boy of illogical privilege who's mother named him Franklin and basically smacked the face of the best president who had the same first name. Franklin took pleasured esteem in his handing out of an extra addition of 50 minutes to Xavier's day agendas. Xavier would be allowed to obtain his computer lab pass but first he was to be escorted to the principal's office in order to confirm his detention with his detention slip that Franklin had issued him. This pair of preteens did not get along worth a hill of manure so the conversation that was to ensue was poor taste to put it in mild wording. "Hey Xavier" wise guy snarls and overconfident Franklin of no confidant confident enough for a trusting began worded corrosion of the true with his first letter and all syllables in which he was speaking "another day in the cafeteria hall my friend, I think that study hall teacher likes you maybe you should stop by and leave an apple on his desk or better yet if you shut your beak once and awhile the wimps won't kick your ass, I say it like it is Xavier you can't avoid him for too much longer it looks like suspension and a sore on your bum bum fine chum." "Yes Franklin, it's been nice falling into another one of your conspiracy traps, you and your assistants of youth trash might like the talk but I will walk the walk whether here nor there scum bum." At this point a handed chicken scratch fight in styles of a cat fight was of commencement. Franklin and Xavier wrestled in motions of hand finger scratching fighting all the way down the hall. "Your mother looks like murder!" "Yeah and yours is so stupid she can't even cough from those cartons your father smokes all day!" "Oh yeah!" the two fighters immature fell to the floor gathering dust on the garments their families were to yell at them for." "Asshole" "dickhead" "lover loser!" "Trash talker!" "balk inspector pecker wrecker" "bloody piggish dick investigator!" the two argued over the pitching duel between Xavier's Tigers and the Braves. Xavier finally managed to throw Franklin aside after a near minute one on one rumble. Franklin walked away knowing he had won another fight that he had actually lost. Xavier fixed his messed up hair from the violent sparring real he had just had to regretfully endure. The red anger of his face faded back to his common Caucasian color and he stepped into the principal's office having realized that his detention slip had ripped during the fight. Xavier strolled into the office as he hoped to be forwarded straight to computer lab class. It was Mister Stone a director and a former youth as one would assume (DUH?) and rumor had it that his last name with a letter added to the end of it whether an R or a D is what he was as a kid. Xavier just assumed the hell with it and he presumed a conversation with the principal "Hi" Mister Stone speaks "Oh Mister Tareynton I see we are esteemed and credited with another wonderful visit form the whiz kid" surprisingly so Mister Stone actually was fond of Xavier and his voice didn't have even a tint of sarcastic measure. "Franklin the Sire out there handed me a detention slip and I don't have it." "Another detention? Xavier look, your not such a bad kid but I'm sorry to tell you I'm not surprised, for one you're in here way too much and reason two on the other hand is that that over privileged little tyke out there is mad that they started you at pitcher on Wednesday. You know my son is in that league, I saw you pitch. So when's the funeral?" Mister Stone laughed aloud as the happy recovered former lush of which he was and Xavier smiled in return. "What are you saying 28 to 4 isn't that bad in little league." Mister Stone chuckles lightly a little more he looks straight eyed into Xavier's face "Don't be discouraged though there's plenty of jobs to be gained in the future at Chico's Bail Bonds you know the sponsor of the bad news bears? "Yes, bad news bares I might have only gone 4 and a 3rd innings but double exes like my name says, you know, lost two girlfriends and like shaggy on Scooby doo says too like zoikes, two exes are better than none and speaking of Nuns I might be going parochial next year." Mister Stone then realized that the period was not even seven minutes in so he continued talking to the section singularity Xavier for a little while. "Alright Xavier" Mister Stone denied the parochial reference from Xavier in his thoughts. Mister Stone continued speaking "Where's your detention slip Xavier?""Uh I don't have it Franklin and I had a bit of a quarrel in the hall as you know and it must have floated away." I suppose your dog ate it or what was that story double X your dog urinated on your homework one time?" Yes, and intuitively so you know my teach said that it must had known something I didn't and it might as well have yellowed and stench stained like triple X style extreme, you know?" "No Xavier double X I don't, and what's with this nickname it's like your some kind of 60's porn star." "Triple X double X singled X marks a spot and hot she was inside for the charming charmers of my satires, you know." "Xavier I know your game you weren't even issued detention, I think that kid is afraid of you anyway and you're backed up for weeks just go today and forget about this one." "I think I will Mister Stone." "No shit? Here's a computer pass whiz kid." Xavier took the computer slip for a lab session of lessened time and exited the office with destination of frontal monitors and computer keyboards. Xavier sat in sector seat frontal of the rows and oars on the theory ship. The theory ship was the lab and Xavier was the mouse in the maze proclaiming amazement. He turned on the monitor. He took the floppy disc out from where he hid it. He switched on the keyboard button. He loaded the data of positive nonsensical antimatter. On the screen was the go to commands of old Atari light capsule box spaces. The color was orange. The numbers had integers equaling to the significance of seven. The pi was forming the sail of the graphics. The obscurity was of specifics. The back round of the screen bore the light of the parted sea. The orange had tinted to red. The developers were watching. The curvature of space was the wind blowing. Solar wind projections objected for the diamond compaction. The buttons of the keyboard were going into action. Fractions and decimal dew were on screen formula with the numbered commands in BASIC language graphic creating. He was elder to the last Emperor. He roared the Ra chant to enemy Emeni false enigma. Tutankhamen laid in triads in stigma triangular. The grams of a purchase are parallel. He disappeared in black hole and was from hell. Caressing the tabs was his decoy. The big screen displayed a convoy. Ill dot.org.to scare the new boy. They drove all the way to a drive in. The asses were lying no jiving. Over was driven and a chemist furlong extremist supreme (supreme mist mystery?). On the screen was a simple symbol boat not of mystery but of imminent history. The sector singular unit boy named Xavier Xevon Tareynton became the motion of primal, astronomy prime mover.

6

AFTER SCHOOL XAVIER was home with Sister Sarah. She was biding her time and Xavier tried to talk her in to attending a skating session on this Friday that was to be of vivid memory to Xavier. Sarah had declared a sibling oath that she would start attending sessions at the rink with Xavier once again after she tended to some matters concerning her new college career. Xavier was slightly disappointed that Sarah would not attend the skate session on this night but this decision was likely of the wise for her anyway because it was heavy metal night at the rink on Fridays. Xavier was to do the usual act of the lazy and let his homework doing routine wait until Sunday night but from unpredictable outcomes ahead he might not have gotten to it anyway. Xavier ate dinner downstairs with the entire sector five piece family of unity liberty pursuing. This eating of a feast on Fridays was a family tradition before the members of it would do the town. This going out on Fridays was still the case for the outgoing grandparents who had by this time reached their status of senior citizenship. Singularity sectioned secular family of the word play play writes with all of them, Sarah, Xavier, the guardian father, grandfather, and grandmother ate in discussions of the era and current events. Xavier was off with father for his ride to the rink. Xavier thought about his dream clairvoyance although he was unaware of what would happen on this night. He sensed a mystery. He was chomping on a piece of Greek Pita and he was chomping at the bit despite. He arrived with father at the rink in the bordering town. The town was an altered state it was across the spanning old dominion faults. Xavier exited the car and said goodbye to the guardian father until pick up at midnight arrived. He stepped through the doorway entrance by the way of an entrance with an upper awning and pathway. He slipped the rink cashier a fin and pocketed fifty cents change. It was not to be another skate night of typical for singular section boys. The boys were to gather mature matters mattered in steps of the paths of wicked way. The theory tightrope was to be walked across in danger life version for virgins. Welcomes way of a starlight traverse with a tight rope to be held and fastened by a trio and then walked across in majesty magical by the three of this outspoken memorable night. A superimposed tribute this night was to be for the Red, White, and Blue. Inside the crowd of the skating rink was in the teenage 80's mindset of the usual. The neon life on ceiling over the skate floor blinked and flashed above the heads of the rounding skaters. Colors of prime mixed with the colors of non explainable energies seemed to send shock waves communicative through the skating crowd. The arcade section was nominal for Xavier as always. Most of the night in the case that he wanted to either play a game at the arcade, grab a slice and a cola with ice, or simply socialize among friends was as seemingly common as living was expected for sector totality and the futures good sector saver saved it was Xavier the boy. An hour passed by and the typical became an emergency broadcast hypothetical. Xavier had just finished a competition round of space invaders with some school friends and others from the neighboring cities and towns. After he counted the quarters he was left with he thought over a slice and cola fix when he heard a familiar voice. This voice was the voice of the frequently serious communicator not to mention a star Braves pitcher in Xavier's league and he was accompanied by the class clown "hey kid thinking about retirement?" Xavier turned his head he looked to his left side and it was Zimmerman the man standing there with Luzzin. These two were aware that Xavier had frequented this joint and they had in good nature of a liking made plans for a joining up with Xavier on this evening for some fun. Little was Xavier aware however that Zimmerman the man had his contraband school bag with him and it was not to be a hanging of the stupid but rather this was to be a meeting of the minds and mission prophecy service of the institute spy world, yes it was the FBI the CIA and the elites of foreigners altogether. Welcome to the save your souls (SOS) morse code of plain called THE MISSION! . . . . Xavier in curious motive questions "What's in the . . . . ? bag?" Zimmerman the man answers "Nuthin" Luzzin reacts further "Yeah Xavier nothing's in the bag but the remedy cure for your lousy pitching performance the other day." Xavier enlarged an eye and raised an eyebrow he speaks "Come off it man, my team is used to losing by touchdowns." Zimmerman the man defending his offense speaks further while Luzzin laughed in his style classic of the class clown he was "yes double x but you gave up four of them and you were playing baseball not football, maybe you should pitch relief or something." eyes gestured blinked hard with the other and Xavier opened them wide and then they went back to normal. Xavier then made a face of wise gut and spoke the manner of it "look, I only pitched 4 and a third and gave up 19 runs, it was 19 to 1 and I thought we might still have a chance for a win." Luzzin and Zimmerman laughed sarcastically and Xavier double x clenched fists of a rage cage and smoke protrusions like conniption matter gaseous of blackish gray was arising in air. His eyes squinted poser style like the heavy metal dudes in picture frames that he listened to when his turtle records were worn from needle scratches. Xavier avoided a cranium top volcanic eruption and as a Tiger he branded determination corruption . . . . hesitation and a twitch he speaks in stern mannerism "UURRRRGGGGHHH!" eyes of double x flashing like his name should had been XXX with a tea cup totaled and Luzzins' eyes showed warfare trauma instantly like Saddam Hussein wearing his under wear on his head, Zimmerman looked for his jaw and chin and he noticed they were laying in front of his front rental buddy skate wheels. Xavier fixes with mind control and his apprehension healed when Zimmerman's jaw and chin complied with reversed gravity bringing his face back to normal making him ugly again but still he was still devastatingly hansom to most nice looking girls. Normalcy became again for the two, or at least that was the case for the deranged world. Traversal boy Xavier double x commenced continuing commentary of a livid lunacy for his remaining season with the Tigers "THOSE BRAVES AINT NUTHIN HRRRGGH HURRGGH" furious pants of a growl form the loins of Xavier's lungs and vocal cords he stated his baseball argument for the tiger life blood furthermore "LOOK, WE WERE 4 AND O AND THEY BEAT US BAD EARLIER THIS SEASON AND FUCKED THINGS UP LIKE THE ASSHOLES THEY ARE, FROM 4 WINS AND THIS LOSS WE ONLY HAD THIS BAD GAME AND WE ARE'NT GIVING UP!" Luzzin made a calamitous comedic expressive facial melting that was not of the apparent embarrassment of which this expressive notion of a look had appeared but more to the effect of unidentifiable affection senses discombobulated. Zimmerman the man states a case for a defending of manure life "so ex-boy what's your fighting team of Tigers record now?" "HUUGHYAAGH! WE WERE 4 AND 1 AND SINCE THOSE BUTHOLES INSTIGATED THE FIXINGS OF A MILLENIUM, WE'VE STRUGGLED SINCE BECAUSE OUR COACHES NEVER HAVE US PRACTICE, WE HAVE A TEAM NOW, WITHOUT OUR NEW PLAYERS AND MYSELF I SAY WE CAN, LAST YEAR THEY WENT 1 and 17, BEFORE I JOINED THE LEAUGE AND BECAME CATCHER AND PITCHER FOR THEM SO TO ANSWER YOUR QUESTION WE'RE 8 WINS AND 8 LOSSES ALRIGHT!" Luzzin made the statement of necessity for Xavier's return to sanity "Zimmerman why don't you let our rated X friend here know what's in the bag?" Zimmerman smirked a sane sided lip curve reminiscent of a quenching for some hot brew and said to Xavier in a happy and ecstatic deep volume voice similar to a whisper with treachery and humor for a good fight "hey Xavier I'll tell you we got a huge full bottle of whiskey and its calling your name." "Is my name written on it?" the three faces of these school friends were overcome with dominating looks of approval for some deadly serious mischief and they darted out the doors of the skating establishment. The planned destination was already set.........a little opening down the side road where they could sit and tip the bottle of a message. This trio resumed the liquor mission and so they made their way down the road while oncoming traffic whizzed by. It appeared that the headlights of the cars were watching as if they were. They were the eyes of some strange life formed mechanical animals. No beeps from the car horns of spies. No creeps from the porn shops disguised. No wink from the man on the moon. It was nearing the end of the end of the school year for the students involved as well as the rest whom were nevertheless still of significant value to the sector that singular unit Xavier was fighting for in survival mode. The three students of a night owl prowling neared the destination and they climbed a small yet steep hill that was strewn with trees and you could smell the pine in air. The green pine tree pricks living were of the pin pricks balanced on the tip of a pin like atoms. The brown ones on ground rested on the hardened soil and in death they were to corrode into the land faults of holistic logistics. A new life form breeding was resulting a minority consultation in quotations negative, positive and neutral. Pro living limb life of the god lambs met in formula triad trio of the try. Luzzin, Zimmerman the man, and Xavier double X sat in the rocky opening among the pines and the trees intensifying the moon beam darkness around with their star material bodies but the light of the moon sent their inward souls into the array of situations elemental meshed into a combination key organized. The bottle was uncorked with an unscrewing analog and the kids in traversing mode began to pass around the message bottle. Conversation started after the first runaround passing of the bottle of this drinking night for these accused punks. They talked about the days of the school year that were vital to the outcomes of their lifetimes and the welfare of their supposed enemies. They commended their friendships fended from the hanging out in woods by a bonfire and the river water reflections. They had witnessed the underworlds of karma. The three acknowledged that manifest destiny was set in stone and differential set outcome by the conspirators to the play writes of the life movie was for the watching over of a hydrogen upcoming life and that the oxygen of combined was making life blood. It was the true creeping death of which had kept them alive. They gained faith in themselves and a possible god by their pride in devout atheism and an effort of man. They felt the liberation gender opposite and inspired the liberal of Xavier in future who was not downplayed for it is true that the liberal can be of any affiliation of the morally correct depending on the situation of an era and regardless of a labeling entitlement. The moon gifted them light from the sun that reflected off of it. The goods were seated and three talked the process in the moon! The spaces between these three spoke the written word of a Poe, sighted the toil conquest tired leg wheel spinners of a Khan, they feared Christ in wise breaths, they rejected the protection of an Alexander and they felt the sins of Julius Caesar. Procrastination denied and the light flakes fell unto them invisible. My god its three more stars. Multitude claims but that would be off subject. Zimmerman the man played announcer as Xavier takes a chugging swig "OOOAAAHHH there goes double x he's downing the hard stuff like a pissed of monsoon eager for next weeks' game and oh he nearly finished a half of the bottle." Luzzin played co-announcer in tribute to another "a battle of epic proportions." "who said that?" Xavier passes the message receiver communication device in the form of a party drink to Luzzin. Luzzin took his time taking swigs of the more experienced drinker and train robber youth of which he was not? On this intervention of a night prowl Xavier steels the microphone but in secret agenda he was to one day obtain the microfilm revealing messages in day time soap operas, he speaks "Luzzin is a fine physical specimen and a hopeful contribution to this drinking league of the stupid, I think he will be rookie of the year, this temporary featherweight has moved on to middle weight and by the time he's in his mid-twenties he'll be a fat ass." "What?" Luzzin makes teen defense for the youngsters of future Alcoholics Anonymous alumni pre mature membership of the not. Luzzin then passes the bottle over to his crime partner Zimmerman. Luzzin was slightly timid on this night and he made quotation fortunate for a cooling of the firewater situation while Zimmerman the man took his turn in the spin the bottle non sexual game of a liking "I hope Xavier and his Tigers kill those Giants next week, go for it double x's." "Most certainly I will Luzzin this buzz I feel has calmed me I feel the soothing of a thousand feathers on my something." Zimmerman the man began to laugh at Xavier and luzzin joined in and Zimmerman quoted "didn't I call Missus Shake a something or something?" "No Zimmerman you asked her why she was being such a something." The bottle was soon empty for the most part and the three of them made way back to the theory pendulum rink of a social crisis. The eyes of the gods were watching and the owl of these woods asked a question........... "who?" Eyeballs of the owl took over the look of worldly existences with the appearance of evil, a gift of wisdom that was to result with the development of life's judgments. The owl witnesses in audio stereophonic of its ear drums on this night for in the midst of this threesome drunk they sang in beauty of the youths overtired the words to America's national anthem, the star spangled banner. A while after Luzzin, Zimmerman the man, and Xavier were homeward bound and they prayed all the way home to get there without parental detection. They scored three safe runs at home.

7

LATE NOVEMBER 2011; Xavier was lying in less than humble home, he was suffering so it was said by some who knew him but the liquor problem he had developed was over rated by some hypocrites. His will was underrated by his unprovoked enemies and this ate at the very flesh of his living spitting image spirit. He had arrested his disease of alcoholism for somewhere near 14 years prior to his falling off of the wagon. Xavier was a dreaming writer of a retort reporting. He was in past of a burden to his causes for self will and his needing of a being someone but in this case he had no choice but to lay down for a very long time. He frequently was venturing out in the cold of an early New England winter and the bottles he had consumed over the past two years since his apparent failed recovery were detrimental to the health of his immune system. Xavier was stricken with the sickness of gastritis and he often had to spit from the acid re flux that his new sickness had led to. Late one night Xavier was lying down. He had just finished off a pint of cheap vodka and he was forced to smoke a cheap brand of cigars for reasons of his needs of an addiction fixing. Xavier was in deathly situation danger it had appeared. It was obvious to him that the surreal feelings he was experiencing resulted from harrowing reality were simply made real by possibilities of origin sources instigated to deceive his mind for a controlling. He was in a must win situation in order to avoid a conversion for a joining of some plot hoods. He was renting a room in another low income home but as always he met his needs and had received some of his needs of necessity. Unfortunately for him in this case and in cases of other situations spawned unto him in forms of downs and his wrong assumption of his failure as a reporter he for once wanted to obtain what he had wanted rather than what he had needed. Xavier was the victim of suckering shots from elites whom desired to rid the last liberal assumed or maybe the last liberal of a threat was more of a correct accusation. Xavier had become an independent by this time and whether one way political, moral outright and ultra, or middle of the road it was not a term system of value to the opinion of this inspired writer destined. In absolute like the drink he sometimes could afford to purchase he had matched with the nick name he was labeled with by the best. He was saved by himself of course but as Jonah had carried on sand at one time his weight was to be carried for a long time. Friends and lovers were of the past and romance was gone so he believed. He met a new friend her name was Renessa and she liked to call him by a new name this name was needed for his recent tragedies. Renessa was to call him Jonah. On the late night of this mentioning his roommate had gone out for a ride and more often than not or maybe in a putting across of more of an exact literal explanation this new home venue for Xavier and his friend roommate of anew had visits frequently from the survivors of this poverty stricken city neighborhood. "Jonah" as will be the name given to Xavier for the remainder of this chapter was resting and watching some local television on the public broadcasting station when an older woman and a younger woman of renowned beauty had in humanity endowed positional esteem in the unwanted soldiers home. Jonah lied in bed baron in the lands as such so it seemed to him, this baron land was only of mind state, minds stated of the liars, the crying dream and the dagger cloak that his true identity of Xavier singled out. The sector was whole and the five jibe of this era was not of cromagnon winds that blew. To the undertaking law of the existences of animal magnetic opposites there was no opposing factor to prevent an attempt for a redeeming invite. The sector that was alive and well and had appeared as a death bed in coffin has the living. The two of the visit to Jonah the alias took the invite from another near death from the potent drugs of the city cabled. A town nearby was the new camp push (Kampuchea) for a cure of the holy. Her name was assumed as Renessa for a carrying. She was a confession of the others and her looks were her output of defense from the plot. She was in safe mode and the mathematics of the databases were justifiably taken care of from spies for Jonah in the accounts in banks internationalist of the Orient coast. Renessa was to symbolize in the mind of Jonah's spot mind attempt number three for the socialite want of the new solar. The trains on track were written as possibilities for a gathering. The airlines were guarded and the post controlled, protected, guided within, and put to use as decoys by the bus systems, the ferry boats, the taxis of another kind for the timer. The underground railroads were limited outbound and so it was the chambers of parallel that are induced from universes alive mid and befell. Renessa had an alias being and the signs tell two of assistance to hold on and another to retreat in supporting the inside. Moon deal; Renessa was to become Dale with a French surname. The town camp bares the name on the steeples of the financial defiance of unknown doers. Jonax, Jonah, Jonas, Judas, Jedidiah, and John of the axis access forms four into five with no asked questions. Renessa was not slow to accompany Xavier and Jonah as she was to call him when they awoke from their night of a first meeting. Jonah wore the crest burden of a victimizing of the innocent. It was a long john top and a pair of boxer shorts, a pajama pair for a poor man. No more shrouds in times of the shadows of changing. This accompaniment virtual was for the two of them not intended or meant to be for the rising of a preference prefixed on the coming times of tragedy for Xavier alias Jonah. For Renessa it was her willingness of acceptance to the realities of the city life that had guided her in attraction to her Jonah. Jonah was her termed name for him a cute anecdote of a nick name a name that reminded her of her past friendships for reasons of back of the mind blurred obscurities. Necessity in the city of her Jonah was for the most part easy to come by due to the past leaderships of this section of New England that the two resided at. This system opposed and was an affront to the system of common term, a notion related to the stereotypical reality truths of rarity that bore the combinations to the time safes of holdings of the citizens ever so victimized by the brutalities of making a living. The opposition system that was established by the local and state governments were indeed the sector of which Xavier Jonah and the members of the sectional five jibe were members of if one chooses to believe so. However the known truth of it was that it was Xavier or Jonah in the callings of Renessa that was the risk tool for the establishment of sector continuance. Singularity boy of the sector five planning moved forward from emotions of his morbid experiences and in deepness thinking of devising his new plans he was forced to let Renessa go her own way one day. Renessa would be subject to interrogation but she was a survivor and the institutions would shelter and clothe her for a small victory in the supporting of the mistakes of Xavier Jonah's reckless abandonment. Jonah became Xavier again and he marched forward in adventure small of walking and a talking, he thought deep in his mind of the liberal arts and he peace marched in violent thoughts defending with a throw when he had to. It was the march of an obeyed new commandment. Hopefully as it was said in casualty the tear would be swept from the facial sides in fates of mercy for him, her, and the rest of the world involved. Xavier had felt the downward plague emotional in his being having found out about Renessa's misfortune. However he was happy to know that the clinics were still intact with the supporting fundamentals set up by the sector he felt for, fought for, and was hoping to reignite. In the form of his personal and out land sighted industry he felt confession and from the profession Renessa would survive from the workings of past sector life and others who had complied with the qualities of the human mixture. Xavier lied down and watched television on the new cable package deal he had subscribed to. It was post election time and he rested with some beers and he enjoyed some of the new times entertainment. He slept and awaited another alias.

8

BACK IN THE past year of 1986 it was early May. The week following the hangovers morning for the three students of the cosmos meeting were on a tare. They had recovered and tended to their duties of a school week. It was Luzzin, Zimmerman the man, and Xavier in the hide out of the boy's room late on a school day. It was the Friday of the following week. Zimmerman the man with Luzzin had decided to give their full support to the cause of the Tiger underdogs of which it might have been but destiny was to be the decider. The pesky Tigers were to play the ferocious Giants and if the Tigers had won after some season downfall slumping trouble they were to earn a spot in the little league pennant. It was Friday afternoon post detention. Detention was let out prematurely on this day due to one of the cool teachers as the kids would term such a person of the education faculty. The three were in the boy's room. Zimmerman the man was puffing on a smoke he bummed from a confidant, Luzzin was devouring a chip bag he kept from lunch period in the school cafeteria, and Xavier was in a mind state like that of the 1978 red sox about to blow a 14 and a half game 1st place lead. Zimmerman the man threw his finished cigarette into the urinal and after Luzzin swallowed his last chip of a bag. They focused full attention and tentative wisdom on Xavier who was in fear of a major choking. Zimmerman and Luzzin looked one another over in a stern stated eyeing of a directive glance. They moved over to trembling Xavier and they commenced to console him in the style of a boxer sitting in his corner after the 11th round. Zimmerman takes control of a situation for his friend and he makes quotation one "Okay, your start was 4 wins and 0 losses right?" "Yes." Zimmerman the man thinks over matters for a moment and quotes his baseball outlook of a situation "Now you can't let the fifth game of this season against the Braves get to your head. Your Tigers are in and I'm not going to tell you what the Giants are saying about how they'd devour your team but Luzzin and I are there for sure." Luzzin speaks "Yeah and I'll make sure I can sneak you one of those 5 cent popcorn bags they sell at concession." "Huh?" Zimmerman speaks the case further "Never mind that Luzzin plays in the city league, they suck over there, now, your tigers were 4 and 1 and from that point your team still had hitting but they have lost their heart it seems." Luzzin interrupts "one of you guys know if they still have slurpees at the store across for the park?" Zimmerman the man with Xavier reacted with a simultaneous comment "LUZZIN SHUT UP!" Zimmerman continues "Okay, the all star picks for your team upset me. These picks were credible but last year they had no catcher. You came in and it was like that! You're a hell of a catcher kid and you will be a pitcher for real." Luzzin makes another wisdom tid bit he was pointing at the floor "is that yours?" Zimmerman the man became annoyed again and Xavier waved a hand in neglecting of a comment useless. Zimmerman gathered his being after recovery and pointed a finger in Xavier's face "alright since the all star game and your absolutely pathetic pitching debut from insults during warm-ups you have heated up and you're on fire. I can't say the same for your team though because after the all star game you have carried the team but your tigers haven't been supporting you enough and your team has not stacked up that many wins since." Luzzin tries again if you want to call the kettle black "do you think this looks good?" Zimmerman the man and Xavier's heads turn looking at Luzzin like an annoying, silly, useless three headed monster. Zimmerman the man took his hand away from his disgusted face and once again he continued a managerial commentary "I tell you for certain double X your coach doesn't do much for the team but he was confident enough to start you against the red sox and your relieving performance wipe out against the odds meaning that shut down of the Yankees was key." "You really think that?" Xavier questioned in no confidence. "Sure Xavier, just get cocky you're good like that." Luzzin was scratching his head by the stall door he commented again "me and Sharon are doin it." "We don't want to hear about your sex life Luzzin." Zimmerman the man said this in rude fashion of this down ward baseball plague to be uplifted to Luzzin while waving a neglectful wave once again. Xavier double X pondered rubbing his chin with his thumb and index finger. He looked over to Luzzin and said with a recovering facial change of the universal wise ass "you can tell us about that if you want Luzzin, short stories aren't so bad." Luzzin reacted "Yeah well, Sharon just some hussy in the sixth grade, you guys are talking baseball, maybe I should have paid attention, she's been on my mind. Win this thing and end Zimmerman's migraine problem before it develops into some freakish brain seizure series and stroke disorder with an ecliptical hernia." Humored laughter took the room mood momentarily and Zimmerman the man asks a question "So, double X what are you going to do about this game tonight, were talking a playoff spot you know?" Xavier rises to the occasion prematurely in sadness of the strong from his life experienced trauma in being a red sox fan "I'll tell you what I'm going to do. But who cares? This is what the Tigers are going to do! Were gonna gather together in fire and we'll be so fired up in revenge for that last whatever the hell it was that the Giants will be mince meat! Guys the game is set for 7 o'clock tonight under the lights too and yes Luzzin popcorn and slurpees but don't poison me with that crap my catching performance must be at the top of its game tonight!" Luzzin said one more fashionable comment of a special day of beautiful afternoon weather for America's pastime of this 80's decade of which they were privileged to grow up during "Well double X your grampa will be here to drive you home and Zimmerman and I have to catch the late bus." Zimmerman the man was in agreement and the three exited the school at normal time of detention dismissal. Three and a half hours passed by and the gathering at the little league town ball park was growing with parents, kid fans of the little league, players in the league concerned with an outcome, some girls for a teasing of Xavier, and some other girls who were there to route on his side or for whatever was the team of their liking choice was to be. Xavier arrived with guardian father and they walked the gravel small stone strewn parking lot whereas Xavier joined his team mates for their pregame meeting. The tigers gathered by the back of their dugout little league style. Some of the nerd kids sat in front Indian style. The cool ones either sat on their asses like lazy studs or stood at attention to the details of the coaching pregame hype up. Other members of the tigers did not know if they were cools or nerds and so they stood near Xavier with life's questionings on their minds. Xavier was listening as always and he did his common pregame practice while he listened holding two bats and swinging them lefty style like he hit and back righty style in a sort of Willamseque exercise back and forth swing of this sporting event pastime for the ages. Xavier had a thought that if the Tigers were to lose that he might aspire to join the Japanese league when he grew up. The coaches called the tally of the batting order and Xavier was to hit in the clean up spot as he always had that season. Almost time for a calling of "play ball" from the umpire and the lights were gleaming for the dandy lion flower watchers in right field. Xavier patted his right fielder friend on back, gave him some advice on the lefty pull hitter the Giants had in their line up and he talked some player coaching to the right fielder who was to take his place in the fourth inning. Xavier eyed the killer giant of a big mouth on the other side and the tough one who competed with him was wary of a four eyed umpire who would call him and Xavier out in blindness of the plate. The players took the field and it was home advantage for the Giants for their stronger record of a one game remained season so it was the tigers who were to field first. Xavier double X caught warm-ups in his catcher's equipment and it was 45 seconds until the calling of "play ball." "COMING DOWN" Xavier yelled to his infield and the practice of the steeling cutoff was thrown in a whizzing after a decent pop in the catchers mitt of Xavier who wore the same number on his little league team as Joe Cronin. The popcorn smelled of aroma fire. The butter on it dripped the laminate drip of constricted time. The lawn chairs for fathers were strong and supportive. The chairs for the ladies of the same making were imperative. The chalk lines on the field were gleaming in limelight. The Tigers saw giants and reddened their stage fright. Out in the outfield the emblems on hats were shining in moonlight. In the infield the shortstop was planning an upset. Double X catcher quarterback was guiding the onset. The sector conservative in public was brewing a new word. The mid grade consoled them and done so in concert. Downplays in game time uplifting these nightlights! Bench warmers were scratching their balls in their skin tights. A sector original was hiding in full bright. The neutrals who were right confided in Tigers. One Luzzin one Zimmerman in silence and trying! One Xavier was out there in outdone misguiding. The giants in mayhem remembered the absurd. The competition spirit that knows them completed compete words. The first pitch was thrown and the baseball was fast for a little league opening toss. The ball came into the outside of the strike zone Xavier lunged for it and the ball hit Xavier right upside the head. Xavier fetched the baseball that had bounced with a distinct ring clang off of the back stop fence pole and he grabbed it fast. The umpire makes the call "STEEERIKE I uh um oh BALL urrgh uh hmmn? BALL ONE!" Xavier knew after pitch number one that he had to have a talk with his pitcher at the mound. Xavier held the baseball in his right bare hand and he walked to his pitcher Tommy the boy. The two spoke to one another in strategic small talk. "What the heck was that?" Xavier asked Tommy. "I don't know man I think the jitters are still with me or something." Said Tommy. "Slow it down if its that bad I know you're a fastball pitcher but this is their on base opening hitter of the lineup, they have good coaching, that was a called ball I can't believe four eyes got it right, the coach knows to have this batter take the first pitch like Boggs used to do, let one go calm if you want and them work back into it, its early so just keep ignoring my fake finger calls and do your thing." Tommy thought it over and responded "Okay." Xavier pulled his mask back over his face and returned behind the plate and went into his crouch squat. Tommy faked a no nod and a yes nod and let out a moderate pitch fast enough for a strike with an attempted swing and definitely slow enough for a controlled in the batters zone strike. "Pop" the prediction was assured correct the giants lead off batter took strike one and the count was 1 ball 1 strike. A few rude chants from the neighborhood bully who was routing for the Giants could be heard and the lawn chair fans of fair-weather let out a simultaneous array of clapping hands alike a lame applause of a golf tournament. Tommy wound up for the next pitch and whizzed a fastball right by the batter and the ball popped into Xavier's catchers mitt with the sound of a whiffing baseball bat, the bat swung around in a 360 degree angle or less but it was enough for this bat to hit Xavier right upside the head. "STEEERIKE TWO!" and the count now stood at 1 ball and 2 strikes. Another pitch from Tommy came in fast again, the pitcher threw with confidence of a legendary Yankee maybe like a John, a Ruth, or a Guidry and the baseball flew perfect right over the plate centered like minotaurs placed correctly. The call came from the umpire "BALL!" Xavier became a livid Tiger ravenous like a mountain lion in hunt of prey. He tore his mask and helmet off of his head and slammed on the dirt. "WHAT THE HELL!" "Ball two kid." "THE BALL HIT MY GLOVE AND I DIDN'T MOVE IT!" "Ball two calm down you." Tommy the boy made hand gesturing for a calming of his catcher and Xavier realized the importance of this game. He put his helmet and mask back on his head and squatted for the next pitch. Tommy winds up and lets out his only other pitch, it was a change up. The ball reached near to the batters box it was low and outside. The batter let off an effort of a swinging and he hit a grounder over to the shortstop. The shortstop fielded the baseball handily and threw a quickie over to first base. The tall twelve year old at first caught the thrown baseball easily beating the runner by a few stretched running paces. Xavier raised his index finger and the Tigers in tradition of a little league game yelled out with him "ONE DOWN." One out and two to go and Tommy, Xavier, and the remainder of the Tigers felt a lessening of the jitters and the game was on. The second batter of the Giants lineup had been preparing in the on deck circle and this third baseman of the hot corner of which it was not was in the case of this little league game of future reminiscence to be a hot corner two times in this game. This giant's third baseman was to make sure his fielding skills matched his team mates heart feels for a winning game. The giant's third baseman stepped into the batter's box and made his stance for a runner and a possible RBI from the next hitters of their lineup. Tommy boy winds up and sends an attempted illegal pitch for this level of league play. The first base umpire was aware of Tommy boy's trickery and high level of pitching ability for an eleven year old so this umpire in detection of this illegal stitch grab by Tommy boy had let Tommy boy and the rest of the tigers know that any such pitches would not be allowed for the remainder of the game. A warning given and in the case of any such pitch attempts as such from Tommy boy the batter would be awarded first base in the form of a balk. Xavier waved off this offset for Tommy boy and this at bat for the giant's third baseman went to a full count over a rather high pitch count including three fouled balls one of which was caught by a lawn chair absent due to a popcorn craving of a stork who had delivered one to many in her times as a town girl. The count was three balls and two strikes and as Xavier became worried that Tommy boys pitch tally was high already for a second at bat that is and he in strategy pregame planning with his pitcher located his catcher's mitt low and away for the hitting swinging style of the examined batter at hand. Tommy boy wound up after an agreement nod of the fake and he threw low and away. A fastball tamed for first inning play jetted and you could hear a whizzing but no whiffing was to happen. The baseball in its spinning jetted into the batter's box and it was hard to judge whether this baseball was in or out of the strike zone. Giant's third baseman eyes the ball and swings hitting the baseball. It was a blooper ball hit into shallow left field. Only the shortstop for the tigers had a chance of retrieval for out number two. The left fielder was blowing a bubble from the big league chew that one of the giants' players had given to the giants before the game, a sensual distraction of tasty flavoring and a saliva gatherer for kids with a common candy store addiction. The chew was distracting enough for no attempt from left field or an error covering for the running shortstop. The Tigers shortstop made an effort diving horizontally after a fast sprinting and the baseball nipped the end of his glove and it fell to the ground. The hit was shallow enough for a first base throwing from the shortness of this blooper hit of which it may have been. A bare hand grab was the only method for this tiger in seeking of Giant prey and so in good judgment of a player he simply decided to keep the ball in his hand as the hitting third baseman for the giants over ran first base in cautionary safety. Safe at first was the obvious call, so obvious that the first base umpire remained silent. The situation under control still, it was in Xavier's judging of this inning so far, and so it was a man on first with one out. The third batter of the giant's lineup was next. It was their pesky pitcher himself. He was hoping to put a runner in scoring position and not swinging away for a home run was a likely choice for him due to his lack of power hitting and his consistency in his having a good batting average. The giants' pitcher walked into the batter's box and made his hitting stance with a determined stone faced look. A few words of trash talking ensued between Xavier the catcher squatting and the hitting pitcher for the giants who was not to be distracted by Xavier's common methods of a friendly insulting complementary for a win took the first pitch and a loud echoing pop was heard throughout the little league ball park. "Strike!" was the call and correct it was but Xavier in such esteem for his pitchers' throw was not as aware as he had been all season. Xavier's unawareness would cost his team at this moment as low and behold the giants' third baseman took off for a stealing of second base. The giants' third baseman was about half way to second base when Xavier although he was fractions of a second late had jumped out of his squatting position and he threw a fireball down to second base with the shortstop covering the second baseman for the tigers for a throw out. The giants' pitcher slid into second base hands first with his arms stretched. Xavier's throw was on the money as always and the second baseman for Xavier's tigers caught the baseball and tagged the runner. Unfortunately for the tigers however the runner was to be called safe. You see, the runner touched second base at the same time as the tagging that was made on his back side. The third base umpire judged the call and shouted out "SAFE!" A little frustration argument jitter quotations came from Tommy boy and some of the tiger infielders but the umpires needed no meeting and the home plate umpire simply ended any argument by calling out "TIE GOES TO THE RUNNER." A man on second base, one out, and the giants pitcher was down in the count no balls and one taken strike. Now it was time for the giants' catcher to take his turn of a first inning at bat. Yes, it was the Xavier nemesis . . . . the catcher of the opposing giants was the cleanup hitter as well, both of these factual baseball player traits were in common for Xavier and this giants' catcher. Yes, to catchers and two power hitting cleanup swingers. The fans looked on in heeded way. The giants cleanup hitter and catcher steps into the batter's box, makes his stance in the style of a Fisk, a fixing of the helmet which he did between every pitch, a batting preparation method that made games last as long as a short millennium. He prepares for Tommy boys wind up and pitch. He recalls the pregame bench warmers itch, he glanced at the pitcher paranoid of gooey Vaseline stitch, he thought of the town witch, he loved the bitch, and he in tribute of the day prepared to swing at the first glitch. Tommy boy became a strategy major for his preparation in opposition of a facing of a cleanup hitter. He nodded two no nods and a yes nod from fingers obsolete. A wind up and a pitch thrown right down the pike. This righty hitter catcher and cleanup lineup representative of the giants at hand swung at another fastball and he pulled a screaming line drive that became a speed velocity grounder demon baseball. By the time the ball had bounced off ground a little more than half way to the third base section it was on fire like a cannon shot. The tigers' third baseman made a valiant stopping of the baseball. He handled this baseball with a diving and a glove pop and catch perfected. He jumped to his feet in a split second and fired the baseball to first. This giants' hitter was called out by one and a half strides. The giants' catcher had fallen victim to his only weakness as a player. This weakness was his lacking of running ability. This out at first was not to be a lost cause however for the wit of the giants' coaching and the craftiness of the base runner they had at second base and so third base was taken from a sprinting of the giants' runner from second base. This play was put into the little league statistic books as a sacrifice hit. A man on third base, two outs, and a lessened pitch count to the relief of Xavier and Tommy boy. Xavier in baseball smarts decided to have another meeting of the minds at the pitcher's mound. Xavier in pacing of a trotting approached the pitchers' mound with the face of a Nixon. Maybe in the future the red sox might have a player with a name similar to that? Well manners, superstition practice of a pastime? World Series win and hocus pocus 1918? The minds met in the on set off set and the lights of the kid park were from the energy of inside and the suns of which had provided it. Xavier gets to the mound and he began to speak to his pitcher. "Okay Tommy we have two outs on these guys, now I know you're doing better and you're more prepared than I was for the disaster we had against these guys when I pitched, but don't fret, that guy at third isn't getting past me as long as you finish off this five slot, when we get him it's swing away time." "Alright Xavier what do you want to do about this five slot in the mean time?" "Well, a base hit and a run scored so we're down one to nothing. We have to get this guy at first, maybe you can get away with a knuckle ball if the umpire doesn't catch you." "My knuckler sucks man! How about one of those little league non-spinning palm ball throws you taught me at the start of the season?" "Yes Tommy that might be an idea the lessened spin can cause a deadened hit like a knuckler." "alright Xavier will do." "Are you sure?" "Yes" and Xavier left the mound went back to his position behind the plate and crouched down giving another fake signal of two fingers. The fifth batter who was the giants' center fielder awaited the next pitch. Tommy boy wound up and made a cautionary palm ball pitch resembling. With the speed of this pitch one would view this slow speed baseball pitch as your typical change up. The giants' fifth batter of the lineup took on the element of a risky surprise and he laid a soft bunt down the third base line. The runner from third base for the giants was a speedster and he took off immediately nearly dismantling the play with is trampling cleat feet as the third baseman and Xavier the catcher were both confused on who was to make the play as if they were partners in doubles tennis dealing with a centered tennis ball in a doubles game. The baseball lost its grounder velocity half way down the third base line. Xavier knew the runner at third had already scored. A distraction no more on third base nevertheless he was left with the decision of his normal act of backing up first base or trying to get this guy out for this ruthless baseball move decided. This bunt had confused the tigers formed certainty of pregame preparations nevertheless it was the slick tigers third baseman who was to field this baseball and make a throwing attempt to first base. The tigers' third baseman fielded the ball handily despite the speed he was required to run at. He threw to first while Xavier threw his mask and helmet on the ground from his livid thoughts with himself for his decision of not backing up first base and his poor decision of chasing down this surprise bunt attempt. The tigers' first baseman handled a decent line drive throw from the panting third baseman. The baseball popped into the tigers' first baseman's glove and the batter of the giants five slot was called out. It was three outs and the end of the top of the first inning with the score the giants 1 and the tigers 0. The bottom of the first inning was to be stinky cologne and it was not halftime. The giants took the field fast. Their pitcher was through with his warm ups after a small tally of warm up throws. The coming down call was made and the giants' second baseman caught the ball thrown from his catcher and the giants relayed their practice infielders throw around relay in perfect execution. The umpire tossed the game ball to the giants' pitcher and play ball was called for the bottom of the first inning. The giants' pitcher was in rare form he had risen to this occasion. This pitcher for the giants had been pressured by his rookie hot headed 10 year old pitcher for another win. A win and it would be a thrusting of this giants' team into the pennant. The greatest team ever assembled was the claim of this ten year old sensation and his team was to see to it that the performance met such qualifications. A little kicking up of some dirt on the mound in front of the rubber and the giants pitcher made pitching formed body language in a bending crouch and an eyeing of the target mitt he was to employ. The mitt was held in the proper location by the nemesis catcher to Xavier double X the tiger. The crowd silenced in anticipation of the first pitch of the bottom of the first inning. The first batter of the tigers' lineup was the second baseman. This tiger second base player was a young boy of a liking to the pastime, and to the rest of his team mates as well. He stepped to the plate and remembered ice cream rewarding feasts afterwards if they were to pull off a win on this night. He wouldn't have to do his homework until Monday morning. The giants' pitcher went into a fast style of a pitchers wind up and threw in the classic style of a maniac. A fast ball this was and with a swift swing at the first pitch a whiff sound could be heard. It was evident from this first pitch that the tigers might have been in for a long night ahead. Batter two in the on deck circle was overtaken with intimidation, he glanced back in concern to the double deck batter of slot three of the tigers lineup and the two of them took coaching advisory. The players on deck and double deck with Xavier still in catchers gear batting fourth and awaiting an outcome began to time the pitchers pitches with a counting for a swinging time clock of which they wanted to achieve a certainty punch out. "Strike one" the call was heard from the umpire. The timers timed and the families of the sons and mothers watched with intensity. The lead off batter for the tigers prepared for the second pitch of the bottom half of this first inning and then came a wind up and another in throwing of a fastball from the giants' star pitcher. Another whizzing of a white blur flew into the mitt of the giants' catcher and another loud pop was heard afar. "Strike two" the call came in from the umpire who had improved his eyesight by removing his spectacle bifocals. The count stood at no balls and two strikes as on deck double deck and the still geared up Xavier had their jaws in dropping mode. Not even an attempt of a swing on this pitch from this giant star player. The coach gave a signal of encouragement and the lead off batter for the tigers once again stepped into the batter's box with courage, he prepared for the next pitch. A whizzing blurred baseball stream again and another loud pop into the mitt of the catcher for the giants and it was strike three called. The lead off tiger batter had swung but he hit nothing. The on deck batter gives a reassuring pat on the back of his teammate as his teammate took a seat back in the dugout. The second batter of the tigers order stepped in for a facing of an obviously red hot starting giants pitcher. More of the same it was as this batter of the two slot was out in four pitches only making contact on one of these pitches with a clang shot off of the back stop. This one non hit of barely any contact was just a foul ball of a hoping for the hitting crew of the tigers who were in first inning dismay. The third batter of the tigers' order was the consistent shortstop. He walked into the batter's box with hopes of bringing his tigers alive and a hit might recover his team from the slump that they had since their 4 and 0 start. Xavier was on deck now and he was only wearing his shin protectors as he took practice swings in the on deck circle. The tigers shortstop took strike one, took a ball, foul tipped in a fighting for his team, took another ball and he had managed to fight his way to a tough full count. The tigers shortstop fouled off one more and the baseball clanged off of a back stop pole making a ringing sound that momentarily sent shock waves through the eardrums of the small little league crowd at hand. A wind up and a pitch and the white blur baseball whizzed by again thus popping into the mitt of the catcher for strike three. Xavier in disgust put the remainder of his catching equipment back on and he looked forward to leading off the bottom of the second inning. The first inning was over and the score still stood at giants 1 tigers 0. The top of the second inning seemed like slow death for the tiger pitcher they called Tommy boy and Xavier wasn't too much different in his feelings for the toiling first half of that inning either. Tommy boy's pitch count was high in this inning as well but it was not as bad as the first inning was. Tommy boy had walked the first batter of this inning and this walk was followed by a double from the underrated seventh hitter of the giants' line up. This seven slot batter for the giants belted a solid line drive to right center making a fine safe sliding into second base crediting himself with an RBI. The batter who led off with a walk had circled three bases with exceeding speed. It did not look very good for the tigers at this juncture. Another earned run for the hungry giants of the night lights and a spark of hope was given to the tigers as their shortstop began to lend some support. The tiger shortstop began quoting to the pitcher Tommy boy and his teammates abroad "tigers never die." Still no outs so far and the eighth and ninth batters of the giants batting order were up next. Xavier had faith in Tommy boy the tiger fighting and the shortstop with others went into crouch stances of attentive heads up baseball and the tigers from this point intended to make a pride striking assault of a comeback. Defensive fielding had to take place if this 2 to 0 deficit was to be tamed for Xavier's at bat leading off the bottom of the second to come. Batters eight and nine were handled well in this no out one on situation for a pitcher. The eight spot grounded to first base for an unassisted play and out number one was made. The nine spot managed to eek out a fluke pop fly to the outfield, the right fielder of the tigers made a fluke catching of a baseball and the spark flame was lit for the tiger team. Unfortunately for Tommy boy and Xavier they now were dealing with a runner on third base who had tagged up after the right fielder catch. A man on third base, two outs, one run was scored in the bottom of the inning and the giants lead off batter was up at the plate again for the second time in two innings. A pitch from Tommy boy and a swing with a one ball and no strike count. Contact is made by the giants' lead off hitter but this contact fell short of the damage that the giants were hoping to further inflict. The second shortstop handled the slow grounder fast enough and he threw the runner out at first handily. One and a half innings done and the score was in the giants favor at 2 to 0. The bottom of the second inning came and other than Xavier getting a lead off double it was followed by a one two three bottom half with Xavier ending up standing at third base which he had managed to steel in rare form. The top of the third was next so Tommy boy and Xavier with the rest of the tigers took the playing field once again. The tigers wanted to dominate the diamond in this case. they had hopes that the lead off batter in the bottom of the third who was the eighth spot of the tigers lineup could spark another flame into the life of this team. All of a sudden something had really gotten into Tommy boy, you might have assumed his first name the same and his last name to be John one might say? Fire brewed in tiger eyes and Tommy ends up striking out the side after a lead off triple that had sent the infield into states of fear and Tommy and Xavier turned into ice bloods. Two and a half innings out of the way and in the bottom of the third eight nine of the order and the lead off batter for the tigers team despite hoping for some life had fallen victim to the red hot giants pitcher going down in the order they came. The giants took a 3-0 lead in the top of the fourth inning due to an infield error. The bottom of the fourth had come and the second half reserves were in already. Batter two of the tiger lineup was to lead off for a rally. Rally cap time had arrived for the tiger bench sitters. Sitting pretty was the near crowd of the blue birds. The crows of the follower riser advisory grew the flowers in their fields. The flower was once a rosebud for the wisest of disguised misers and given unto the symbol of the tiger was the red risen lions. Bottom four and inside out the tigers' baseball caps in a line on their dugout bench. The entire tiger team made a crying for the wolves sleeping. The batter was up for the bottom of the fourth in this six inning duel. The two spot of the tigers line up finally got to the giants pitcher, something no player on the tigers had done so far in this game other than Xavier. A soft blooper single sparking some tiger life into their blood as it began to boil and the ice bloods of Tommy boy and Xavier cooled the feel of the eyes blazed of this fire. Low key motions of tigers in motions, baseballs' heroic emotions, and small crowd commotion gave the team player at bat commencement as this shortstop sparker stepped to the plate. A 3-2 full count for the third time came for the fighting batter of this at bat followed by a slamming crack outbound to deep center field. The ball jetted outward and hit a wooden advertisement located on the center field fence. A triple for the shortstop and the tiger dugout cheers aloud with stomping feet and the rally was on. Xavier had taken off all catching gear and he entered the batters box on the lefty side of which this cleanup power lefty always had hit. He takes his stance and awaited the next pitch. Three spot of the order the shortstop at large stands at third base, he was pleased to have earned another RBI bringing the score to 3-1. No outs thus far and clean up four spot awaited with anticipation for a strike down the pike. A fast ball of a woven spinning sped straight forward and a first pitch swing from Xavier makes solid contact! A loud aluminum bat and baseball clank sounded. Xavier knocked the ball in a pull hit to right field. The ball flew so high into the night skylights of the kid park that this small white speck of a ball had disappeared in the black sky. The baseball came back into eyesight it was falling with speedy velocity down the right field foul line. Chasing towards the short outfield fence was the small right fielder reserve for the giants. He neared the fence and the ball falling but his efforts were to be of no avail. The baseball clanked off of the right field foul pole. A two run home run for Xavier and the tiger team this was. The tiger bench and the tiger parents and friends went into frenzied madness and Xavier rounded the bases with the shortstop congratulating him at home plate. This home run tied the game at three runs a piece and the tiger players remembered to remain low key although the excitement of the moment was uncanny and to be remembered. Still no outs and the giants coaching squad felt the pressure. A meeting took place at the pitchers mound. It seemed that the star pitchers' one hitter through three was not to be the positive outcome that the giants were hoping for. "What's going on out here?" the giants head coach questioned the star pitcher at this mound meeting. "I've been throwing my arm out this inning but I have some left." Coach speaks "There's no outs and you just got shellacked I'm going to have to put you in the outfield now." The giant's pitcher became angry and he thought things over "I have to confess that I threw some spit balls back in the first, this team is the comeback of the year but I can handle it coach." The coach of the giants thought momentarily and made a decision "This next guy gets on and I'm pulling you for sure, you will be in right field and I'm bringing in our second baseman who's been bitching for a win like this all season." The giants head coach patted his pitchers hat head and went back to the dugout. Bases clear no outs, bottom four, 3 to 3 and the five spot for the tigers steps up. The five spot batter did not fair so well although he didn't strike out a grounder to short was fielded like a pro and he was easily thrown out at first base. Batter six reached from a nervous balk but the coach of the giants saw improvement but he had signaled to his second baseman that he might be called in. The seven slot spot hitter walked giving the tigers a first and second base taking with still just one out. After this given up walk the giants' coach patted the back of his forearm and the second baseman walked the short distance to the mound and threw a small series of warm up pitches. The pitcher star had been sent to left field position. The emotion was not dead for the tiger team but the frenzied feeling went into neutral. The tigers concentrated on what was to be done next. Warm ups were done and no relay throw for an infield due to the runners at first and second base. The new pitcher was ready and the last batter of the tigers order stood in the box with an unorthodox straight standing batting stance. A pitch thrown with two strikes and a surprise fluke single hit went luckily through first and second. Now the bases were loaded with one out. The lead off batter was off of his game, he made a tough at bat for an intimidating day so far of 0 for 2. Another full count was reached and an amazing foul ball hit took place. Tigers lead off hitter hit the ball backwards over the back stop and concession stand into the parking lot. Xavier looked on and commented in humor "that one would have been out of here backwards." Looks of approving agreement from the coaches of the tigers back at Xavier and the next pitch was taken low and away. "BALL FOUR TAKE YOUR BASE!" celebration came from the dugout again as the runners advanced and the walk brought home the go ahead run. The bottom of the fourth inning would end with a fierce determined strikeout but the tigers managed to score another run beforehand. End of four and the score was tigers 5 giants 3. The fifth inning was preceded by what would be considered the seventh inning stretch in a major league nine inning outing. Festivities were special on this little league night in this town for the special one game playoff of which it was. The public address system of the kid park made celebratory tradition of a country with the words of the park announcer speaking through it with your minor microphone ringing and static voice coverings obscure. The fourth inning stretch ended and the coach of the tigers had felt that it was due time to have a pitching change. A bench warmer in usual games was to replace Tommy boy at the pitcher position in positron and Tommy boy would still be needed for a possible hit for a win or an insurance run. The tigers coaching staff met and decided that Tommy boy would take his other position at first base. This reserve took the mound and began his warm up pitches. Ten pitches of a warming up and the reserve pitcher let the last one fly. A loud pop into the catcher's mitt of the reserve catcher and it was once again time for baseball. Work was still cut out for the tiger team despite a two run advantage. In this top of the fifth Xavier was at first forced to field some beginning wild pitches of this replacements pitching start. A walk starts of the inning followed by a double play of rare form for a little league outing and things were looking up for this tiger team. Because of the young age of this pitcher aged at only ten it was a fact that he would only be acquired for minimal relief. With a no on and two out advantage some of the more powerful hitters for the giants were to get at bats. Consecutive doubles knocked in one run cutting the tiger lead to 5-4. The last batter of the inning wore on the arm of this ten year old boy young for a pitcher in this level of play. Coaching batting strategy was taken by the last batter as he took the first pitch and the second pitch was a called strike with an iffy location. A couple inside pitches a foul ball at the back stop and finally the kid got the batter out with an infield fly. The third baseman was to call this straight up in the air shot and he did so like a pro waving his shortstop to the left of him away. He made the catch handily and the tigers went into the bottom fifth leading 5-4. The giants' pitcher who had replaced their star starter gained stature and he was getting to the tiger team's esteem as he needed to. A certainty momentum swing despite the fact that his team was behind. He went forward pitching a 1, 2, 3 inning including two strikeouts. Top of the sixth was coming and the giants only needed one run for a tie and two to go ahead. The minimal relief reserve wanted to go back out but it would be another that would be chosen to replace him. The third baseman came into to pitch for the top sixth. Xavier might have been a choice for replacement at this time but coaching felt a win was more than possible and that it might be better to have Xavier start game one of the pennant and to save as much of him as possible. Warm up pitches taken and Xavier threw to second base for the final infield relay of the tiger day. Sixth inning pay ball time and batter one of the top of the sixth for the giants walked up to home plate for a lead off hit. A lead off hit it was. Yes, a sharply hit ball into right center and a solid leadoff single for the first giant batter of this last inning. The second batter of this inning came up to bat and Xavier was looking out for a steel of second base with side eye vision. Another pitch after a foul tip and a sacrifice moved the runner to second. One out and a runner on second base and the new pitcher adjusted his hat preparing for a closing to a needed tiger win. The next batter of the giant order ripped a crack of a line drive to the gap of left center field. A relay from the deep outfield was of commencement and the tiger cutoff man performed his task of the cutoff catch at second with exact perfection. The lead runner was heading to home plate but a play of wit with the word maybe added to it was executed. The hitter had gotten selfish and he wanted a triple instead of a double so instead of finishing the relay to home for a Xavier tag out an easy trick toss and tag was made on the runner advancing to third. This made it two outs with no runners on and the score was now tied at 5-5. Tiger coaching approached the mound and this was a rare case. A talk ensued between the new pitcher who had been the evening's third baseman, Xavier, and the head coach of this tiger team. Decision made, and Xavier agreed to come in if any runners got on base within the remainder of this top of the sixth inning. Some kicking of the dirt in front of the rubber, Xavier crouches into his catching position, the infield and the outfield tiger players squatted in baseball fielding stance preparation and the tiger coaches look on in hope for a last at bat succession. The star of the giants was the nemesis player in this case and he was the opposite fashioned player to Xavier in ways of the qualities of their work in the pass time game. He batted righty, Xavier batted lefty, he was a slow runner and a power house, Xavier was a fast runner with dexterity and a power hitter despite, this nemesis was a smart experienced type of catcher who acquired knowledge from work, Xavier was simply a natural, but Xavier would have to live up to his nick name of power lefty of which his nemesis had respectfully termed him during the season for in this top of the sixth the pressure was on all involved. The pitcher winds up and threw an opening pitch that the batter just took for strike one. Another pitch came and it was inside and taken for a ball. With the count at one ball and one strike the catcher for the giants did the millennium routine dragging on the minutes of baseball nerved and anxious intense. With helmet fastened in place and a one and one count the pitcher wound up and threw another fastball. Down the pike this fastball came with heat and a pure swift swing from this giant made contact and he belted the baseball into the deep outfield. Down came the baseball and it hit a tree in back of the fence for an automatic home run. The giants celebrate in what appeared as a mean team gesture but that is the way of the game and the name of the game was written in minds planning as Xavier looked to the unknown player of the team in right field as the replacement he was, the two of them felt some pain and Xavier made a hand gesture request. A raised hand from Xavier and the coaches agreed with Xavier that it was time for him to pitch for a final out. Two outs, no runners on base, and the giants had taken a one run lead with this home run of giants' heroics of a moment and tiger dismay. Xavier takes the mound for proper. He wields baseball in hand and he felt the stitches of it sternly and firmly hard with the thin yet strong muscles of his fingering. The reserve catcher was in and crouching. Xavier bent in crouch not slouching. A series of three throws met the mitts arrival. The next inning to come and a new giant and tiger created rival. "STRIKE THREE" three straight perfect whizzing past the batter Xavier had faced and the top of the sixth was over. Bottom of the sixth was here and two with other molded a new escape for a win and survival. The giants took the field for the bottom of this sixth inning. Xavier was hoping for another at bat and . . . . chance for victory and it was a run to tie two runs to win so he began pacing in nervous habit. The new pitcher who had gotten off to a rocky start for his giants team was still on. Xavier was not an easily intimidated kid but momentum shifted like wind in a hole filled tunnel when this kid heats up. The first at bat for the tigers in this last-up for them was a virtual joke of a dying cause. The pitcher had matched Xavier's top of the sixth strike out with one of his own. Three pitches three strikes and a rare relay of inspiration was a throwing throw around of the tiger's non-existent poise at this point. The second spot of the order was 0 for 2 with a walk, he was next at bat with one down but before him was the first slot who had game statistics identical. A series of pitches it took in this case but no play on wisdom ball game day for the tiger life remains dismayed. A shallow pop fly was called in the air and caught by the shortstop for the giants. Two outs, no runners on base, and the replacement right fielder who had been eyeing Xavier beforehand got ready to step up. Xavier began to talk with him before his at bat while the giants reserves were on the bench chanting the word over and over in reminiscence of a Chicago "shanana hey hey goodbye" chanting and singing. The word rattled the two in talking over a clutch pulling out of a baseball miracle and the giants bench continued in unison repeating of a death chant "HISTORY!" "HISTORY!" "HISTORY!" "HISTORY" and the two ball players decided the scenario. The reserve right fielder stepped into the batter's box. Xavier had suggested a bunt and the boy they called Bill in a kidding liked the idea but he was to opt according to the pitches of which he received. Fought hard he did with a pitch count tally of 8 pitches and a full count. A few swings were taken in this at bat for Bill. So was he to swing away and outrun against odds? Was he to bunt and outrun against even worse odds? Was ball four going to be thrown? A wind up and an illegal curve for this league undetected by the umpires flew slow and in side. Bill was in gear and he lays a perfect bunt down the first base line that was strange from the way the curve ball made it spin and stop in the right place halfway down the first base base line. The giants' pitcher covered first as the first baseman and the catcher for the giants collided in confusion of the play. Bill reached first but this collision was not ruled as an error. A runner was on and Xavier was up. This was a chance for a tie or a walk off winning home run worth two. Xavier decided not to take the first pitch so he swung for the fence on this first pitch and the bat caught the bottom half of the ball. In field pop fly of roughly 30 feet in midair fell downward in normal velocity and the catch was made by the giants' pitcher. Pop into a glove and the giants celebrate further. The game was over and the Tigers knew they had made a valiant effort and a pass standard season comeback team they were for sure. Xavier and the right fielder who was held at first base in a hoping for a clutch win took it like the boys they were. Teams gathered back in their dugouts and the tradition line went across the field whereas all of the players slapped hands and said to one another "good game." And so they did. Xavier left a while after for his sector home with father guardian. They walked out to the parking lot and low and behold it was Zimmerman the man with Luzzin and they seemed to be a bit under the influence on this baseball night. Zimmerman with class of a fellow player said to Xavier "good game kid." Luzzin exposed a beverage for a person of 21 years of age or older that was hidden behind his back. Luzzin looked at Zimmerman the man like a wise guy in humor of a friendly ragging and he looked back at Xavier and said "Don't forget to tell your father about detentions next week." The guardian looked at a fearing son and asked him "Xavier did you get another week of detention?" Xavier answered with a yes and guardian father smacked him upside the head. And so it was a final tally Giants 6 tigers 5.

9

IN PLASMA THE guesses made of the gaseous minding endorphin blew in the formation of paper torn confetti for the new order confederates. The merits of the prophetic poems grew time in tours of those hidden for industrial in a city rising. Disguised was the prince vagabond in anti to a doomsday machine. Resolute was the deceived who led him in the future. She was guided in guiding of the primitive mover astronomical. Negative upheavals became of sterile hardness. Positive downplay felt the healing of evil good. The Eden lots of stone were disintegrating for the home stand. The pirates learn the new words. The army of growth termed the owing birds. In flight was the ostrich possum sculpted on scalp from the seeking of new clay. And the trinity gone mad soothed souls from the facilities of a boy's room educational faculty. "Guys?" Xavier refers to Luzzin and Zimmerman the man in reference of a downward Monday morning. "Yes Xavier what's wrong?" "I'm just kind of upset about something?" Zimmerman the man knew for certain that Xavier was going to be very upset on this depressing morning from his over the weekend loss to the giants. Luzzin could be overheard farting while he defecated in the graffiti strewn stall at the other end of the bathroom and he asked a question "where the hell is the toilet paper?" Xavier in such a depressed state of mind could not answer Luzzin as he and Zimmerman the man ignored him and Zimmerman begins to give his condolences "I suppose you're in mourning over the game you guys blew on Friday huh?" "Well any respectable pro would be wouldn't they?" "Yes Xavier just look of the good old sox it hasn't been since 1918 since a World Series champion title for them.

Do you think Yaz, Fisk, Lynn, Evans or Rice for that matter never felt this way?" "Yeah I know it wasn't that good for them last season but the 1986 official season started in April and hey May was good. They could heal my baseball depression it has only been 68 years know what I'm sayin?" Before Zimmerman could respond with anything at all Luzzin slammed open a stall door in livid fury and pain with his corduroys hanging as if his zipper did not work "You'd think the custodial staff could put some god damn tee pee in these stalls over the weekend!" he whispered in angered talking volume and the two of the baseball audio talking took Luzzin's self talk rhetorical as a directive comment to themselves in personal. Zimmerman tried to raz Xavier to somehow improve double x's depression "You had to pop fly for a third out didn't you? A pop up sucks in that scenario you know? A pop out, like your pop when he has his weekends?" Luzzin found his tee pee fix and joined his two friends, he added to the humor and thus he opened a bad can of worms "A pop up? What great ever popped up in the clutch?" A conniption was nature's option at this point but another one might ruin the red sox season in this year of 86 so Xavier simply let loose in angered quotations "HHGGYYAAAGH! WHAT DID YAZ DO IN HIS FIRST CLUTCH SITUATION? ANSWER HE POPPED UP, IN 1978 WHAT DID HE DO? HE POPPED UP, AND WHAT HAPPENED AT THE END HE POPPED UP!" Zimmerman the man and Luzzin looked on in fear of a shocking moment expected and said together a question "Yaz popped up?" "NO ASSHOLES I DID!" Zimmerman the man and Luzzin felt the fueled fire of yesteryear and the three who planned a possible switching to parochial school next year dreamed the revenge of year 1967's impossible dream. Xavier had not exceeded his inner goals of a personal endearing. Commanded he was inherently so and as his inner soul had bent and curved with universal genuine a non existent clairvoyance magical non existent did exist. Geniuses posed as enemies but friends they indeed were forthright and although skepticism dominated his days, the originality of the sector, and his family members including the sixth of the jibe his mother felt the times of the burdened neighbors anew to be honored with inheritances. God contemplated a will thought Xavier and so it was as the week passed by Xavier would take into consideration his feeble priorities and in his self questionings of his parent's parental teachings of maturity he confided in grandfather and grandmother thus opting to attend parochial school once the pro baseball summer and the summer school vacation ended. Xavier awaited the bell on the last day of the seventh grade, he focused a vow of vile intentions to an ultimate outcome, he moved as a diagonal pawn killing towards the queen only to see a sighting he had seen on any given day, and so the truth shall set us free. The bell rang and the students and teachers said their goodbyes. Xavier after school had managed to convince Zimmerman the man and Luzzin who lived in the proper district to join him and attend parochial school with him for the eighth grade. The dream was still alive.

10

XAVIER IN HIS seven year recreation process of molecular renewal of his stem cell life had confided in the cruelty of the seasons of the school year. He was to reach his first year of his teen years over the summer. In the passing of paces of his ventures he imaged in more than hindsight outcomes of his services completed in futures time. From his other self the alias inspired clues for his safety whereof this alias for Xavier had placed in wordings of public scriptures, entertainments, graffiti, and in the basic decoy articles of media gurus for the people of an ultimate oneness; a sector whole of sectors inclusive of the sector of the five jibe and as a whole in methods of sanity this was the cleansing of deceivers. Such outcomes were unfortunately taken into consideration by Xavier's supposed enemies as a back down. Intuitive to damnation was his new burden but undone was an unwilling transport karma plot intended to dignify the absolution existences of natural evil in the ultimate view of the good it truly is. For forbidden evil morbid a match from heaven with hell grew within the no plot escapist of Xavier a beginning of an anesthesia, a deoxyribonucleic bonding of water, prosthetic, workers for a new world order, those who were to soothe the order and see to it a taming existence within, trust, seven virtues, seven deadly sins, an eighth connection, and an added eighth to the seven wonders of the world, significance, an era of the something, the nothingness of lies from pains intended, summits, diplomacy abroad global, a fighting of phobias, inspirations contaminated by resulted falsehood beliefs and vice versa positives of tyrants with unseen values discredited, leaders, followers, and the average person affected by all of the above. Insurmountable uncertainty was set in the future from a head laceration and an injection smart, indescribable, and this matter of the subjective object created by true evils of no end undignified with this action by modes parallel was set on a setting. Only the grams of an owing of a net weight two fold in the paid credit for Xavier in receiving could send him in the direction correctly as this matter from outer universal informed was a hope material gathered elemental, it would defy the object set in an incubator for reduction. Nevertheless the central gland of Xavier's brain was to defy the created object as well for they did not know who or what he was. Lowness of the gram from outside the existence of escaping dusts in solar winds outbound would cling to the back triad connection to the brain and the spine giving evidence of uni-gender persona and everlasting relations to the serums pro and con. The cling was magnetized to the part of a mind making the difference for a reference. This would be the line of opposite reactions of time conception's understandings by both sexes. The object was a complexity algorithm growth of programming, it was made from the silica turned to silicon but the cactus trips of the realist lovers had made devising and the family of the sun sees value in Lincoln subconsciously and the cities of land and the cities sights in payments that were currency thus had the value of the nothing man. Mockery dealer called boy grew in sanity illusive and he slept in the center of mayhem sectors of a bordering ruler, he dreamed the dreams of a chameleon. The object was a computer chip placed in the head. This object was not to be victorious as expected for the existence of holy was whole and escaped the alias had done and he won again, but he still could not afford his bus fair. The operation injection into the cranium was mystery of a process. The excess of the process made something brew a womb victim. The victim in prison defied the existence of something and in the form of nothingness was an era. An error was the era termed. The claiming dawn's vitamins vitality underworlds are inspired by the grub worm. Storms for the merit credits sent shots into a lightning flash and the thunder was pushed to the future. Optimism pathetic was new torture in a falling of a fall season. Reasons would not be heard by the origin religious lie. The X marked the name of a Xavier back in time and in year 1996 A.D. the microchip device was set for a delusion caused but the delusion alias moved through time and dimensions reflecting no dementia, and so it was in his head and so in 2011 A.D. the alias was a revenge victim stigmatized from re flux pain, addiction, and gastritis. He this Xavier alias she called Jonah rested after the dismissal of Renessa and in his resting for a recovery a new clue was discovered sent back from year of 2019 A.D. A savior guide knew of a prophecy of 2020 privatized, hidden, and obscured. This communicated in avenging the unfounded revenge against Xavier Alias Jonah in 2011 A.D. by an opposite method and the testing tourists on a side envisioned the unit member of the five and the one who had carried on the meaning of oneness. Xavier in views of an original waits as a patient patiently for a rescue from an S.O.S. he sent in 2009 A.D. Greenhouses were of affect for the gardens above and in due time the common time bonded of no years existed equal to universal time, they were made into a noun matter of solid state anticipation. A blackout; A decoy or a saving of the wrath child? The peacemakers walk in the direction of a black light and a skull shot saw the mind of a cured plague. A screen, a reel, an auditory audio reporting was to send the information and Xavier Alias Jonah had witnessed a blackout.

11

IT WAS THE year of 2011 Renessa had left with some stolen items for her safety, a cell phone, a gun, and a garment of her liking. She had left her boyfriend Jonah with the memory of an embracing and the hazed garments of a mater. In the questionings downed by plagues the horrors of drawn negative photon picture frame simulated stimuli with similarity to hell's gates, she wandered waiting in a foot pace dramatic! The alley way strewn with heroin syringes and bottles was the stone setting. Mortified was she on her sensuality peering a scorn to her will and the night that was of sub zero weather in lateness of a winter that made her reality demonic and original. Vision she was despite her incisions in her brain as it was and in dangers of her kind it was her Jonah. He in sedation had followed her on her leaving. He sighted a still guard of the downs mystery, a leading of inner minds guided to a purpose of the X man. Jonah peace walks with insufficient blows to the skulls alive. Prayers of Hitler and Pran argued with the cats of vile ages and in the dark of lunacy sanity lunar a twinkle solid of masses gastric sent light of red to blue in the hands of a clock tower. The gun was a gun for definition of the bay girl and the curse curvature crusted the land of the south east. A wind blew in the location of this freezing night and the Jesus stain of the escape white sheet met the dawn light of a darkened section. Ex double x alias Jonah runs after the girl Renessa and timed her eyeballs for in light they were to embrace once again. The gun was a foil and the communication device was the new defense for the covenant. Conversion planes of a peninsula and a desolate developing bordered within and a flowed folding of a new globe. A garden snake representation slicker like an eel in waters foaming and the cored colored owing of the new dawn left the professionals in the esteemed right of the victim of the assault on a just on with the symbol of the dead termed not deemed able exhaled with four letters written in blood! D.O.W.N. the initials stood for dawns over wars neutral. Hopes in vision were the eyes of all beheld. The representative garden tool eel transferred inheritance cosmically in comic. The Town underrated timed things with the name of the brother. The mother grieved the dry cut clotting in her inexperience. The mater sent something and inns of uncommon wealth took a breath of neutral matter. The cats scattered, serums battered creating the man of the minute it was the wielder of a spoon and the white felines strayed the crusted peninsula called Cape Cod at noon time. Luck dogs, big hogs, smogs, and two brothers of the anti click witnessed the skipping of the princess frogs. For the X man now termed by a short love affair he in upward tempo terms terminated acclaims identity as the Jonah he was for only the brother to this son had seen the green minnows who sought a new dawn and dusk. Night grew the chlorine unclear if sterilization could and it had floated. The stench marsh pool was a moat and the sheep, shepherd, and goat spread into the orange and soon to be red horizon in rare form. Tomorrow had arrived and it already seemed like yesterday. Torn eye cat up at bat hits a grand slam. Back in the dark of urban mania growing the hysteria of mass bred this lady. Jonah made a final pass at her and when Renessa made her safety call Jonah fell into a deep sleep of a silent night in the room of a new set original time forming new born for sky world temptations. The bottles replaced the candled and a pair of sneakers becoming stained are worn sandals and a white robe was stripped as a t shirt from a peasant by another visitor her name was Nikita and she would not fall short of inner glory and true self satisfaction. Mind you the guard with the sneaking and the sand was nor, nil, and lesser but confession to a confidant aided as all let them eat cake. Kind feel made a slice of cake a bread as if it were a multiplicity of a fish. Old men of a seizing saw sights in easy and forgiveness is easy. A rose dropped and the drips drifted and caught the drift and felt the gifted as two moved closer to the bond and may have been like the spy of the same name. Sunday morning arrived and Xavier alias Jonah shook the hand of Bill W once again. A new star and another David makes seven a trinity three and a ministry outlook made hope for a world to stand in unification. B.E.A.U.T.I.F.I.C.A.T.I.O.N . . . . . . initials-bonded education affection under time if fighting is controlled at times in oblivious notions! That was a potion. "Thank you." 2?

12

THE SUMMER OF 1986 might had been reminiscent, a backlash brew in aged stigmatized eye lids but the lids of the beer cans were uncorked for the two young illegals who saw a river revere and in their stares they had invited Xavier up into the stairways of the ominous sky worlds, it was to be discovered by the wanna be trinity of Xavier, Zimmerman the man, and Luzzin that eyes inside are blazing fire and that the last temptation is acquired from the memories of our lifetimes nostalgic. The clocks were ticking and the tocks in between guarded as if they were the black centers of enlarged in eyes and hazel actions of change surrounding since the times of the sand ventures and the prisms in the third dimension. Colors of a globe and the smells are of familiarity. June passed by very fast, so fast it might had made even the great Albert Einstein reconsider his term for fast time passing with stern and vivid sweat toiled realizations. July might had been a god send but it was the oneness of Xavier as an individual and solstice time of June that had fended and gossip had began among those of a new walk and talk. A lingo was created dismantled and underrated it had faded and so it was that a message was sent in the form of a letter. The young man of a new age teen spat on some glue and in an enveloped message with some cooperation from the guidance and the advisories of four members of the jibe primarily sister Sarah this letter was stamped and sent to the parochial faculty of the nearby private school that was to sadly close down some ten years later. Xavier had decided that he would take on a more mature attitude during this upcoming school year and with healthier habits he thought it possible for himself to achieve a sufficient enough grade point average so that he would pass an entrance test and attend either the affiliate parochial high school or to the rather he could consider attending the all boys high school that was rumored to be in the city that was a spark to its twin nearby and had become the birthplace of the industrial revolution of the United States of America, mind you this was of the era of the originals. August passed as fast as June and Xavier who had since decided to at least drop his corny and conceited nickname of double X. He was practicing his power lefty batting swing. Xavier loved his red sox but he was not hesitant to try hard for the senior league team he was to be picked by, rumor had it that he was being eyed by a team he despised none other than the senior league evil empire "YES" the Yankees. If X marked the spot Xavier would be the newest member of a rebel force. On an early September morning Xavier awakened with anticipation in groggy motions of your common tired bed stretching of the arms. Hopped out of bed he did in almost literal fashion so literal that when he stood on his two hind legs he straightened, and he was willing to try to touch his toes. From this enthusiasm for this upcoming scholar to be he believed he would in an attempt that had passed his common attempts prior wield the simplicity of a time key. They were feeble attempts if one was overly critical. Running and batting practice would prove to be more of a payoff. Parochial school with religion for a class and Xavier wondered if his friends whom he had only conversed with once during this legend summer were going to show. After all Xavier had realized beforehand that school was one of the last priorities on minds of vision children. Downstairs he skip hopped in the new blue parochial uniform with a tie. Out the front door of his good old fashioned house with the thought "they don't make them like they used to." Through the neighborhood of written love letters Xavier might have buttoned his cardigan required but the September New England air was not of a chill and he did not want the weekend to come too fast. It was only a half mile walk on this nice day in fall. Through this acre he stepped near a steeple and his persona grew in times of tectonic Korea under seas. He passed a gold dome and stared at others entering the other private school schoolyard halfway through it was to be his first of school years timed routine walks. A fastening of his tie, a brushing of his blue button down of which he had not removed every pin from its packaging, a frustration with his grandmother for a non allowance of his common brown boat shoes and his more with it parochial uniform blue corduroys. There was to be twelve other students in his class so he was told several days ago by the teacher he was to meet on this day. Of course he hoped for his school chums of the year before but nevertheless his dawning and what he was donning lifted the origin heights, it shined on his hair lightening it. Into the lot Xavier peered as he swallowed the last gulp down of the 50 cent hot dog with ketchup, mustard, and relish leaving a tiny drip stain on his heart. If A equaled C the studious one knew a perfect tie fastening this was Omar, if any one could see the non graduate she might had sealed the new words, if the basketball was flat Wayne would have been there the night before, if the beautiful one was staring the stars would gather this was Nina, if the Bears were to challenge the home team that year the refrigerator would be challenged by Flip the freezer but the geezer had yelled too much, if Lauren was around you might not see her but the snowballs of ice would sting from the dynamics of her throwing, if an apple was on the teachers desk Guido would eat it after he gave it, if the janitor was around the apple would one day be investigated, the prognosticate two predicted? If the other girl named Lauren was there you could here the words of a Journey, if Tamera had been nearby a yelling would become your sonata, if Xavier had talked with Stacy the right to bare arms most definitely remained, she was the devil. Small talk ensued between Xavier and his friend find acquaintance anew. It was Wayne, he in courtesy of a meeting of the minds of saint hoods counting to twelve with the thirteenth writing the letters on her ceiling made Xavier comfortable and welcomed as if waited on at the local eatery called "Eat at Joes." Kindergarten through eight was unorthodox to the new student of a morning walk but orthodox and a parish would teach the atheist, the believers, the caring, and the wanderers of choices elsewhere new religion old religion what's the difference? "What's the difference?" A line was called to formation by the front doors of this elementary parliamentary result happy, and so the leaser on ceiling made ways in minds for legends on walls of stalls. Her depression would awaken the angels. Eleven in line standing a band of kids set to judge commandments. "One more time and you can put it out." Zimmerman the man tossed cigarette on sidewalk to Zimmerman liking. A mild surprise entered the line. Zimmerman and Luzzin stepped in slapstick silent like a Chaplin. One monk moment punk saw time in fractions. One class seriousness comic intention at his side knew practices of the stepping paths that lay. Xavier sighted them as the lines walked in after the sound of the school buzzer and jokingly called out "Look its Harpo and Groucho!" Thirteen students entered this old brick school.

13

FLASHED FORWARD BACK into the year of 2011 1985 was on Xavier's dark dream mind sedated and 1986 success was rendered incomprehensible and futile. The nostalgia of that time had left him devouring past devising of his mind's dreams to and fro. Henceforth momentum had shimmered in forms of a memoir flash forward. A déjà vu this was not! Picture frames with broken glass had sadly been covered with the dusts materialized beyond incoming existences. This shattered dream had taken a toll but in others he might see the true meanings of his past and his past statements are termed as quotations deemed in dismayed morbid time with undying will and so the hovering remnant noun called human fulfillment takes solid form. Renessa was unfortunately gone and soon he would meet with others who are there for him, a boy by the name of Cooper and two of a moment still are anonymous for a reason. Xavier still felt like her Jonah and despite his being stranded on this theoretical island a rescue attempt had been made by a stroke of luck. Her Jonah had not earned his short lived freeing from a mending hand lend and the efforts he made for survival following his 39th birthday just might had led to inspiration from such mishaps that distracted him, angered slams of devices, advisory commissions, and the down terms of his times. Coop had parachuted like a drawn butterfly it reminded her Jonah of the mystery actions unknown of one D.B. Cooper. 1995; "SLAM!" an angered young man at a New York bus station slammed down the pay phone he had used to call a local figure. This Alienated youngster aged in his early twenties was the death pledge to the combine of disguises. He was the pro to a Gordian knot passage ala pencil vein of the I.A. otherwise known as the international alliance. Alienated pathetic hypothetical and not theoretical. His council was the anti-number a down five lie and a single numeral to be filled by an Englishman, a Cambodian, and an anonymous figure astray. 555-1212 was a number known to an American for a long time but the information profound was not astounding. The peasant was filled with holes. Out for a sneaking seek of a mystic find this youngster wandered in stomping rage and he was magnetized like the origin mammal evolution in eon neon natural. Amid the dew mist of the past hour that made his skin feel the feelings familiar in stimulation, it was live and he spotted his secret taking at the corner of a five and dime. Into a beat up moving truck formerly owned by a moving company he turned the key lock like an escape artist Italian with the proper utensil of a thief. Inside were the weapons of a practice and with the jump start required he drove forward calmly enough. He rounded the corner into a lighted dark night New York Street. The modes modular were obtained and the screens inside lit the fires of hydrogen peroxide oxygen. Democratic Kampuchea 1949; a planning required early very early to say the least might have not been enough nevertheless backwards communication ala presto! Key dreams from the jack traitor trade and the maze is fucked up. Straight line stupidity strategy of the time was perception for a match flame. It flew on some wood edifice and a pacifist pessimist sprinted home to his anonymity with bright lights inside. The picket sign could not and the flame from silk cloth made at Silicon Valley was deemed inefficient for a defense plot. The future moved prime numbers on screens and the decoy straight line saw no result. A transport domestic import export sent the hydrogen peroxide for some wound wiping and some pain did soothe. No move "DAGGER ONE SENDS FILIPINE GROOVE!" "SLAM" after a yelling into a phone. Dial tone silent and New Years 2012 was to be festive for the driver of a truck. Decent months remembered and a print from a sprinting became at midnight.

14

THOU ART THING might be a terminology old school for the fools of the minority combines but the sectioned secular five jibe was in from a pass move. Demented not, cemented around from corners odd on a five fingered star symbol is not the fear symbol nor is it a symbolized phobia. Claustraphobia forum surrounded utopia it was. Seven was a numeral significant for the symbols doped up on the other side of the city but the five jibe erased petty matters on this day and so it was that such amusing happenings like the big wheel race became feeble on mind. The sectioned secular five were in, out, and about and so it was in this case of past phenomena futuristic that a realistic tom fool named Xavier Xevon Tareynton of the liberty humanities was to have the experience of lessons survived in the days of his early youth. Father guardian, mother who was not of the sector, Sister Sarah, and Xavier were to fall victim to a plot and experience this lesson. In it was a blackout. It was still summer but late summer mind you and to the flock's underworld of the sensationalist crows they bore colors on prisms. The full moon night was to become the only lighting of this neighborhood. "What was that?" Sister Sarah asked curiously with puzzled expression. A sound of a clanking was heard outside as family ate dinner in common ending of their work week routine. Lines of aged wrinkles intrusive to a man's aura, a look of knowledge, subconscious discontent, and nonsensical surety was on father guardian's face. Wide eyes from father, a brow bending like a man from mother and a neck and head spin turn from Xavier nearly giving him whiplash and thus awakening him from a supper time daydream. Cat scratch fight outside and an ending to a trash can top fall clank, and a 90 degree spinning. Theorized as a top spindle of the sort a creator of a sound as advanced nature and the unexplained had spoken with whispering wind resulted. The result was this sound a pottery Vaseline glistening and the jelly on bread faded to the petroleum of which this Vaseline was in texture and color in shadows fallen. Lights out, and in a split second the starting of what was to be a lengthy neighborhood blackout was of immediate commencement. Sister Sarah's face was faded in darkness as only dim light from outside coming from a glowing powered down streetlight, it curved her outline for what seemed to be less than a second. All of the lights were out and nothing was visible other than their even darker outlines of their beings. "Huuuh!" mother takes inward gasps and exhales them as one maintaining immediate composure. "What happened?" cried Xavier in trembling anxious fear of a post infancy nerve. Father interrupts and ends the panic in the darkened room. "Oh no it looks like a power outage I know this house like the back of my hand it's been a while that we've been living here, the flashlight is in our bedroom sweetness I'll go get it." "Yes but hurry up I'll keep an eye on the kids." "Yeah good one in this blackness you'd be lucky to find your own head." "Just get it be careful though and thank you the kids and I will be fine." "Yes?" sarcasm frustration from the mouth of the father. Father guardian carefully made his way to the parents bedroom while the other three of a family waited nervous and patiently. He slowly and carefully opened his bedroom door having only knocked down a few petty items along the way. "Oh yeah batteries!" father guardian came to a vivid down of a stupidity realization as he had noticed that the emergency flashlight for such occasions was empty so he retrieved some large triple A batteries after emptying three dresser draws thus leaving a pile of his wife's clothes strewn across their bedroom floor along with some picture albums and a collection of bills and mortgage receipts. "Here they are!" father's discovery somehow made the others recover even better from the room they were sitting in down the short hall of their fairly new home of just over a year and a half. They had been making seemingly rude requests from the kitchen where they had been eating. Sarah was of maturity and bravery for this situation and Xavier was off even for a seven year old asking his mother if he could have a bowl of coffee ice cream for desert. She told him to shut up and a light of a flashlight stream came around the hall corner and back into the kitchen. It looked like success so far but in father celebration be-stilled he made a necessary commentary. "Good for now but something is spooky here its like déjà vu or something, kids keep an eye on your mother I have to go to the god damn cellar where the candles are." with the emergency flashlight in hand father guardian walked to the back deck and down the steep stairs walking fast aided only by the light of the moon. Father entered the cellar and retrieved some old candles of safe quality, they were set in glass surrounding molds whereas the wax would not drip causing anything to burn by an off chance, of course the wide frame of the candles of this old box set would prevent them from tipping over. Father bolted back up the deck's steep stairs so fast for a even a man of 35 years of age that he was panting when finally with a lighter from his pants pocket he lit a candle. The family was in for a romance four way to be remembered. Xavier commented with enthusiasm for a friendly fixing of this local neighborhood ordeal. "Dad what happened to all the lights?" "The neighbors lights in front and the back of our house appear to be out too so we must make a go of it." "Oh?" Sarah made an expressive question sound. Father joked for a moment to better their moods "How about a nice game of monopoly?" "Xavier's face shined in the light of the flame and asked "Why don't we play twenty questions?"

15

FOLLOWING THE FURY telecommunications slam in New York City 1995 the thief of a computer truck whom had met vital escape was watching the screens in a secret hidden location. Disguised as a furniture moving company truck the interior of this vehicle was not obvious to your average onlooker New Yorker or tourist for any matter. The screen displays were to be judged and coded carefully and the level of needed extreme caution had been intensifying despite a mobile stable venture accomplished by the alias driver thief and others in misery mystery set in locations placed as objective motive motion spies who to put it in the most easily explained of descriptions were located according to the moral cause. Injustice to his will was not his problem and misguided was this unit. Their spy forum presented to him was obscurity in instruction. To put that one in simple terms this driver who had slammed to end a message with exclamation expletive was out for a friend and his gullible persona was used to attract his loyalty. The sector and the combines watching would see to it that he was satisfied with all of his decisions. An old style modem screen display with your 1970's and 80's style green screen lit up a top row above a key pad set. Telecommunications were premature relative to the time of this alias truck thief as well as his abilities in certain aspects pertinent to the grid control requirements he was set to put into a placement. A send key was vital to a signal and the satellites that he had now discovered were being used by spies for illegal operations, they were now for a short time his new found possessions for a move in this cause. Case in point was send 2 of which was not set as a decoy schematics communication. A weapon of control, a seeming soul life possession of beings using individuals as chess pieces, and a back off was unfortunately to be rendering imminent from this truck thief's over abundant caution. There had appeared to be a problem with push send 3, an apparent intercept had corroded the anti plot. The scores for the total population was objective 1 but indignity, defiance to the teachers undone from the times of terminal downs, and uses of basics but not in computer terms it was ultimately downplayed. The result of such downward motions had ruined the images and scorned reputations of those who had origin wisdom and ability for resolution absolution leadership. The human race was that of a bee hive and the queen bee was torn. Assumed accidental gravity faults conspiracies of within making all revolt against the grain of human instincts, learned judgment, and common sense. A 4th send had to happen in order to defy the intention of a time alteration blackout. Grids grind and explosions would never happen but in a lessening of a taking out of our vitals another blackout move might happen. Times of axis earth accesses assessed and from a new perspective the driver thief drove to another location and the time was running short. A quick call to nobody resumed an important telephone conversation between two of sacred. The thief dials a number and no one answers. "Hello?" "Trade jack Mack asshole!" "What?" "Objective motion undone flaunting feathers downgrade mechanism 1." "Accepted will dues and the send off was a success excluding number 3." "Code play set to mechanism two outdone is in initiatives intended." "Do you have coordinates of data set to the wave signal algorithm pacing." "Yes but the gravitation related to our term logistics set the grids on collection action branches coded in fives, old school, and send 3 missed illegal Silicon Valley." "I take this as a no?" "Send access of open number codes and send my regards to the others." "Others?" and a laugh of dominating purposeful amusement contained belched. The conversation ended and the truck thief had detected some interference defiant and he became paranoid of authorities. In an extreme state of panic he spotted some blue lights in the distance and although he believed he was undetected he peeled out in this panic state with plans to destroy or sufficiently hide and abandon the computer truck that he had stolen from under their noses. Another consideration if there was time was that probably and more than likely it could have been a motive for this thief was to dismantle the equipment in the truck. Due to the severe situation and his limitation of time for a completion of the objective an abandonment of the vehicle was more likely to be the resulting act. Justice was hoped for of course and in this taking of liberty a clever move was needed in crunch time. He decided to take a risk and he headed to a location obscure, adequate, and where he would have the means for a dismantling and an abandonment of the vehicle figuratively in the least. The driving thief who had slammed expletive defiance at overlord authorities slowed down at a less populated and less thickly settled area of the metro land he drove through. Down to around a 15 MPH cruising amid wide spread street lights he drove into his set plan destination, it was an obscured for a large city gas station hidden by a water way and a tall grass rat infested field. At this station was a booth for purpose of self serve two over head thick ceiling dwellings similar to a bank safe wall in terms of mass and rows of four rectangle shaped lights over head that hung from chains over the gas station pumps. The lot of the station was empty at this late hour and only the cashier in the booth was to be seen other than an obscure figure walking aside tall grass in the direction of lighted unknown venues. The driver thief pulled to the side undetected so it was believed. Aside the station in clear view of the working cashier the truck thief sat behind the wheel of this stolen vehicle. Through the window he quickly gave the cashier a deception glance and as he started scratching at the hairs of his left temple the cashier exited the gas station booth with poor tact of secrecy, he could not help but to stare into the face of the driver thief. The Bronx was across a field, the station worker made a signal of a back off wave saying "its okay" as he and the driver who was now outside of the computer truck had with mission plan secrecy grabbed a hard plastic gas container he planned to fill for a fire starting. Following a casual payment to the cashier the gas container was filled and the driver thief then jogged fast to the truck. He entered the back of it and he poured out the gas all around the interior making sure that certain silica melt mechanism devices would be devoured material as well. A nitroglycerin stick with bonded twist wick and a manual pull cork for confusion was to be used for an explosion and the fire would be enough for a dismantling thus a cutting off of processes communications algorithmic was iminence execution and a style of such a word soon would send blue and white screens into reaction chains tombs in expo exploded. Quick wick despite and a spark signal from a cooperative cashier. The driver threw a light into open back doors and he as well as this supposed cashier employed ran from this momentary explosion in sprinting style of on the run fugitive maniacs. The cashier was well ahead of the driver who was running in the same direction and in a moment so fast it seemed to happen within seconds ago. The truck lit into fire simultaneously and the truck exploded with intense ear popping decibel shock level. All that was left was a charcoal truck, a cutoff of pain in futures results, sector breaths afar of a stay alive intent, a running pair, one Caucasian illegal alien out of a job and a misguide guider upgraded who lost his ride home. At the mid section of the field was a roadway and there stood a yellow yield sign, the illegal alien who was the counterpart to this plan stopped sprinting inches from this street sign nearly colliding into this street sign. At the location of the yield sign the alien awaited the thief who ran after him. The unemployed alien had spat on the pole of the yield sign in exhalation he panted moaning in chest pain from cold weather and a fear run. The thief arrived one moment later and the two of this real life cloak and dagger had their meeting. The out of a job alien spoke first while fire blazed a little over 150 yards back "Last time for a favor Mack." Mack the now identified thieve ploy panted just the same "you owed me one but never mind that, the bitch you often refer to too is presently placed in secret location in a small town far north of here." "I'm not worried she will meet with our prime mover in the city north in a couple of decades, this takes some time, you know?" Mack beckoned to his alien partner of the night with a more calming manner of a panting and breathing "Back home must had been hard for her your favor is rare we don't usually get this from your people since the days of the law." Alien alienated attempted to speak for alien nation true dream but the two who had been running were about to fall victim to a mistake. "What the?" A rustle sound was heard from the tall grass brush at the road side Mack looked down and went into shock as a rat scampered in brush distracting this meeting. Near to the moving rat however the walker sighted obscure just minutes back was set on the ground in a laying down position with a scope and rifle. Two shots fired the first hit the heart location of Mack's chest and blood exploded in a glob, he fell to the ground. The second shot was off by a little causing a shoulder injury to the illegal alien, he fell to his knees and the hit man rose from the tall grass and neared him in seconds. "Any last words?" "K" and an immediate shot to the skull and only a sounded out letter, a syllable fraction of confusion, debate, and a death for the cause of a future bonding was yet not foiled. Mack as role of alias was embryo kin and the fallen was of the eon fabled dream. Death was fast, ended from fire was futures electronic mailings for evil, and as was the sky on this night black sleep had overtaken them.

16

FLICKER FLAME FLAMBOYANT boy and girl had been sitting in the night light of the waxen candle. Manitoba was memory afar and in the old nightmares father guardian had heard of a sent crash and summer dreams deadened in stained sadness was above gladness for unrelated in corpses of a dawn was a calling. The evidence on this earlier date prior to the wells of swelling burns on a bridge had justified a phase shift on set to a three way matching. Cameras microfilms odd of an old timer, pore tear pours called sweat made time symmetrical for the beads on a gypsy. The strangers on strange land had recognized the ignorance of the messiahs silent and so it was that the readings of the topology tectonics phonics continued. In darkness flickered the flame of enlightened the seemingly foiled foursome talked the ways of the knowing concepts of a special night. Fear had slightly overtaken them. Sister Sarah watched the brother work as the liars weaved webs of truthful. Youths wronged, energy derived was cut of for the prongs of new time old time and so it was that the 1980's were reflected by a deathly sacrifice of two in future for this was now the time theorized by two of death's flesh wound as the new 1960's. 1995 was a watch watcher watching and in a slamming call communications the pride sin deadly was of a new life above. The conversation between the four was inherent of the sector wisdom and so it was said in the names of unknown legend that the memoirs of a nighttime brought the new dawn into a day and dusk whereas the water falling had answered the calls of the three true who had been answering the questions counting to nearly twenty. On question 18 of the second game of twenty questions came the question of a downed dream of a square north of two deaths, this was old time Harvard Square where born was those of self sacrifice. "Was he the other one who was shot ma?" "Yes and that's 18 you have two more questions if need be, Sarah can you answer who this was?" "Bobby Kennedy?" Father guardian was stumped he knew this answer and from a blow of no sense what so ever the candle blew out and Father just lit another. Anew was another lightening forthwith it was a mover in hopes of ultimatum grand. "That's right Sarah the man was harassed but the living dream never shall die." 1995 done and fears Kamakazi style were not to be warned enough in 2001. 1986 might be hardened dismal but at 13 to 1 odds to a liking of two downed and dead from a shooting a 1 symbol on true philanthropy sparked no nonsense into minds of the youths called stupid by generators and not the hearts of the generations past. Lights on were not yet possible and from the intense felling swelled mind of the under country guards the family had stayed up until the middle of the night. By the time the morning came the blackout was lightened and a meeting making of the outside personas met for future wells swell and metro. Hetero Homos sexual dames, the games of time brought courage to the young but a taking of a craft reminds those across the board of true theft and conceit is to be a "rest in war" burial R.I.P. R.A.W. R.O.W. R.I.W no to bloodshed? Rests in pieces (A) rested, roped at wounds, roar on wills, rye in white breading and a now know knew two and bloods shed tears for a liberty lesson learned. Sector down and addition arts breed humane original political die roll and a dying yesterday. Sunrise of a new day a wound healed by flows for gone and the written wet rodents of the Angeles lost symbols of dead prevented invented therefore the experiences of life had come and gone for some but for all was the promise unkempt. Days doomed in gloom called another and from a well built bridge was the sighting. Vision in morbid made a bid and the acid of a ripping made peace pipes in the tee pees. It was the tents of the dog wind the old war abound sent a new send in the form of four legs walking. A penny, the city in the city termed as a pen, phenomenon, and a camp befell in pity to those of the chemical growth. The binding of the awl tool all was named for the accidents inside existence it was gowth. The new day came in old times remembered like that of the depression togetherness time. On this day of no mourning and sunshine mornings natures nurturing light shined in hairs for the time of a yarn wool day. City cancels slightly limited it was for the center section of which this residence could see drew the rays of a felt late summer tanning sensual. A bus dove landed for the hell's of the pigeons of New York. There was no bench to sit on for the meeting simplicity and the not to be wasted spirit minds dense termed terminal and populous small. A quest of a bonfire from outer realms instructed wise hood and blame was becoming. The years fade but as for this year of 1980 a question started the motioning sun further upward in lighted night flamed. 1980 quartz melts of the bled hearts together they spoke shifting the owed eighth of futures a nine shot and one was speaking to ears uncut. 1980 depended on the binoculars for nighttime vision for the toned bridges burning and computes a bridge. 1980 . . . . .0891 . . . . rhythm algor . . . . isms spasm in Spain . . . .1986.

17

THE DAYS OF Renessa were of the past and others who had seen her knew she had mailed the scorning of the thorns into the minds of revolution bloods for the roses of the dead. Grids already grind and in the resembled night sky it was possible that a star of no twinkle had begun to twinkle in coldness lighted frontiers. The implosion just might have happened. Nevertheless minds of forces reminded the significant numerical transformed as the new breed for the key to it all grew from abandonment, seen men, women, children and marshes. The explosion would never happen. A lie, a truth, a guessing new guess concern absurd, the blizzard of satellite three in eyes owed. Now the wombs bow to man divided by an A figured algebra problem and frankly the moats of the castles anew in death were the marshes of parallel pools. Weather lies, United Nations, or Moons in mid afternoon it was not Kent in a booth or sainthood ages for the wanderer of Santiago Chile. Lady Maria wad hiding for the brown delivery and from the United Kingdom came Keys for her Jonah of Xenon. Xavier in embarrassment of his name looked down the sights of the queen's lane and saw corrosion, it was England her name was Katy what a shame. Shamed was not the word for her or him and for them in meeting again they loved from an open window. Next door on the third floor was an open door and diagonally next to the hall radiator was her Jonahs doorway that happened to be unlocked on this day of return. The year was 1994 and in late January of 1993 the two had met in envy stare at a local diagnostic clinic. The sending of a mad slam was soon to be a continued life for her Jonah on the isle of his stranded times. There she was and there he lay in his bed. He was waiting for the summer of futures hoping to arrive. A minority local get together was taking place in the apartment diagonal from him. After sighting his old friend find on her way inside and after a wave of friendliness amid winter snow her laughter could be heard slightly over fine times and spirits. A day glow shine was reflecting on the window top and snow so after a breath of healthy cold air he shut his window to a mere feel of a few and far between winter wind crackling vibration. He looked to the wood of his door frame and lit his last cigarette for the day until he could cross the street to the corner liquor store for another pack. Before nearly falling asleep and a pushing out of a filtered generic he awakened completely from the slamming open of his unlocked door, the door knob had hit the wall leaving a dent on the off white painted wall. It was her, the old friend from Jedidiah and the England old land. No key needed on this day of Renessa's younger years for the elder one in care of a mother with partners in love for a day and the end of their lifetimes taught the teachings in dates to her Jonah's time of manifest destiny. No words said and Katy stripped her clothes off at the bathroom door. Slow stripping in the venue of the liberty new way and her Jonah was male queen. The sex about to happen was a deliverance of the stroke stork and the X spot was to be uncorked. Xavier Xevon Xenon in on was on her and empathetic mother slow stripped into compassion for this lover. Erect pensive senile for no isle this was and the middle aged Katy befell and he was from a place insane in terms where he was, heaven and hell. The two lied down together and with politeness impolite she gestured a glance and this boy of a man stripped down his denims. The couple of one day became intimate and caressing and the act was of passionate commencement. A slip out during and a funny commentary "lost ya dick" no embarrassment and an answer came in no time. He spoke to her with sarcasm undetectable and confidence in his gene pool "I didn't lose my dick its right here." And he put it in again. The love making was nowhere it was passion totally resulting in some small talk. Katy sent Xavier out for a pack of menthols after an intensity orgasmatron. "What do you think is better the cigarette after the sex or the sex?" "The cigarette!" "Nice answer you are quite a domineering woman." "Gracias huggabear don't forget to count your hatches before they chicken." "Chicken is my favorite next to spinach." "Don't piss me off!" "I like you too." And the two of them sucked their menthols down in mid afternoon serene. "A Jazz band is opening up for a Polish Polka band at Sluts Are Us tomorrow." "Sounds nice and messy." "Four polka members went down on me once." "there's nothing like a bonfire on a tin can muffin." "Mockery side kicks made a bread and butter sandwich." "A sandwich or a sandwich?" "Crazy daddy long lez legs made some pegs for arms and me legs?" "Hamai chamina damina cum in her?" "What's this Chinese?" "No Kampuchan dairy dust love lust bred some swill in my bust." "Russian, Swahili, Maine or Filipe?" "Coffee tea and my milk mystic will do fine." "Okay then let's fake a shower." Xavier and Katy made way to the bathroom door where she had stripped down to her thighs beforehand. She turned on the waterway fountain for a cleaning and the two of them sponged themselves until the soap had run out. What a shame, saddened in times of one year left. Happiness pouring of afar had come and gone for the time of a missing. Missing however Katy was not and "not to be forgotten" might have been a quote shamed if Xavier had said it. Habits of the neighborhood he had avoided for the time being and somehow as Katy passed away some time after. The hereafter was not remembered with laughter on a new day despite a pleasant awakening and a failure to communicate. Damnation of the times for it was in a Sun obituary the sad news of Katy's passing on. Xavier had heard news of this unfortunate news for him and others of his neighborhood and so it was that her Jonah would be a troop for a new justification but just what was to be the deciphering difference? Time healed the wounds for him as he did not regret their day together and his telling her of the tragedy of his time. And so it was that on the day of this involvement that the true cause of a writing spree would unfold in his personal ambitions. Days would come and go and melted snow had led him to the former American capitol. New York destination and undying adaptations adapted. The figurines were stoned in deception as the commons back home held the growing seeds of another true finding. Revenge did not behold him but right or wrong for such reasons of no blame could only be settled in the thorns on a blondes rose. Xavier Her Jonah recalled his inside and remembered as well the attack mode resisting. Insistence instantly strained a strong storm and aimed towards the culprits of the instigating switchers. The wizard and witch tribute the bitch but where she went off the something of which had arrived in enlightened days on snowy terrain was a printing. The true lie of summer made the loser of Xavier win. Dawn time upward or what's the difference she might say as would he. The pigeons flew and the cares caressed her. Katy gone at 36 Katy's dawn at 37 Katy's gone what a shame.

18

BLACK OUT ONE in 1980 A.D. forced inducement mechanism 1 2 3 4 and five mates assess cue moves and checked in for a sign of posted scriptures anti to the back doors of this vicinity gleaming on a sunshine day. Night was far off and the conversation of the morning after undertook forums over the Pacific falling and the Atlantic was calling. Slam 1 was outdone and was set off course. Bats bated in mastery misery and had exterminated conquests of man and the others of angels deceived the black door, the whore, the old man of fathers and natures coursed. Recourse required to the mandatory abuses courses and a countdown undid it. Outside at the no bench sun spot Xavier met for a meeting with an imagery, it was him. Sighted on cold icy terrain was no pain sighted and in tight was the other anti to the lit flicker aura this was to evil believers. Xavier in his mind had started talking to himself in senses of all five of them, May hems, stems, a sewed hem mended pretended and scented of the nose and stars see man he talked aloud to a voice. The vice was cut into fours and it was dripping symbols, a thimble, terror, the mirror sound whispered to the viceroy named Xavier Xevon Tareynton. "Got a test Monday and watch out for papers to be signed." Xavier gasped at this voice in his head he was not yet deemed with gifts of communications to crying authorities and he studied his surrounding environment crying coded mechanism 2. "Paging mister pig boy spaghetti eyes you're a little tyke for a visit tonight." "Basketball is my dream." Xavier looks downward in hopes of infancy mercy and he remembers age three. "You incompetent moronic young fool a loathe loaf might be your demise and your cool whip will curse you." Anecdote antidote quoting flowed in prediction and a whipping for the enemy made the boy add addition arts, the artist took no prisoners. Xavier was bored and he on this Saturday the second day of this neighborhood blackout decided to knock the wiffle ball around for a while and then he went upstairs and grabbed his basketball. He practiced dribbling and the chains of the liar drip dropped into Xavier's brain and his strains inward glandular setting his mind onset for a centering. Dome light, flat earth, Sabbath day, Horizontal pronto world reporting your non confession, the profession, time travel, and defenses were taken on withstood. Moonlight night was turning to dusk and mother was under an order request he heard her sweet voice calling "its late Xavier time to come in." the others entered but who were they? He or it? Ill stricken electric the prongs pony rode songs and flaunted brains were resolute and neon life undaunted. "My ways take on your house is haunted." The family four lit up again with a spark and flicker flame on candle they knew the door was locked and did not fear the ding dong. The conversation of voice interference interface shadowed the corners of the winged falcon, it turned into a cancer, scorpion eyes upon dominated a galactic inward universal law, the pellets became the holes inside and the lines of a face glanced into Transylvania written it was outside of a mind and the black hole called deranged for a foe friend framed. Enraged was mechanical and four more quotations were then spoken inside his tormented mind while Xavier paced aimlessly through the darkened halls of his home, he followed the voices of three inside with flick flames on you. "Fire came and your bird is the angel in the pillow." "Demons defend you." Xavier cried inside supposedly. A voice gulped and the memory was to be unjustly criticized in lies of not a soul for caring. "Your gate source will be your doom." Voices or the voiced frequent frequency said to the boy. 8 o'clock on a summer dusk of the dawns light saw near darkness completed Xavier rounded the corner he saw fear, a pulled out chair from dad, and he was seated. The sky cheated. The stars overhead competed. Supernova secrets completed in the dawns of the heaven hell. Water well sells a dell bay graveyard and the cursed draft card bewitching sewed the stitching. A boy named Xavier made the draft with quotation four of the steps' insanity bereft. "Greeted." Time has a way of birthing another. Father guardian spoke in tradition, Sarah sat silently peering at mother, and Xavier after a greeting sat with family in the dark glow room with a candle. Greeted was greetings on a draft card, fire was an uncontrollable weapon, serpents spited the demon word. The gate source was of late. Big or small the sending was the beginning of the . . . . end. Deafened ears and ignorance to a child sends the bidding. Sister Sarah asked for another chance to win with another game of twenty questions. The night was too far gone in another hour so the four of them went to bed. Splashes went onto land and the tom fool was the justified jester born again. "Okay Sarah last chance it's your turn." "Umm was he a member of a sectioned council?" "Yes" father guardian interrupted. Xavier excited blurted out "Tip O'neil?" That's right Xavier I'm so proud liar of you. "Thank you, can I have another grape freeze pop before I go to sleep?" In the dark room of flickering shimmer shining Xavier was denied a last treat by the guardian. Mother and Sister Sarah expressed emotion of wanting for Xavier and although he had one already and despite a melting from the energy blackout another strange drink was served by mother. A quick downing grape flavored liquid ensued, was downed and off to bed went Xavier. In his room he laid in sterilization stimuli awaiting the senses scents incomprehensible. A year back he heard something by his side while lying down on pills and surviving. Contributions west of where he was aided was safety of those in black lit traps. No escape for them they blessed the lucky dog war times. Sensed insensitive comprehended together the sound lingered with twinges of death day cartilage that melted into dirt grains. He this boy aged just over seven years saw the light fading absence on night two of a blackout. Spent time for sectionals undoing coded blames identified, it was enhancement sensationalists themselves, a guarding stand still and wills of the neighborhood boys nourished from a jar ajar times of escape plan pore holes. May the Vikings of continuum row from wars in astronomy-normalcy beyond and the craters were still hidden. Foes for the deoxyribonucleic liquid lie down. Sought fighters caught in sourced man ships and the ghosts became fleshed completely in dimensions. Third world country, third world blood wolves gaining meat, groove hooves moves up one of mirages. Back was the price cost original leaving equal value to living lives, the boy slept in pitch black! It was now an even match. Unrelated and supposed location of a Metropolitan city 2012; the supposed adult aged delinquent juvenile lowlife was laying in alcohol post seizure phase aftereffect. Her Jonah who is Xavier lied down in a depressed state as he avoided such a name that seemed to him to resemble the most broken of men on some given days. After a spree of killing in his mind and after his new Karma insane had overcome insurmountable odds one time in measures of fair play he was resting while awaiting the upcoming election. Another had left him and yet another who aided him was left outside in the cold for survival of the fittest. The two of this recent time exerted spy times, winded the watches of water ways. Smooth on the outside and her Jonah was to miss them. He finally fell asleep and due to sedation effects he had no choice but to miss voting day that was held weeks prior and days. Her Jonah could not dream and in his blackened sleeping time he only replenished despite his inadequacies of actual inward entrances. He awakened and outside of his window he could see that the sky was still black and he was confused as to his lacking ability to acknowledge anything for the short time of his present depression. A news reel came on his still activating television screen. The report flashed on and a local news break in the middle of a commercial interruption and this announcement caught Xavier's attention. Reporting quotes went as follows "A blackout has struck the outer section of the city and it has effected two blocks leaving thousands left in the dark." Xavier having paid attention to this news break reported he was unable to pay attention altogether. He remembered well the blackout of which he had experienced as a youngster back in the old hood, he was trying tribulation. Xavier in his new state of paranoia was a disrespected person and despite this he in deadly pride so it had seemed pointed to the screen as the news break had ended and with a stiff index finger he in a way played the lottery Russian roulette style. With pointed finger Xavier in roll of her Jonah said sternly, loudly, and proudly enough to be an honorable man "BLACKOUT!" the news break was over. Her Jonah rolled over and began snoring, he finally in sedation fell into actual sleep of a non alcohol fainting.

19

WHETHER IT WAS the fainter, painters, or the adolescent it was to be seen in the year 1986 that artistry of no details are obscure in beginnings whereas the globs are thrown onto the canvas and thus our art forms fall short and are criticized before and after. Nevertheless it is the artist who feels the pain and the collectors of the now ill forgotten worthiness that shall return the losing arts to the times of our miracles perceived. Accepted as the artist is, was, and may ever be it was 1986 year of that the thirteen students of Xavier Xevon Tareynton's eighth grade graduating class that built over the waters of flowing deepness and although water under the bridge is often shallow the 13 together including Xavier, Zimmerman the man, and Luzzin were in for a possibility. Stark reminder of course was most definitely plagued, the young Xavier who was at a ripened 13 years old had felt as such. The class had entered their eighth grade homeroom and this particular parochial school was different from public school for sure. Eighth graders as well as kindergarten through seventh grade students had to spend their entire school days in the same homeroom that they would enter and be seated in for the entire nine months of school days from September 1986 until June 1987. First day of school roll call and intros were made and over the course of this first school day the kids as well as the fourteenth member who was a well respected teacher in the parochial school system all became acquainted. Zimmerman the man, Luzzin, and Xavier with Wayne wound down the clock towering over the American flag above, beyond, and over to the right hand side of the back wall next to the chalk board. Wayne having retrieved the clock by stepping upon a school chair held the classroom clock in his hand and he asked Zimmerman the man which way to turn the back knob on the back of the clock for an exact fixing. The time was apparently set back from a lacking wind up. Luzzin made commentary referring to Xavier the new boy and as the four students waited for the first lunch cafeteria break of the year. Xavier jokingly referred to the clock as Big Ben of the United Kingdom. In reference to this ridiculously off kilter clock analogy compared Wayne looking over at Luzzin and Xavier who had just made this non humorous joke had winked a left eye at Zimmerman standing there and said to him "This clock is not Big Ben it's Tiny Ben New England." The four then waited for lunch and parochial recess as Nina fixed her hair with a pocket mirror, Guido was brushing off a trapper keeper for a no dust shine as Tamera talked to Omar concerning his future and Stacy was sketching a portrait of the stone structured local city hall. Lunch and recess came and went and so the first day was a success. Xavier had considered his first day consulted by the authorities of sky worlds and so now it was off to his home where he would see father guardian after he returned home from work, Sister Sarah was not to be back until later she was searching for a college recruiter at an education facility on the other side of town, grandfather and grandmother just awaited his return home on this first new day of parochial school for Xavier they wanted to ask him how he felt about the decided advice of this parochial recommendation for him. Xavier arrived and met with four of the five jibe did his homework, ate his dinner, watched two of his favorite satires, and threw on the night red sox home game it was the 3rd and final game of a 3 game home stand. The red sox were on a 4 game winning streak. Weeks passed by and the eighth grade elementary of the venue educational was sweet breeze and the dew of the sunshine had formulated the outcomes of the lanes lesson in religion classes. Studies and satires as well as the weekend roller rink tradition was still very important to Xavier of course. His sox in this 1986 baseball season were fairing well in competition and Xavier thought that they might have a shot at the pennant this year. The World Series title on the other hand might have been slightly out of reach. Xavier was a fan of his satires but on weekends he liked to watch some of the classic television programs on the classic television channel and soon while viewing one particular episode he had a clairvoyant sighting that just fell short. On a bright sunshine Saturday afternoon Xavier was watching the classic show "lost in space" and near the climax of this episode that was either about a clairvoyant one or a time traveler a coincidence would inspire him as a baseball fan. A question was asked to the one who might have known the future back in the decade of which this show aired "So if you do know the future then tell me who won the World series in 1986?" the answer came "the Boston red sox." Xavier was predominantly determined for his own teams' season in the senior league he was playing for. He was hot as a starting catcher and he was to make the all star team. He might possibly pitch if he did better over his next few games. On a Monday in October the school day was just another ordinary day. Lunchtime came and Xavier was eating with Luzzin, Zimmerman the man, Omar, flip, and Guido was minus an apple. Some scag commentary came into play "Had to quit at 4 and 7 this year huh Xavier?" "Yes, but I fared well in the all star game at least." On an off note as Guido sipped a coconut juice, Omar was feeling his back head section of a shave around the ears and Luzzin provoked Zimmerman the man to do some scagging on Xavier, Wayne noticed and he as the basketball dude was not one to feel guilty enough not to do some laughing along. Luzzin shoved a sliding pastry snack at Zimmerman and he commenced with the festivities. "Xavier do you swallow?" Xavier looked around for a second or three and tensed his face into embarrassment. "What do you mean?" "Swallow you know? It's just a question Xavier, do you swallow?" "Uh I don't know? What do you mean?" Guido sipped, Omar raised his eye brows, while Wayne was laughing a little with Luzzin. "Once again Xavier just tell me do you swallow?" Xavier's brow curved in stern face of and I don't know look and he answers "What would I be swallowing?" "Xavier just answer do you swallow?" A few light laughs and Guido became disgusted. Xavier answered again "Do you mean food?" the others laughed a little harder and Zimmerman the man just told Xavier to forget about it. Xavier starts to tell a weird story in the form of a question. "You know how when you wake up in the morning and you have like a gross mouth and then you've got that white stuff that you have to scrape off of your lips with your thumbnail?" Guido made a face expressed with serious concern like a coach or something, Wayne with Flip, Luzzin, and Zimmerman the man who just sat there said to Xavier as if he were a freakish boy "I don't wake up with any white stuff on my lips." Xavier states a case "Everyone does it is from all of the dust in the air, maybe there is more where I sleep at my back porch." "White stuff?" Guido said looking at Xavier as if he'd be committed one day. "Wayne questioned Xavier "How the hell does someone wake up with white stuff on their lips it can't be from dust." Xavier "it's from sleeping with your mouth open." Luzzin made brows inward diagonal and asked Xavier "Does any one else live with you Xavier "No just my dad." They all burst out laughing as they had realized an unintentional dirty joke so Zimmerman the adolescent asked in humors for a crew "Did he swallow? The buzzer sounds and it was K through 8 recess time.

20

FENCED IN WAS Renessa her Jonah although confiding in her had been deemed powerless to aid her needs anymore. She was in the dismal of a new sparked to life city. The city was of the torn heart a jugular like laceration major bleeding had sent her Jonah away long ago. The gas had melted the actual culprit. Claims of mystery made history and the eastern gaseous good beast inside hand made this maiden from the neck up. Outplayed by her was her Jonah. The garment of her liking had kept her warm she had witnesses around who over on the other side of the section of the city resulted the Bokator fighting art form and with it some had defended. Hands made the fair lady the maiden and the angel dying knew of the arts of the weapon that she might have had to use in defense on this night of dismal reversing to an uprising. Downed, underrated, disrespected, the sleep shall project them. From the fenced in spot of which she was standing was a fake threatening on straight line command. Repossession repetition she dialed a number when she had realized a car of possible hood thieves who might have opposed her. Neutral down a hill side on the other side of the canteen a disguise wound up dead. Cameo chameleons victimizing or victim was the question asked in a day-mare but the day was night and the night was holding the key for one of the twin city. Renessa wanted to take out the gun she had held although the thought of violence was vile to her. In fears defense all real of surety something entered the realm and at the helm in REM sleep. It was not Jonah but it was father guardian who in his future selfishness something had remained from the past. The past lingered inside of him thus causing an intention. He did stray the neuron and in his brain the back of it aided injury. A sound was heard far off it was yet another explosion in the new spark city that happened. Renessa with a gun, sleep fun, slipped notes, quotes, father asleep, impostor awake? The impostor was father and in the name of the dead and the beauty of the living the gun was of no use for homicide a distraction guides a way. Over yonder on the ground it was not a green glass vile like in superman but it was a dead rose that made a fossil like shape in the snow. The gun was away and the new hoping guide did return but it was not an Anna or a Consuela her name was Maria again she saw the dark at the end of the tunnel and walked to the fossil and the sun on the other side of the new earth sent an array "it was my ray" so this is written and sewed is the soiled rose. Renessa was to be picked up by a trustee maybe she could see the ghosts of Salem in her travels after all the graves of the city held ground and digs dug up were defied. A gig for the local semi small time fame underground band was featured at a renowned club in a far off section of town. Renessa was picked up by her ride call and they took her by for an unknown intention. Upon arrival the club venue was entered and the attendance was more than steady on this night. She decided it would be wise to leave certain items inside of her friend's car and so she did. Inside were no sightings significant. The sounds of the music were deafening melodrama after a drink or two with some acquaintances. A face on the other side by a back wall was familiar to Renessa. Little did she realize however that an octagon, a parallelogram spin fall, and a three dimensional prism spectrum disguised what was a face of ancestors to Salem or better yet "witch town." The octagon made an 8 side 3 by 4 in the paragons undone. The prism triad shape on side 4 in a 3rd dimension was not completely visible yet no colors spun into dome club light whereas senses made light invisible. 5 of 6 on parallel over gram measures had fallen into a near square rectangle and the degrees equaled to kinetics. Octagon, paragon, parallelogram, pyramid, ohms are invisible. Renessa and her Jonah mates invisible visibility plus time and at the Pentagon was collecting new outer information. The last chords were played and the words "thank you good night we love you all" sent Renessa out, she remembered the face of the match to a wizard spelling and in paranoia she made sure she still had her gun. Empty chambers, a winter night went into the next morning. The scorns of the proof prophets lost a non existing dune doomsday. A melting bullet of marble and lead was saved in a gun. Red roses for the dead! It was late Renessa was being driven home and her Jonah dreamed a dream. Amid the dust life of a sky world was a unification post assembly. Members counting to 11 of them each represented among them. The council's members held a politician, a pleasant man, a pleased lady, a dingo that was spore spawn freedom cat mixture, a dictator former army captain, an elite, a bird of a feather, the corded energy of a continent, an incompetent man, an incompetent woman, and lady of the veil Maria for bridals chilling. Santiago pawn swan poem sent a message in this dream to her Jonah and alias Xavier woke up as if from a nightmare to find out from another news reel that was playing on his television saying that the blackout was in a more severe stated emergency due to cold weather and after affects. No festival for sure but the festivities safely died down for Renessa. She had fallen asleep herself having heard the news from another anonymous source. The dream might have been about the upward council.

21

THE ABOVE COUNCIL resolution is minor theme in the eyes of the perceived and whether it is then or now . . . . ? Pagan defined (a word taken offensively at times) or new words often defined for a new creation same yet different yet same it was and still is. A mortality resurrection was hoped for before the second shot from the hit man killing the driver thief and the illegal alien who was his counterpart. The two of them just laid in death from it, it meaning the death shots to the two and the set back to vital quotation starting with a key to a grand dream. The hit man after eliminating these two for a cause concerning injustice just left behind their bodies in the freezing cold New York night. The hit man then strayed off in any direction of destination unknown. The computer truck was destroyed and the burning charcoaled it altogether. Any possible objects capable of communication for hackers on the side of the soon to be evil dawn were rendered still uncorrected or inept of corrosion. This shot plot might have saddened able bodied pro for a dream so in fable time he was off. On the other side of the Bronx rat field it was his computer van and some vital components inside including a screen that was now inactive and cutoff from some satellite relative sending schemes. Bright blue and blank was this useless screen he turned a key and drove to New Jersey finding a spot for sufficient seclusion. He wrapped himself in a blanket and slept for nearly three hours and when he awakened the sun was in mid rise on a bright enough for a scenic mystic morning. Upon awakening the hit man unwrapped himself from his thermal blanket. He was slightly shivering just short of intense quivering. The heat of the van he was driving was off formed for the texture of the cold air, his sleeping time for these three hours lessened. Unsurprisingly so the climate was cold enough for him to see his breath. Despite this cold weather factor he was more than sure that the equipment he had inside was sturdy enough to withstand any possible damages. He started the van and with a turn of his key ignition, Ignition was immediate. Five minutes for a warming up and from the side of an old Jersey freeway semi diagonal on a road he drove off. He passed through some side streets with seemingly aimless intent. Onlookers were nonexistent he was aware as he drove on. Down a ways away he passes near the old Giants Stadium. It had appeared that in his trickery drive he may have driven in a circle. Glancing over to his right side through the van window he could see the amazing view of New York City from New Jersey and he was in awe at the sight of horizon to horizon scenery of sights for the ages, an edifice and growth industrial etcetera. The spread of sky scrapers as far as one could see boggled a mind to this town foreigner. It was just like looking out at a beach and wondering what was beyond the visions' ending. Down the road he drove on and a left turning into deeper New Jersey a few turns of rights and lefts. With less than a quarter of a gas tank full he pulled into another gas station surrounded by pedestrians and civilization. It was 9 A.M. by this time a morning cup of Joe was in order. As far as this hit man was aware he was not being followed. However it is true that his foreigner inexperience might cost him because about 30 miles back from where he was laid out two are dead and a now black burnt out van is outbound with evidence. He put on his sunglasses and made sure his clothes were changed. He threw on a cap and went inside a mini store for a filling of wake up juice. As a non member of any American affiliation so it was announced in alchemy he purchases a newspaper, a plain cruller, and a large coffee light with some disguise, and his rifle equipment mount, scope, and his cartridge cases for extremities if he needed to use an automatic. The hit man in his smarts for a stranger in these surroundings beheld decided to wait for a while to check if anyone was on to him. An unfolding of a paper the man stepped out of the van and after a swig of his coffee and a swallowing of his last bite of a cruller he placed his beverage on his van hood so it didn't topple over and spill. The hit man just stood taking sips reading the sports section. The computer van's radio was playing. The window was rolled down just enough to hear the words of the classic Christmas song with the words "do you know what I know" and "do you hear what I hear" it sounded déjà vu significant with its rumbling in and out over static from the cheap sounding van's radio, this song was playing on a popular New York radio station. The hit man was biding his time just checking the scores of the world soccer league. A few sips and a sighting made by him without any aiding of clairvoyant factors interfering of origin. Minds mended minded and beheld a timely and imminent immediate happening. This happening would be seen by the innocent people of the present placement of this occurring roundabout. Little did this hit man realize it was the car across the street that haunted him! A blue shit box with a New Jersey license plate. On the front bumper was a bumper sticker that read the classic quote of an 80's supposed mockery "Shit Happens." The hit man mysteriously had come to the realization that a young lady in this car was staring at him. The hit man was not sure of any outright self suspicion due to a pair of dark sunglasses she was wearing. She looked downward momentarily and took off her glasses with a staring vivid, anti-charisma, and more intense, it was inquisition for definite. The hit man began to react with as little panic as possible. He poured out the remainder of his coffee beverage on the station parking lot pavement. It splashed a merit demerit. Hit man tossed a cup in the general direction of the trash barrel. While opening the door to the computer van he looked back at the lady who he had realized appeared to be of an Asian descent. She did not have the common eyes of Asians featured. They were more oval than one might expect. The lady stared. She smiled slyly and with a clever and satisfied look she returned to her rage. By the time our hit man realized this he was one foot into the open door of the computer van. Lady calmly and surely put her sunglasses back on. The obvious motive was the bumper sticker notice and so it was that this look of confidence was because of the factor that this lady was simply the spy game dagger jab trick move decoy. Decoy stares, van door stairs, scares, pedestrian bus fares, a sudden screeching from an unexpected direction and a loud car engine multitude massive in cubic inches motoring loud like a disturbing motorcycle drive by. It was time to say goodbye. A power house motor car of strong muscled steel American made and bought for sure sped directly into the direction of the computer Van's driver side door. A seemingly stupid plan of attack seeing that this van was in fact a normal sized van and not a mini one. At about 10 feet away the hit man driver had begun to panic so he abruptly turned his head to the right and south to get a grab chance at an automatic with cartridges that to his misfortune were not applied. At this point the Asian lady or whatever ethnicity she was of for an important matter peeled out immediately and she too started to floor it right at the other front side of the parked computer van. A thunder crash and the driver hit man fall dives to the floor, frisking the floor and tossing his automatic and cartridges in a bag to the side, he frisk frenzied for his rifle that he had separated and set apart from its scope and rifle stand. The thunderous lightning crash pushed the computer van to the right a shocking three feet and the lady in kamakazi style via Japanese mode crashed into the front driver side corner denting the van so bad it made post car crash sounds before this scene was over with "CRASH!" tic toc tic toc "CRASH!" tic toc tic toc . . . .

"EUEAUURRHUEUAHKA" the inside sounds miraculously came from the Goliath van in its death as the vehicle it was. Goliath van downed and so the two David cars did some damage for definite means of new definition, it must had been our communication fast style. This examination is evident from examining the attack tactic of a Japanese death crash. The hit man was in back with half of his legs and feet in between the two front seats. The bag with the automatic and cartridges was kicked backwards with his bottom heel towards the lower part of the front van dash board by a console. He continued to drastically feel around inwardly with his hands acting with his arms as spasms that were panic induced. The two cars that had bombarded the computer van emptied out. Surprisingly so the lady exited her car first. The lady could exit fast because she had on her a pistol with a full twelve gauge round therefore she was prepared for this occasion happening. From the muscle machine the driver of it exited his vehicle a moment after he had on him an old fashioned revolver with 6 bullets full. In the back of the van was a scurrying around. The hit man gets to his rifle with rifle stand and scope. The stand and the scope for a long range shot was not a necessary commodity for the hit man in a case as deadly as such. The lady and the man from the other car who was also a loner on this morning coffee newspaper chase run signaled to one another and they both ducked moved bobbed and weaved by each front side of the computer van for a mass killing. The killing mind you was not to be fulfilling but thrilling, chilling, and willing was the word of the morning whistling wind. A shot came from the inside. A bolt sound prior to a millisecond soft dense click trigger flicker came from the ceiling of the computer van. A hard denting bang and hollow boom sounded and the shot fired from inside went up and out through the roof of this van. At the moment the hole was made and the sound was heard, the hit man pulled the door opener on the left van back door, he swung the right door open for a shielding. The right side door swung open out and around completing what was a virtual 180 degree angle. A shot immediately came from the lady. The shot of a bullet from her pistol hit the right side back window of the open door swinging. The bullet left a spider web like round shatter print she immediately ducked and turned back around to round this van and moved in from the other side. With the rifle inside shot the hit man scampered with a plan, he jumped outside on his two feet landing like a thrown cat using the left side door as a shield himself. The man who drove car two moved in towards an almost straight narrow left hand side back van door. The hit man with rifle in hand had to make a maneuver or it was foils rats again. The lady was ducking down by the left front headlight that was smashed dented by car two. She could see the other driver shot crash guy of her signaling lying down spying style by the corner at the back of the van, he had gotten down like so for a sneak shot at the hit man. While all of this was happening a call was made by one of many now hidden for safety onlookers. A police siren could be heard afar but this did not cause this shootout to end fast. Another shot was fired, it was a loud shot from the revolver the lying spying guy was aiming. A poor angle of an aim caused the shot to fizz shot past the hit man as the hit man jumped up with the rifle wrapped around his left shoulder onto the ajar back van door that was not hit and shattered with a web shatter glass look like the other back van door. In mid jump he latch grasped the inside back of this now swinging outward van door, the van door was swung and stopped and the fizz shot hit the back tail pipe from the unbalanced shot of which was feebly attempted. The tailpipe came loose with the shot and fell to the ground with a clank. Driver two reacted to this door swing he had seen that the hit man was holding it with a tight clenching. Driver two rolled under the computer van fire safety style and the lady fired three fast pistol shots at the swung open door. Two shots fired hit the door and could not, the bullets could not move through it. The third fired pistol shot was fired at the hit mans head that the lady could quickly have a glimpse of when the hit man had looked at her through the back door van window to estimate his plan for an escape or a one shot one kill deal but the 2 to 1 odds held this hit man at a standstill. The bullet from her third shot nailed the window shattering it altogether unlike the shot she had shot at the other window of the other back side van door. 8 bullets left for the lady, 5 bullets left for one shot one kill guy was his known tally from his past shooting spree endeavors, the result was holy roller driver man of crash car two now was down to 5 bullets in his too loud for public revolver. 8, 5, and 5 three alive, a dead van, as for the cars it was a suicide solution. Holy Roller on the other side got to his feet fast with discombobulated absent coordination. He moved around to the front of the computer van, overtly side skipped with a foot slide swiping across the front of the van, he peeked around the corner and planned to back up the lady from behind. The hit man had a tired arm so he let his feet hit the pavement fast and then he jumped back up, held the broken window frame causing a thin slice glass cut laceration on his hand. The hit man hung from the now moving door. He hung out in a dangle angled unorthodox dangling and his left side was exposed. He aimed the rifle still with its strap on his back, he was still able to aim the rifle at the lady releasing the strap hold. The hit man was holding his left index on a trigger while his right hand spurt some drips of red. A red line liquid drip quickly slid down his now bare forearm like slow lightning and a drop poured. The lady was down on her right side knee and her back foot on the left side was on a high heel toe tip with her left knee sternly gripping paved cemented ground. Two near simultaneous shots were fired by two enemies of the morning. The rifle held by the hit man and the pistol of the lady shot off fired shots so close together in a timed fragment that it was indecipherable for a nearby 20/20 vision witness to determine who had fired off first. The pistol fired shot by the lady pierced the hit mans left bicep. He angle dangled and he dropped. Nevertheless he managed to miraculously for his own sake pry with a gravitation pulling aid. The rifle strap went backwards while he was falling to the station lot pavement. His lie landed lying but still he was not dying. Incidentally this hit man's fired shot whizzed past the lady who amazingly with either a particular Asian art move or your basic complex tai chi reflex movement amazingly jolted up her right arm straight at the sky resulting in her pointing her pistol straight up at this same sky of above. The bullet from the rifle shot made a bang whiz sound whereas the bullet of a firing had bounced up from its hit cement spot roughly 7 feet past driver two who was behind the lady ready for his non lacking back up of his girl. Sirens aloud were nearing and the lady with her crash partner immediately bolted away towards the grass at the end of the station lot. Over to the destination of this two person bolt sprint was a convenient escape vehicle so convenient it made the sky worlds wonder about the persona auras abound, a universe, and the deep holes of no convict times in convection upheaval dawns. Timing was in sink and a signal was sent to these two unseen from a youngster at the store mart door. The youngster of young driving age held up a beverage as if to give a toast and cheers. A running car, two ran from the star, car door ajar, and the keys were turned in ignition. The lady and the guy hopped into their new Honda for a leave take and lady peeled out pushing pedal to the metal. It was too bad for the hit man though because the two who were professional form for the shit that happened most certainly weren't out of the woods yet. They in this time for a shot kill and attempted murder were on for another wild goose chase if the police could detect them. The hit man was tempted to resist arrest but injuries plagued him, he just laid there screaming, panting, breathing with a loosened rifle, a dead nearby van of a nutty scene, and his right hand was relief for the time being. He was using it to clench grab his bicep bullet wound bleeding. Four cruisers sped into the station mart store lot. All of them peeled out in a fast skidding. The hit man got on his knees, dropped the rifle, stifled, he would have placed is injured arms and hands behind his head but he could not do so. The police cautiously ran over to him and put him under arrest. A paddy wagon took him away and authorities were to find a solution. The computer van however left some evidence behind although it was no day of completed foul play. Two cruisers of the four were sent to chase the two spy escapees. A distraction call was made by the youth who had made the gesture signal at the store mart. A sending out and a mere pest chase from a cruiser was not very hard for the lady to maneuver away from with a couple of lefts and a right turn. Onto another back road and back across the state border into New York

State the lady with guy driver two rode onward. Outbound onto a freeway the two of them in victory celebration sang along with a Christmas jingle tune "giddie up giddie up lets go lets look at the show you know it's lovely weather for a sleigh ride together with you, I'm glad were together for a sleigh ride together with you." Their happiness was pure glory and the two of them fell in love with the new dream. They drove off and on the back of their new Honda car were two bumper stickers one that said "honk if you're an asshole" and the other for the pedestrian drivers abroad it said in plain bold print "SHIT HAPPENS."

22

IN RELATION TO the blackout experienced by the sector sectioned immediate family in 1980 the metropolitan city blackout of 2012 candidly candle wire matched unfathomably even to the cleverest of puzzle solvers or spy game code deciphers. Waxen wood of a polished haze glaze showing the darkness from the light of the hydro-gem blue to black sky effects. Sound effects or after effects of lightning strikes from a craft hood made the hammers of a nailing undying trusted. The match between the sparking city small neighborhood blackout of 1980 and the 2012 metropolitan blackout was a scenery ploy to wandering fearful pedestrians for 2012 mind you but as for the 1980 small scale occurrence the matching of certain factors uplifted the alias absolute to Xavier. This match is related directly to the computer vehicles, meaning the truck and the van whereas two were struck down, two allies unknown were inspired inspiration, another smart one was handy with a signal and a leaving of an escape vehicle, and another who was tempted had given in so he was wounded by a bullet, arrested, turned over to authorities. thus this computer van man had melted and disappeared as if he were sand to glass in an hour. First in a match examination is the vital signs of the computer truck driven by alias alas impostor friends if one wanted to be malign in contentment. The computer van that was driven by the instigated instigator investigated investigating young men who fell into the hands of the authorities as well. He was hell well kept in interrogation. In there you will see his reason for possible ploy hood investigation. The computer truck; key turn modern modem art again is the sky high night time mockery true and eventually there was a crash. "SLAM!" was the sound of the New York City pay phone. In deaths toned the cores of applause blown sewn and terrible burdens to the plan in early on metro way is this. The van incident that was there and the computer truck terminally burned. The raw affront against the four involved split into halves. Molds in pains of a cut and bruise against her. Traffic of the personal rage of stop and go was gone making one paranoid of a new becoming ghost town. Brawn taken by needless byes of narcotics buys to the van driver a heroin fixing said. The habit recommended only by those of bad wishes for your outcome. Truth be told the driver of the van in this face, body, and soul match vehicular was not taking in a syringe push to the rather he searched out the morning habits with learned caution and no negativity. The heat of a fire and the warm breath, a death push trigger pull and horns of bull's bullets need not. No bullshit, the candles lit in 1980 matched 2012 so van and truck did not fail. Door swing, one ring, hand sting, and a Christmas sing thing. The burning charcoal truck; down avenues of a New Jersey town the van driver wants a starry way. Not straying too far from the direction of a finding was time unwinding. Another key turning of an ignition is your art. Los Angeles over seas a Cape Cod north but Nord was written on sign meaning the same in French. Melting phase shift entrance dimension north, north east, and outright west made same places make no senses. Addition arts counted to four and a unit made five. Gone in hours our soldiers of this playing rode the dark horse. Sources course was off course of course and even worse was the curses to timidity times. The art of a written word, mad art life articles and particles came together like hour glass sand. Then as we all shall see the sail of the computerized boat on a madness ocean astronomical. It was commanded a go to. The manifest destiny comes true for the planners of the day. Sing song of one way and the day happened. Smart one handy; a wide nose breathes in a healthy breath and noses knows an answer. The train on the New Jersey tracks let in a smart one handy. A signal given approving a void to a situation for the eaves dropping lanes of this guy in the sky and the signal is in you. Yesterday or tomorrow do as a number system, do as a letter, done as a destination. Times of who, what, where, when, why, and how came into the bibliography founded found city of subjects. What we have here is some brave subject matter. Scatter plot cosmopolitan metropolitan fallen. The tempted; a man in financial debt intuitively attracted or better yet she was magnetized to the throne of decency outcome. This mind you was not animal magnetism or an optimistic outlook meaning that the outcomes of the throne holders in vein do induce the primary goal for the animals to adhere to, a connecting unifying oath. Outcast spaced and dramatized are the good adjective representations of improvisation for such attractions. Therefore attackers become the followers and forthwith the unifying oath simply becomes the guiding lit flame spark bonfire of night time attraction. This will lead to the underworld passer by. The drivers in this scenario and their options for hand tools assist for a better and more perfect world. The gun meshed rose is the mixture serum of evil and good, morality and confusion, mistakes and imperfections. Metropolitan blackout; 1980-2012 tempest storm back out, the jetty rocks stack out, lack out and the instant changes come to the insides of souls. Introvert minded caller of a slamming phone in the heart of a city the tempest within calmed, with the storm eye and extroversion this was secluded. He was the walker nevertheless he was aware of the danger involved with the parental advisory of "never walk out in the eye of the storm." Sand to glass man and the melting hearts on mind tamed for it was the dog peace in pieces that melted the brains of out future leaders. Stone cold stoned by the jetty itself the casting of the true cast of no acting theatrical. Practicality sanity on mind means introversion to the beyond. The just one might have assumed typicality on heart is no find of your needs and all you might ever want in the temples of necessary downs. No faults for the garbage dump and the burials for metro add and subtract the environmental gram life future of metropolitan searching. The match made in hell was lit in the non Catholicism place a sector home. Bound for out of bounds dubious devious and venomous was the flame but the conversation pertaining to questions counting to an owing brewed the cuckoo screw and the loose screw is turned back in place with a screwdriver. The duo of the fan shit that happened made more of it. They as said drove away victorious fleeing from the friend who is another alias to Xavier. They had a sing song floating and when not safe they tread water. Brother, sister, father, mother with no blanket fears for smothered. Code cipher decipher hypothetical furor hit a lair and no dragons. Lag sag the duo drove on and the battle of nowhere was in the bag.

23

A LARGE FRAMED MAN standing approximately '6' '2' of no identity known was walking the dark starlit streets of metro black light. With him he had no forms of identification for a detecting by the authorities of either the national, state, or local city government systems. No picture Identification or bank card, no need for such items because although the blue lights of police were around for assistance this man's expertise as an escape trade jack, this fallout was virtually impossible, although with his style of a mover a win was by that of teeth skin or a game winning shot at the buzzer. Undefeated, mistreated, and defeat in onslaughts were erased by his brain anti matter for what actually mattered. The matter was a long ago, super imposed message test for a sighting he was to be informed somehow. Maybe the energy from a generator that lit some windows or a victory sign at the post buzzer garden floor could flash point a pinning of bite holes. Back in 1980 it was late morning and by major coincidence the light of the day for the blackout of 1980 was a relative equinox resulting when examined in detail. When the sun was to go down in 1980 the sun would somehow win a matching eclipse and rise in 2012. Nonsense how is this explained? Such an equinox situation has to be set, however the silicon reflective matched and the man in charge of something in 2012 matched the boy Xavier in 1980. They moved in unison coincidences. The large framed man walked on down a usually crowded street. He turned a corner to an avenue, cut across a back alley to a way. The temperature was low to say the least, a possibility of frostbite lingered yet he took caution and fortunately for him and other he took precaution as well. He donned a pair of night goggles for vision in the more dark places. In his paces he saw the chaser of a villain but on this night tactics surreal were his foundation and heroics had to be put on the back burner, however he was in for a real barn burner modem story of the sort. Xavier put on his clothes, a pair of gray kid 80's corduroys, a beige sports jersey, and his old beat up Olympiad sneakers with the necessary garments. On this possible last morning of an old time blackout he had slept until about 11 A.M. on this Sunday and likely the solution to the 1980 blackout was to come to surface. Haunting whether it was theory to a hellish way or a conspiracy made by demons of the past it was the haunting intrusive messages that defied passageways for Xavier. This boy who was to be the moving stronghold of locale and defiance to any worldly immoral deviation was onward in a scheme genuine. Xavier passed on a late fixing of a breakfast for himself and he in weekend privilege freedoms from his considerations went out for this walk. Luckily for him and the unidentified man in 2012 Xavier on the outside this separated alternate deuce were to be of safety, the wise, and was to move swiftly because of his life of worthy parental guidance. Out the door it was for Xavier and the walking was destiny's choice. The man in 2012 passed on at the end of the way where he saw some innocent by stander pedestrians on this dark and freezing night. Chaotic would be best for a description nevertheless the pedestrian life was even lesser than few and far between. Unidentified man reset his night binocular vision goggles on his head with a hand fixing. He blew out breath of visible carbon dioxide and he found what he was searching for. At the helm of a building grid mother board sort of speak was a silver handle. The motherboard was attached to the back of a building that was not of any particular significance. He pried it open with expert tactic while feeling frustrated that he was unable to locate any nearby manual grid control fastenings such as a power plant in a town. He rubbed hands together after he took off his gloves, he reapplied the gloves and started to pull on some wires that were strangely mixed with some electronics as well as some electrical work. A motive was inept in detection especially to a jack of either electrical or electronics work at this time, especially for a fixing of a blackout situation but the motive as imposed might had been newer than earlier thought especially when a superimposed objective is met. On the other side of the snow static channel bar Xavier was wandering his neighborhood in this 1980 daylight time of a blackout. Down the main street he walked and around the way into the neighborhood park where he met with a friend at the basketball court for a game of horse. After playing a quick game Xavier left his friend and headed back in the general direction of his home. A picture window of a humble home must have had their generator in check and prepared beforehand. Inside this picture window was your basic color bar with nothing written on it in cable bold at all. The residents of this venue wandered around, three of them in total a father, wife and son. The father tinkered with the basics of the television and managed to receive a local channel. On the television screen was a scene from a movie with castaways stranded inside of a ship lost at sea. The antenna on this television shot a visible jolt of electricity and the screen went black, Xavier saw some significance but he could not put his finger on it. Xavier called it a morning well spent and walked back home. A shutting of the door to the grid control and a spark into action was achieved by the unidentified walker of the 2012 blackout night. Unfortunately although of minor consequence for him was the misfortune of his inability to properly refasten the grid control door. The motherboard was tampered with by him with rare expertise. It took the man nearly a half an hour due to conditions of lighting and weather nevertheless a situation unannounced led him to believe his efforts had paid off. In around five minutes red lights and a fire engine siren was heard rounding a corner. By a bay side a non blackout situation unaffected by this blackout situation beholding was handled. It appears that a crime of theft and assault and battery was being executed on a small boat at a dock at the edge of this metropolitan area. This was step one of the night's achievements for this unidentifiable man. A solved crime eventually when police became involved and the result was a wonder ploy about the local governmental conspiracy possible. The walker of the night refastened his vision goggles and in primal he stepped indoors for warmth at a convenient 24 hour sheltering. Soon he would be off for objective two. Xavier runs upstairs hearing the sounds of his liking. Sister Sarah was hacking on her acoustic and she had managed to completely learn an entire song. Mother stood strong for the sector sectioned on this likely final grand finale blackout day and night. Sun set with a superimposed posted signal and in 2012 the sun was to rise in a matching of this understanding strangeness but due to common sense understandings of orthodoxies the goggle walker was not to allow a finale until other tasks were completed. At the sector home another candle flame happened. The four played another family game and the Christmas song duo slept in an alternate year.

24

IN THE ALTERNATE year it was the holiday season. The duo member's crash driver one was another parent to the perceptive eyed as likely an Asian. His name was Kyle and the lady was Malinda. Prior to the altercation and their inducing the result of their alternate ending they in top secret were stricken with temptations ill defined by the logic of ordinary everyday living. Preparation was to be candid and they had felt unfortunate to be appointed with dealing with such a grotesque situation. Kyle was a surprisingly mild man who in the opinion of his partner in assistance to the ploy directive is very shy especially when it came to absolute imperative motive. Supplemented by the natural art forms and her appreciation for her times of living as well as other appreciation for histories of the past might have defied her true not yet found self. Self searching of souls is required in such cases of a necessary duo. The kind heart of Kyle is not as apparent to Malinda which was not the case in vice versa reverse. Suffice it to say it was and is in the case of this story line that Malinda and Kyle in endeavors errands mysterious are two souls of patience way. Their expertise was a virtuoso and the art form talents of Malinda would be considered a god send. Done over in time the two were out of time, they believed but in timing ticking talks they had erased any doubts in their minds caused by talkers who talked a talk but did not walk the walk. The duo was not a couple of intimacy or an item. In fact they were purely professional. Two professionals one would be led to assume with confidence and the claims of the down time fell with the tai chi arts and an aiming up with warning. "We are the neo neon dust life save our souls" but it might in literal terms be save their souls. The explosion must never happen. Kyle and Malinda growing on a tree "KAY EYE EL EL EYE END JEE" Malinda and Kyle sign in singing songs "PAY I EL EYE END JEE" constricted, restricted, con convicted, predicted, rendition, mandatory petition, superstition, competition, born for a mission, "ESS I END JEE I END JEE." "Uuaah!" Kyle wakes up from a mild scary dream of childhood nursery rime playing. Malinda was awake in the back of the hatch back Honda lying across from him in fetal position. The duo of Malinda and Kyle had escaped in times trialing for a new race. They consulted one another with confidence and so they still confided in the dream they had loved. Above mothers looked into the crystal ball of techno wizardry and witchcraft and they saw the intentions of the sick, the misguidance of confidence, pride, envy, lust, and greed. Denial from others who were their equals did not downgrade this duo. The duo held it together and they in secret ploy schematics process of a taking took out the interfering plot hood to the goal. Soul is a word indeed that binds them in times of their hardships and so these strangers in a strange land landed on a slab of a new commandment. Respect thyself in honor for self and others. The prejudice held back and the faults are not important so no finger was pointing. The confidant let loose a done tempo and a new purpose is anointed. Kyle became a man. Malinda was a lady, she intercepted a call in tempest tempo like an algorithm computer glitch. She listened intently to the following............... "Deoxyribonucleic or human DNA for short had strewn a protection glaze among the new lives. Lying down was the tempest beast in east of a figure with no determined direction. Trigger pulls of the lying dragging man's hamstring and his fibula sterilized. Humanized demonized for a prize with eyes watching over us and them. Wrath gas made a neo-town similar to a Chinatown. Anno Domini met minors they timed communications defying and correcting mistakes. Before Christ suffers a threatening aftermath. One is credited he debt debut debacles but embedded the information in pinprick holes on tongues aiding first the sponge fist between ears. The lagging lair layer lying lunar life filled strife. Anew a new meaning of wife and with the times commits comet strength. A striving mode shift survival out does all opposed. Liturgy explains it, logistics rearrange it and the derivation Lucifer cannot change shit. Cape Cod, Yucitan Peninsula, Florida, Gulf of California land, are sticking out like sore thumbs. Japan, New Zealand, Great Britain, Korea, Ireland, Cuba, and Indonesia are all tectonic upward stands for the repo man." Malinda had to wait momentarily it appeared that the algorithm talk paused for a reboot debugging search for a possible fatal error in fetal. Protection guided the duo of Kyle and Malinda to some of these places and inward to a maze. They are not amazed, phased, or pacifists nor will they be engaged, their weapons maybe probable for disengage nevertheless rages race for a race not to be erased, Malinda continues to listen with her headset. The algorithm speaking intensified counting out letters as initials quoted. "T.R.A.C.E.D.! . . . . ? Terror Rats Art Collecting Education Devices. G.R.A.C.E.! . . . . ? Given Rats All Credit Educate! . . . . ? E.R.A.S.E.! . . . . Eastern Rats All Stay Erect." Malinda ended a phone conversation with a sigh and said to the other of the game "Yes this is the call I want traced operator."

25

CANDLE WAX DRIP drops from the lighting of the Sunday night candlelight slid inside the glass candle holder surrounding. What to say when one asked what of it was it. Two hoped on an issue of what father guardian of the sector said was likely in confident agreement with mother "Yes I believe that the blackout will end tonight." Mother with father guardian, Sister Sarah, and Xavier sent wishes upward, downward and in whatever direction possible that was in the situation sensational fallen sun night of this 1980 blackout. The candle case had held enough candles in it to last another night and on this last night possibility of a lighted neighborhood a gift was given for the convenience of the sector 3/4ths family of the dying to be living meaning of liberty. The gift was a temporary borrow lend to be exact. It was a battery powered transistor radio. News had still been applicable and taken in by father guardian and mother not to mention the youngsters of the family. News had it that the authorities in charge would be able to finish tending to this minor state of emergency in completion on this Sunday night. Happily for Sister Sarah and Xavier school cancellations were happening and within an hour it was announced that both of the schools that they attended would be canceled on this upcoming Monday. The light of the candle was sufficient enough for Sarah to do some show and tell. Her room was located at the end of the kitchen they sat in and she had left her acoustic mounted in the corner of the room by the refrigerator and pantry room right next to her bedroom door. Sister Sarah with father's approval and mother too as well as a curious but envious Xavier. Sarah went over to where her acoustic guitar was and grabbed it in the dimness lighting of flamed so that she could play the first song she had ever learned completely all the way through. She brought it back to her chair at the table, she made sure her guitar strap was correctly fastened and she tuned up and began to play. She played the rhythm with proper tempo, all three of a songs chords with near perfection. A not overly impressive rendition of a popular 80's song instilled with some finger picking acoustic detail. When Sarah had finished she smiled and the sectioned sector two who were watching clapped with esteem for the girl. Xavier looked on into the candle fire flame and with bright eyes he said in a funny for a young boy's tone "look at the fire!" Conversation became nostalgic, reminiscent and renowned. Topics mentioned for family bonding such fascination deemed subjects such as past lives, Nostradamus, history via political, folklore, current events etcetera. "Okay kids why don't we play a game of twenty questions like we did before?" Sister Sarah took off her guitar strap and acoustic she had been holding and slightly playing with during the family talk they were having. Father guardian was pleased surprisingly, this was not a game that he always wanted to play. Xavier without hesitation said "yes ma lets play." They four immediate of this jibe sector sectioned were not as wary as before, they were used to the situation. The four of them agreed altogether with a couple of approval nods that it would be nice to play and in doing so they just might set the timing straight for the posted days for prevention of elimination dawns. "I'll go first. "Father guardian enthused decided to get the question ball rolling. "Alright Sarah you can ask the first question." "Is this person a living American male?" "No" Sarah's brows bent semi triangular but you could not see them in the dim candle lit room. "Okay my question." mother said and then she asked question two "How about just an American deceased male?" "Yes and congratulations ding bat." Mother laughed from father guardian's friendly yet wise pun. "You got one, yes, it is a dead American man, Xavier it is your turn to ask a question so go." "umm umm umm umm umm mum?" Xavier mumbled nonsense from post infancy trauma and mother said to Xavier while rolling eyes in the dark "What Xavier?" Can I have a grape freeze pop?" "There not frozen and a drink like that is bad for you why don't you have a warm cola?" "Okay" Mother got up momentarily and grabbed Xavier a cola from the emergency cooler. Father guardian wanted badly to get on with the game and with temperament and pleasure at the fact that he had given himself permission to take a sick day the next day, he simply insisted "Xavier your question ask or I'll belt you." Mother laughs again as Sarah took esteem in family humor and togetherness. Xavier asked his question "Is he a baseball player?" Father gave off a stern stable and calamitous humored "No." Mother smiled wide and she interrupted "my turn" Father responded with witty sarcasm humored still "Okay ding bat do you know the answer?" Mother laughed again and said to him "No but I can ask another question if a ding bat can do such a thing?" Father responds "Okay let's see how you fair, what is your question?" "Lets see this is an alive American man or boy that died young although that is not likely, and he is definitely not a baseball player, and Xavier I think you have been collecting to many of those flea market baseball cards lately." Father interrupted impatiently "Question please!" Mother laughed a lightly and nervously uncomfortable and she asked "is he one of your personal inspirations?" "Yes he is but what does that tell the kids honey. That was such an unfair question only you benefit from it for the answer. I want Xavier to win for once." Mother speaks and Sarah pats Xavier on his back to give him some confidence boosting but he didn't care all that much at all for a win on his horrible record at twenty questions. "Okay" Mother said to father as she swallowed nervously and continued speaking. "I can fix this if this man is a dead American man and one of your inspirations it must be something to do with your past work. "Yes honey the kids are aware enough, it was a politician. Sarah was next and she asked how many questions have we done so far? Father guardian responds "That one made four so there are sixteen possible questions left before one of you finally figure out who this guy is" father's impatience annoyed a presently disabled Xavier. It was Sarah's turn she asked "Was he a president?" Father very pleased smiled and responded "Yes Sarah this man was an American President and he was oops no extra clues, Xavier that makes five your turn. Xavier scratched his head confused at why they were playing and this pre-pre-adolescent asks his next question of a family time killing tradition "Is this that guy you worked with" "no Xavier be your age not your shoe size." Mother laughed again and Sarah made an expression like a girl who was sick of homeroom on the first day of high school. Mother interrupted "His shoe size is just about the same of his age hypocrite." Father laughed a little seeing the lightness of the mild mood of the candle room and he looked to Xavier anticipating and hopeful. Xavier finally responded and tried to ask another question after a minor break in the room mood for four. Sarah interrupted in hopes to end the game she felt was pretty stupid "game rule Xavier mistake questions count that makes six of them mom it's your turn again." Mother responded with no disappointment, she had taken Xavier's mistake inconsequential lightly, she speaks another question that did not pertain "I forgot do answers count as questions?" Father guardian guards game rule number three and says stern while holding back laughter in mystery of a finding "yes that is the way this game is played family, darling wife your turn." Wife Mother Hubbard responds with question seven "is it John Fitzgerald Kennedy?" "No that makes eight questions now" Sarah barked out annoyed. "Unfortunately for you Sarah it is your turn, forget about your stupid guitar and get on with it" mother said in her manner of undetectable usual lazy neglect for her daughter. Sarah stretched her arms and then she went back into a slouching position in her chair like a guy and asked the next question "Ah a twentieth century president? "Yes" father said as he slammed a fist on the kitchen table enthused but he might had hit the table a little too hard because he shook it nearly knocking over the glass encased lit candle. Father gives the next authoritative instruction "Mother Hubbard of the cupboard your turn." Mother with pride for the five jibe and in representation for herself and the other family members including the dreaded mother in law and the charming grandfather and also as the strong point sixth prided member of the sector family asks question number nine "Okay let me get this right here, this is an American President of the 20th century, the one were in right now kids, this president is not John Kennedy and we have also determined that you never worked with him" laughs "and this is not the present president I presume nor is it one that is alive.

Father interrupts "Well what are you waiting for Christmas?" "I think it, I know it, and this isn't fair because I know he was an inspiration to you. Why don't I ask another question and let one of the kids get it?" Father responded "yes that would be the fairest thing to do." Okay here is a rhetorical one since I know the answer, this will be vague though, I am routing for you Xavier." Sister Sarah rolled her eyes again and let out a breath of minor annoyance flaunted strong with patience for the blackout special situation of this family dealing. Mother continues and she immediately asked "Is this president responsible for the establishment of workers Unions in America for your future pension and things like that?" Father responded and he was pleasured inside appropriately "Yes this would be that president Miss Hubbard." "Miss Hubbard?" "Would ding bat be better?" Comments disregarded and father let the kids know that the questions were half way through for the game. Father guardian saw Xavier who was mad that his turn was skipped had had his chance "I don't know but I must guess that it was someone." Mother looked on and Sister Sarah, encouraged Xavier with one of her looks "Roosevelt." Father responds with happiness "Yes, that's great Xavier but was it Teddy or Franklin?" "Teddy?" "No Xavier it was the other one father said not disappointed. Xavier then asked "what was the other ones name?" Mother interrupted and told Xavier "Franklin" "Huh?" "Franklin Delano Roosevelt was the name you wanted, we know you meant him so you get the win Xavier." Family was pleased for the candlelight moment of common liking. "Well, not bad it only took eleven questions for that one." Father approves of family game performances and he in good nature of a good man of the present time at least tried to think of how to pass the time for the remainder of this blackout night. The candle blew out from a mystery gust and they were left in the darkness sitting.

26

DESTITUTE JETS WERE all the same so it had appeared. The prostitutes offered the dome chain star game so the floaters aimed. Landing crashes invoke passionate dead souls molded with a smooth soothing. The skulls in between life and death, good and evil, lightness and darkness, matter and anti to it had witnesses in formulas solid as they are. The witnesses mold the combine of disguises. The trade jacks mended sewn wool for prices. The command post saw a new ghost. The compost introduced a hoax host. The hexes identify in sexes. The south and west sided with Texas. The dawn looker saw writing in books. The new queens are taken by the rooks. The knighted are sighted on a day. They flighted Cronkited Apollo and Clarke stars. The airplanes that went down were like cars. The people inside them were from Mars. Savior days of no dazed and blinded, we have found ourselves, life becomes sound. New clay is profound. In tones the apples ate Mars scars. In bones the cell life mates Pluto. A figure of 8 is reduced to a standstill. A young man flicked paper on window sills. The center of a system made light life. The marriage outlook flew outright. Together they were in damns of the willing. Two rings and a new world and married to thrilling. Out is the price, pretty and nice, we all thought twice, and it past hysteria for merrier pass and choose it flints amuse. The fallen were paranormal pentagram material indescribable unless elemental is absolved. Solvers salute with flags in daylight but ever wicked of the weighing sounds the siren of the escaping jailbird brings absurdity into the simplest. This would be doubt for the most complex minds making perfect sense. This explanation has to do with the expletive explained thoroughly beforehand to the New York City slamming of a pay phone. Upon escaping and the involvement of one who was at the steering wheel helm of the truck disguised for furniture moving, this is far from common knowledge to the employees of our governments investigation agencies. Proficient sufficiency is insignificant for the slammer jammer who slammed down a communication device. Efficient policy tells those who know of the ploy defense to a plot of evil that sufficient, proficient, or efficient are not qualifying but sensationalism magnificent is the unfortunate matter of the truth of this slamming, and all relates to the big bang star scatter. Nevertheless the truck driver lost his vehicle to a morality bandit but as credited to a selfish inside all was not wrong or negative for the loser of this computer truck. When the truck was stolen the watchers were not the disciples and the last stand was a gun. It was the roses for the dead however that stifled and the rifle is obtained by the hit man who eliminated the thief ploy boy of the disguised truck. Two pretended to celebrate an early Hanukkah and they found the spirit of Christmas with a downing sing song upgraded. The two who had been assassinated were found dead on the side of the road some time after their demise approximately two hours if one wanted to be retentive. The burning truck in disguise was obvious motive for police and other investigation authorities to make this advance and discovery. From this unavoidable mishap for the hit man driver of the computer van an investigation was executed. It was the use of certain devices by the Christmas song duo that aided them in their need to devise their retaliatory strike. The crashes at the other more less obscured in a more thickly settled and inhabited area were subject to investigation too of course. Suffice it to state the investigations ended up linked to one another and the duo unfortunately were perceived as either individuality of international ties thus an accessing of the government or those who had crossed a line and had taken the law into their own hands. This would have been a defiance of United States law and basically it would have also been defiance to the logistics of international physical sciences of law or simply the way it works. The duo was aware they that they were in a situation that required tricky maneuver and clever modes, methods, and intricate tactics of disguise. Four possibilities of disguise types had been discovered. Skin replacement was one that wore on their minds but they however had come to the vivid realization that they were fighting for a worthy purpose, this last statement is the poster post script for the meaning definition of understatement. Another disguise was impostor replacement used with a lie and an instigation positive in aspect outcome. Impostor replacement when used by the opposition meaning those subversive of evil or those of natural and uncompromising evil must not get their brain paws on such ideas although some believed they had already. A third mode of disguise was optical illusion sensual formula. Optical illusion sensual formula can and oftentimes is considered both the third and fourth mode of disguises. The problem with optical illusion sensual formula from a perspective in the taking into account as consideration is that at first it is non formula chemistry of mind matter and non solid therefore it is simply the first phase of two phases. Phase two takes time and if in the wrong hands could be inevitable and dangerous something like actual cloning, but there is a difference. Simplicity in action is the mode play ploy faults supportive for the duo and their own vocation education of their arts, thus shall combine with art of souls introduced. They will not fail! The duo will, shall, and did or whatever time scope out look that a reader adventurer prefers to move in prime with the mover. The rovers of dead and the times written on pages just might be the shocking surprise to the outcome. The sector sectioned is neutral on this matter for a time but the section of the writing on black white and read will also be surprise in virtual vital virtuoso modular involved in a theory. What is the question Kyle might ask Malinda, what is the answer would be her question in the form of an answer days or years beforehand. Nevertheless no plot defies the ploy boy, he is set in times of modern modem play for assistance with expertise of the heaven falcon. Development theory cannot, will not retain, but obtain a vital sign it does. This is a sign of the times.

27

AT THE 24 hour sheltering was a calendar displaying on its small top pages interesting posters. A history on a topic on a photograph of a small scale excerpt relating to the subject of the historical landmark snap shot within borders of this now metropolitan sector city. This sighted casual find was pleasantry glimpsed for a moment. The unidentified man with night goggles noticed something important to the importance involved on this freezing dark blackout night. The venue of this sheltering was intended for the blackout emergency. The blackout was only to last one and a half days and most of the people who resided did so due to where they were at the time of this minor emergency. The venue on subject was an old high school powered by some generator activity and due to location this old abandoned high school sheltering it had some power from outside sources of locale including telecommunications. In this old high school by a hung up picture that displayed all of the presidents of the 20th century was a hung up American flag. Onlookers looked to the stars and stripes on old glory. The flag made the onlookers open inside thinking back to the year and the day of United States turmoil eleven years before this blackout night. What was noticed interestingly enough for a fear feel feeling of frightening déjà vu was an old style phone answered by a woman with one of those familiar faces. The woman answered the phone after two rings. She paused listening intently. While she was listening intently just so and justified her face grew into a melting downward sexed, stable, unable and hopeful for enabled. She did so with wide eyes and surprised in definition timed surreal. The woman after listening for one minute excluding several umms and ahhs spoke softly to the person on the other line. "But!" she realized her angered tone and decided wisely to speak softly. Only the woman was heard by the unidentified man so he in attention and with intuition listened inconspicuously. "I" . . . . "you can't do" . . . . "NO!" . . . . I can't get that?" . . . .Yes and he's crooked I won't do it." . . . ."Newport street yes." . . . . "Then get another job!" and the déjà vu ended with a moderate phone slam. Unidentified walker man had some knowledge in pertinence to what this conversation might have entailed. He knew some of the problems of local crooked police and the local government. This necessary eaves dropping caused him to realize what he must do. He had his carry miniature knapsack bag with his night goggles and the blackout was still prominent. He got his mind together and made the decision that it was time for him to obligate himself to objective number two. Out a doorway and into the dark night way he put his night vision goggles back on his head with a fastening. The unidentified walker had heard through the grapevine that one of his possible alias' once frequented Newport Street. He was not sure just what an alias was in the case of the story of blackout but it likely had to do with the disguises of combined combination to the pre-explained scenarios concerning modern phenomenon such as optical illusion sensual formula or skin replacement cheat tactics. It was an issue of enemy fear tactics in this case of a possible Newport Street scenario real. The unidentified goggle walker knew for near certain of crooked police work having something to do with actions taken somewhere on a road off of Newport Street. He walked on with needed sight, his peripheral was limited from the vision scope goggle binoculars he was donning, so he had to turn his head in a manner of seeming paranoia more often than not and common. Corrected would be the word on the night of this 2012 blackout and objective might be the word for the blackout of 1980. Small neighborhood importance an underrated fan phase hazy glaze of the evil maze amazed. Some traces of some sort of green like chemical was detected on the ground by the unidentified walker. If the cards were to be played correctly by him he would end up the hero of this blackout night but her Jonah and the point made by a sedated pointing bonded the joints and cartilage spots for the body of this man. The sands of a plow truck had laid its grain and the walker was forced due to icy ways to walk nearly in the middle of a back way street. He picked up a green granule of dirt and sand and wondered if it was a clue. A clue for certain this rock green grain granule was but certain factors were puzzling. Back in the time of 1989 another who was a member of the combine of disguises played a roll. A sector ploy opposition of inner conspiracies who was well versed in schematics this member was. This was the 1989 member of the devised ploy advisory commission. A commissar in denial served trial far away.

Just how this trial with a commissar became relative to the blackout story is far fetched yet when the evidence in this trial is examined far fetched takes on the meaning of undeniable evidence. Proven providence evident to the judge and the commissar involved although not directly related to the circumstantial evidence found and displayed in exhibits of this trial, his denial had diminished for a while and so it was that a coast European had the means to make a cut off of a mad scientist who was devising some sort of plan to fuse a carbon combination with nitroglycerin and other chemicals with a color haze sensuality sent through it, thus defying periodic elemental rules of scientific fair play. Whether the commissar mattered or not is mostly mystery to a judge and jury in America but the foreign court responsible saw his misery as a direct tie to his relationship with this man. A few containment vile cases for liquid toxins of this magic potion were packaged and sent to those who were qualified for an examination of it. A vile got into some dirty hands thus it becomes evidence that the dirty granule that dirtied the right glove of the unidentified walker was this magic potion. Modern day wizardry mended the frock hemming of the donning women innocent enough as the members they were of the craft. Yes, the magic potion was green and not the material elements of a wizard spell. 1989 time ploy boys rearrange time on a silica sand fault and reflection birthed life out and about within but the movements were strong and cold. Green was the colored haze glaze for writing words, walking and speaking them. Times of timid walkers saw con victory so history was outdone in tyranny. "Stare at me." a young boy of 16 took a monopoly boardwalk walk to a talking phase they realized in partnership what the words "do you know what I know" mean. "Come on right into my left cornea look." A noticing of action phase shifted bodies and souls and the spit spirit lingered so in 2012 the boy who was the man fingered at a screen. His genes toxic, his means ironic, poisoned he was not from the tonic he drank it was the diluted decomposed green gue. "What is it?" "Oh nothing I just wanted to see what it would be like to look into the eye of a mockery." Back in the future year of 2012 the unidentified walker went into a corner and took out his cell phone and lit his flash light in purple. He examined the green rock granule with the knowledge he had retained sending purple light through it. In this examination he saw a mixed color mostly grayish but the color had a tinted blue florescence. It was determined by the unidentified walker that the green on the granule of rock and sand was this substance indeed. He, due to this examination fastened his night vision binocular goggles once again and he started to look around on the street way that was only parallel with Newport Street. In his looking investigation of this green gue clue he noticed that some drip drops and one glob were strewn in moderate separation on the street way ground. He followed the evidence spots of green and around a corner he walked right onto

Newport Street. Down away past more unlit venues still he had seen near an old dominion with a neon sign that would normally be lit up there were some pedestrians over yonder. These pedestrians were in rare form seeing that most of the population of this city section in a blackout and declared state of emergency were inside of their homes at this time. When he moved he moved carefully and soon got over to the place of which they were standing. He had to peek around a corner into the opening of an alley way. A bonfire was lit and the pedestrians by this bonfire seemed unaware that the identified walker was even an existing member of the human race. Unidentified walker stalked one, he suspected as she wandered in a stray. An array of light in sky made a flashing apparent like that of a gaseous astronomy photo of nebulae in purple. The girl was far, he could not recognize just what her features were like seeing the darkness of the night and the fact that he had to place his vision binoculars back around his neck. When he moved close enough to her he saw a face of familiarity, it was an elderly woman with no graying, a deceiving made by biology sciences leading the unidentified walker to believe something. This something was true it was . . . . a disguised woman he questioned her thoroughly although she was shy from the street smarts she had and the severity of a blackout situation just made matters worse. He found what he was looking for another clue. In his questioning she had informed him that the old coffee house had an employee who might have ties with a culprit of long ago. The unidentified walker man worked further in manual modes he might have liked to access a portable modem screen nevertheless he had seen to it that she was not a culprit but to the rather she was simply an informant of mystery to a blackout case to be resolved. Whether the walker or the unidentified walker of many names termed to this story had completed objective two was to be determined. One thing was possible for certain however. The green substance might lead to a reason unrelated to a blackout, the woman might know a scientist or a commissar in the past, talking on a phone at the temporary sheltering might mean that a mandatory nonsensical evacuation might have taken place, regardless of this it was observed in an assumed motive to a ploy boy watching a television screen that conversations and lies defied lead to good or evil. Reality however told the unidentified walker that motive two was not fathomable, so whether such evidence would lead the solvent to a solution had to remain a secret for the time being. Be as it may the compost was defeated and the dawn of light was to make way with more motives caused for the unidentified walker. He settled for this clue in his mind and the time had been getting late it was now about 1 A.M. and the light of day for a cure was still far off for him and Metropolitan madness calm when considered in absolution thinking. The unidentified walker set his night vision binoculars back in the placement of his knapsack bag, it rounded a shoulder. The walker of the blackout night headed back to the temporary sheltering, it took him about a half an hour to get there. Attention for him was vital at this new point in time.

28

THE MORNING EIGHTH grade buzzer went off and it was a half a day but Luzzin and Xavier liked the weather. Zimmerman the man was not available on this day because he had been attending school on this half a day. It was morning and on Xavier's common walk to school, he ran into Luzzin with another who was with him, a sixth grader. 1986 early October they wished it was snowing but the red sox had to play and wild horses or even rain would not stop Xavier from watching his home team from getting that pennant. "Xavier me and Chuck are skipping today it is a half a day, why don't you come with us?" "I don't know man I missed some days already I don't think I should." Chuck spoke up like the menace he was "Come on Xavier it's a half a day and we won't get caught, no friend of mine is going to be a chicken man." Xavier decided that since it was a half a day and he did not have his bag with him that a nice day of hooky wouldn't be such a bad idea. The three of them agreed to make a school skip day of it and head out to Luzzin's house for some kid fun. Down a way they went the three of them two big shot eight graders and a sixth grade peon. The eon day was no play for the prayers of the dark light nights. The common prey of children of the down social scene looked down at them from the north but the births afar sent just ones along in dew of this mystic morning. The morning mist mystic tic toc on clocks and in a walking the three school skippers of this day went under a bridge, as the motor cars sped by some were beeping and some were sending messages form the maker senders of our love letters, they have our number. Soon they arrived at Luzzin's house for some morning Joe. Xavier was not particularly a coffee drinker nevertheless with Xavier's wisdom and bologna to put it straight he knew that the sixth grade big shot who always went by the name of Chuck should have one for a wake up calling. After all the common drink for Luzzin, Zimmerman the man, and Xavier was commonly yellow carbonation, a beverage inexpensive with potatoes as an ingredient, or some whiskey on rare occasions. Underage drinking is commonplace in American society but the experiences of your lives may be guided by them if kept in moderation so as the slogan states "to each his own." No advisory of wisdom for the three came from above and Luzzin brought out some desert food it was time for cookies and milk. Around 9:30 the mist of a freakish half an hour phase died down and it was skies of blue for the daytime. The three finished their snack and health calcium fixing and Chuck thought it would be about the right time for some good old fashioned complaining. Chuck started to plan a complaint scheme as Xavier looked around noticing a family picture on the wall in Luzzin's home. It was not the entire family of Luzzin's in this photograph but rather it was his parent's marriage picture. Xavier pointed at the picture of Luzzin's mother and father and asked "who's that?" A moderate clean cut young man donning old 50's decade nerd glasses standing with a moderate lady of your common look was in this picture frame. Xavier in rudeness said ignorantly to Luzzin "your father was a nerd huh?" Luzzin reacted "WHAT!" "I" Luzzin cut Xavier's next word off "don't call my father no nerd man if you do I might have one of your baseball player hissy fits and one of those conniptions you have might be in order too." Xavier went to comment in an apology that would have been false and insincere but Chuck in bad humor saved the day for the assholes. Chuck speaks "NERD! He's a nerd! He's a nerd tird of the dumb ass word!" Chuck got up from the chair he was in that might as well be a high chair and started dancing in the style of a teasing razzing. He spoke with ominous wisdom in art of the wise guys in the sixth grade "Nerds worse had heard the bird word and fur comes to the boys of my ass class in this state of the cool kid mind and Xavier you are buying me a sandwich later. Luzzin walked over to Chuck with one of those orange street cones they would set for cars in a lot. He held it like a megaphone and before Chuck could muster another word of the wise Luzzin lifted the cone like the megaphone and said into it and when he spoke the word that changed the world, it sounded loud in stereo surround sound. He spoke loudly into it "F##K Y#U" oops expletive corrective. Xavier laughed and the three decided to head outside for some hooky school skipping good old fashioned fun. Down another street and walk way by an old cemetery and the city's most popular ice cream parlor Chuck had an idea. "Guys lets hop one of those freight trains or a moving truck or something if we do so we might get to the other side of town." Xavier rolled his eyes and had a fast change of heart when he heard the local city freights over by a way beyond the new gas station auto body and the apartment buildings that were sadly demolished and replaced that his mother lived at as a youngster. The old terrace place was the romance novel lifeblood noble and novel for the new blood boy joining. The parents of her Jonah alias Xavier had met the days of love lives. Although they barely knew one another the times of romance ways were not seen in full until examples set in the fables of the dreamers. Apple core dreamer on another side bent in stride and asked the question of the quench quest of why. The industry stable within the city heeded way for the twenty questions answered for the new blood was socially secure in his born life of trails, truths, triumphs magnificent, and burdened times. "Hey look there's the local freights going by, convenient as this day is for an advantage taking I say s##t man lets go hop one." Chuck advised his friends with inexperienced pride for his class clown persona. "I don't know Luzzin here might be a scared 'e' cat." Xavier said, "Shut up Xave" Luzzin started to walk towards the freight trains anyway but the three of them realized that there was not enough time to catch these freights unless they ran for it and that was not in the cards of a dealt hand. The three walked further and grabbed some lunch at the parlor, Luzzin paid for hot fudge sundaes around the house and Chuck reminded Xavier that he wanted a sandwich after their day was over. Later on there was a golden opportunity for them. A moving parcel delivery truck was parked outside of a local convenience store. The driver let the motor run while he stepped inside to make one of his daily deliveries. Before he stepped inside the store he saw that Chuck and Xavier were getting ready to buggy hop the delivery truck. The delivery man was far from stupid and he was able to tell that the two were going to attempt a hopping ride either from their faces conniving or Luzzin was a tattle tale who felt in the mood to go against his way. The motive plan was set in stone, Xavier and Chuck had determined in commanding nods of agreement that they were to hop this truck when the driver was to come back outside and get behind the wheel. Luzzin with a sly happy smile stood against the wall of this convenience store and pretended to assist the kid crime as an accomplice. The delivery truck driver came out and was going to get behind the wheel but his suspicion guided his smarts of the not to be foiled one day mind. Luzzin saw that Xavier with Chuck were behind the truck already, he told them the coast was clear and to get ready to hop it. Hoping for a hopping the driver moved towards the back of his truck with a hop skip and jump figuratively speaking of course. The two of an attempted hopping were fortunately off course on this day because as Luzzin began to nearly laugh the driver stepped around the back of the truck and he caught them red handed standing on the back metal panel holding on to a grasping bar. "I TOLD YOU GUYS TO GET THE HELL AWAY FROM THE TRUCK NOW GET THE F##K OUT OF HERE!" quick hop skip hops and the two were off and running for no reason at all. Luzzin laughed hard and the driver got back in his delivery truck and he drove off to another delivery mission on this beautiful sunshine day. Three of them got back together after a two man running spree and it was now early afternoon. Parochial school was out earlier that day at 10:30 just a few hours back. Time passed and the three decided to go home for the day. Luzzin went his way and Xavier agreed with Chuck's unsubstantial order of buying him a sandwich. The two of them ventured to a downtown area whereas Xavier tried to talk Chuck into going into a fast food joint or maybe grabbing a slice of pizza. Chuck in non compliance of a social youth low life talked Xavier into going to the local deli. When they walked by the deli restaurant Chuck tried to annoy his friend by saying "Smell that food ummmn." Chuck then made smelling sounds inhalations with his strengthened nostrils. They went inside and Xavier realized he was just short of some sandwich money. Xavier compromised and so he decided to buy the two of them each a large sized coffee. When they went outside Chuck asked if Xavier had any more cash and Xavier became frustrated with Chuck. Xavier started to speak and all of a sudden Chuck broke into a fit of rage. Chuck threw his large coffee at Xavier and it landed all over the ground making a splattering stain "YOUR QUEER!" "What?" "I SAID YOUR FUCKIN QUEER ARIGHT!" Chuck made a left hand swiping gesture brushing Xavier aside. Xavier shrugged his shoulders and basically blew Chuck off for the day. He stopped at the boys club and showered. After a nice hot steamy shower he walked home. It was a beautiful day but a nice snow day in December might have been better. As Xavier walked home he thought about the red sox and his hoping for a pennant title.

29

RENESSA WAS LONG gone and the times of morbid hell were still prominent for Xavier her Jonah in his sedated life state. The Christmas duo was in hiding in their time frame. They had felt the feel of lingering demons and in their stated goals of prime the two of them accessed methods of just survival of the fittest and they were the finest. The eight grade parochial classroom was to be abandoned one day long after this class graduated. The entire class had won the hearts of past generations in deepness of the dreaming minds. As for the hit man van driver he would be subject to containment in the proper facilities but beforehand he was subject to interrogations. The others involved all followed the path of righteousness or so we would like to believe. Nevertheless the blackout story takes a turn into modem modes of lying defiance defined and the lies that diminish our truths downplay the question of the answers to a solution. In other words the answer lives lies and they rest in waiting days of manifest destiny, a resulted solution set in stone. Dawn light certainly awaits the metropolitan city place but in the other city that sparked a flame in 1980 it is legend tale that the very same year of 1980 caused our true lighting of a candle flame for the mystery tragedy protecting in 1989 and the town grew on the branch in the formula striping strip. Xavier her Jonah rested in sedation in the 2nd decade of the 21st century we all know. The bleeding heart causes who never really intended to bleed for a cause paused unintended and thought hard they never pretended. Because of the terrible burdens in the lives of all of those involved in the blackout story it was said as a given that a bond was the time fault spring to the well fountains streaming and gleaming in the days of all burdens for the counted motorways of a vision. The cities paid a price and with a city a dime was worth a fortune. Where was the happening concern for the kindles cradled in a hospital? A trend all spindle winter sprinter ran like Kinta. Santa Maria via mama Mia see her free, deep in times thought do key pure lure of your liars lying lairs. Santiago Chile 1879 A.D.; Maria a new born in a refugee camp had made an accidental discovery. At the ripe age of 9 she had been a member of another family due to abandonment unavoidable. Her mind from dreams in line with Jungian anima animus of a mind outlook in the dream world unconscious had her realize from premonitions her intention in life. The creation of her must lead to something? So it was said by some of knowledge . . . . but she was now the dreamer of the dwarf star 9 (at least for the time being that is) Raging rated rather. She had now visualized herself as the destroyer. Voyager and other hazards to the astronomical of what's out there had in the future with NASA discovered 8 brown new brown dwarf stars. A fuel mileage hazard gaseous clay of a molding folded and the dwarfs of the outer domain could not combine like skin pores or convective pebbles on a needle pin tip meshed with a grown light semen material elemental. Maria had learned from her guardian to mend and sew. She sat in feeble fable mending a hem. Since age 4 she had remembered her dreaming of a nova birth. To her the birth of a star could happen in other ways and not from an explosion. Corroded was this dream and from a choice she did not have she as roll of the destroyer could not hope for her nova or to be more accurate a brown dwarf mini star. Her new intent from this age of 8 was to create black light energy to decompose the outer realm. She felt the healing of some pains in her times as a youngster playing with her small group of fellow refused friends. Intention in her tent had dominated her so she became a dominatrix in her early teens. 8/100ths is the numerator and denominator for a qualifying brown dwarf star. Reduced that is 2/25ths. Take away pint point 5 and its 1/13ths or one 13 or won 13. The dominatrix Maria tried to be as dominant but she was only potential for a numerator over a denominator. The white light of half life was set to her. Domination was to be denied by her and Maria knew this even at her young age. She finished sewing and put her materials away for another day. The others at the camp oftentimes shunned her. Maria however is woman's troop leader. The heroin young and new born Maria is and only is the dust of an angel who was once a demon who could induce the semen for a sun time November. Meanwhile forward tasking and flash fan phased into 2012 was unto postmodern Renessa. Renessa had found evidence for her infant unborn and if pregnancy was in volition than the violent potential of pro choice was wrong in such a case as this would be. This of course was a personal decision and the matter after a womb mended the woman strong it was Renessa, she became old iron side as a battleship, friendly yet she was cunning in her ways for the defending of a litter theoretical by motherhood protection of her own. Now was a time of century centurion relations across a plane of time. Tomorrow was not as promising as yesterday but today brought nudity unashamed by the cloth De Vinci promises that are so ever, whatever, and forever may be from angels and a feather.

30

A THIRD MOTIVE IN the making might seem tragic magic of universal formed statics but statistics rendered the odds in favor of the unidentified walker and none other than Xavier her Jonah. This of course did not seem to be a reality glimpse of non fiction and the friction from an escape and her Jonah led him to his other disguise as the underdog Dog Star dog war life spewed in dew and the dues were adding up. Hammer of sick ill stricken sickles in red and gold symbols drew breaths for the hopes of the people inside the Gorbachev new sign. No liars, so the tires tread on tiers and the wolves let go like the compromising porpoise; the drool spit spun in pinwheels. The rounding up of slay attempted adaption of the sort would always lead to the mystery of what is actually behind closed doors. The door in this case was the mortuary living and a new understanding had to be forced. Locked in placement of a death trap was the possibility in Xavier her Jonah's mind. Her Jonah was locked in his home after Renessa had gone away. Xavier was to be eradicated, his beliefs abolished, and the foundations of his dreams diminished slowly inside. In plain English the plot against him and the leaving of his others left him demolished. Behind padlock and key was where he or she was supposed to be undone. Outcomes showed the peacetime. He or she meaning a switch trick was pulled in the dynamics of a conning, a ploy, and a plot. Messages were sent to Jonah on sides of techno color high def. Processes of it all and in this switch inside, it was Xavier her Jonah behind the wall with the padlock set. A locksmith sent was the trick move but the sent was scented and the intruder was to be another spy opposition. The intruder had come from the west intuitively not. Regardless she showed at the doorway and became part of the Jonax conversation. Her Jonah or Xavier; Jonah, Judas, Jedidiah, Jonax or John it was simply code names for one and a mimic of voices. He took the day between the intruder and Her Jonah code named take your pick. Three knocks and the running up the stairs happened. The intruder felt the phases shift and others on the outside were intended for her backup. "Knock knock knock" on the door and Jonax conversation came in. JONAX CONVERSATION; Jonax in a Russian accent like a woman "I can't hear you maybe you should knock with your passport fisted." Jedidiah like a young man and another accent Israeli "die this intruder will for such defiance" he spoke softly to Jonax supposedly and they listened intently. The intruder woman speaks from outside the padlock door "I have been seeking one Jonax he is supposed to be a relative of my predecessor to this cloak and dagger game." Jedidiah next "No can do my will stays with the night lights and the protector is known to us and not your government." The intruder woman speaks again with nerve for a plot and ploy taking into a Swiss account "Money is the talker! You know the walk now talk it and I will head to my home country." Jonax as a woman spoke with charismatic expertise "The boss is not very happy nor will his be again if we don't send you back and don't try to use our local police." Woman intruder again "What's the deal do we have a bargain for the lives of the two dead or a ploy for the two alive? You think I don't know about them from 1996 New Jersey or someplace else?" Judas does a fake cough and an expressive exhale recognizable but different on a given clue from the other voices. The cough is followed by a throat clearing and Jonax spoke again "no bargain you shall not find the seeking. The duo is somewhere you will never know and we are still bitter for the loss of two of our best players." The intruder gasps with surprised accumulated acclamation expletive style "No f#####g con job on your personal agendas I see but when it comes to this dream you might be set to a throwing theory of abandonment! Your duo got the best of us." Jedidiah made the last word for this matter of a section segmented "my way is the highway, I did stay in the places bound and three squares a day is fine by me." Judas in the same recognizable voice as his cough and outward gasp put in his two cents "the downed are up there an if I go up myself I will see the dream, I do have faith that I will see our two deceased as well." A last word from the woman intruder "So be it! I remind you that there is more where it came from and we own a good portion of your authorities. Cats out of the bag! You win this one." The intruder left and when the door slammed outside, her Jonah as his true self none other than Xavier original exhaled in relief. He had faked the voices and the Russian Jonax woman, it was the hardest one for him to muster. He washed his hands of the mission for a night and silent sleeping he was. Her Jonah slept serene and silent because of the sickness he was inflicted with. The sickness had affected his breathing and due to other factors of his past behaviors his cardiovascular condition was suffering otherwise. Upon awakening he was so sedated that he did not realize the time frame of common. He was unsure of the year, his silence was haunting him, he was reflecting and he thought over another shot at a writing career, and the voice faking Jonax conversation he had the day before seemed like a dream itself. The days of the no lanes for the wicked only showed a possibility of change and there was another far ahead, he must aid the babies of a new time and marry the love that was set to defeat him. We will see what happens next but what happens next has nothing to do with grids grinding or an explosion to happen. It was in all fact of nurtured nature and supernatural if one wanted to reflect on sciences spiritual, physical, mental, and religious. Prestige was on set for no downgrades downplayed and the ploy hit the plot on its weak spot while it lay. Down for a counting and at sins of seven and virtues of the same numeral the significance of the number seven brought the babies to a land isle with approval from all involved. Disapproval needed to be sewn and a shine light took the good crown. Do not be deceived by your own decoys.

31

DECOY MEN AND women were considered expendable but the children were part of the white cloud sacred cloth. A beagle and a shepherd combined into a spotted leopard. No matter how enforced the laws international were to be the audience for Xavier her Jonah was truth, lie, deceit and genuine in one. The audience was the laughing hyena. This audience would have appreciated his output input but only the communications of certain data was passing through what is called the bar gate. The bar gate was a blocker to any decoys that in explanation would be termed as a word adjective, verb at times or adverb but not a noun. Phantoms decoys made boy and the boy grew into Xavier her Jonah. The lady became woman and woman returned to lady and saw the human value in the white cloud cloth of their young. The Christmas duo made it past New Years Eve into 1997 and they entered the combine of disguises. Enterprise chaotic in action, the duo made some dough from the payoff involved and they acted as if the combinations of the locksmiths were plentiful. Kyle and Malinda felt splendid winter feelings. It was a bitter cold January as one would expect. Projections from Kyle had off set Malinda's able bodied ways thus he was weakened and so it was that she was still the driver of whatever cockpit they would undertake for a necessary joy ride, an action commodity that the two of them were familiar with for sure. February came and others including Xavier did their parts in their active duty involvements. Kyle had noticed along the freeway when the two of the duo were heading south a town with a clever name, they were to hide in Kill Devil of the Carolinas. In Kill Devil was a stereotype type O assumed. Ashamed as was his partner in this spy game non game she was Malinda and she unlike Kyle was not just a leader of this duo in dynamics but she had been watching the watchers from afar. Henceforth was missing from her friend and co worker Kyle. He was a drive for the required prestige, a commitment to the higher committees condemned in damnation and deterred he was to the aiding of nations. These nations were plagued by a notion rule of no emotion. The tempest crucifixes had lost ground and from the metal of which they were elementary composed the woods unpolished outdid time and off set a minding mind, this was the mind of a newly hospitalized 1997 Xavier Xevon Tareynton. He had moved to the metropolitan city and the duo had to live on in Kill Devil. A morning stretch and yawning came from Malinda in a separate bed from Kyle who had been enjoying a few nips he had purchased from a small liquor store near a beachfront. The duo was to theoretically set camp and in doing so the two of them had found a quaint parking area with rental space. Their phony identifications should have been enough to do the trick but it came down to Kyle's outstanding ability to adapt to given surroundings. He faked his way in with some small talk American lingo methods. The duo sent signals from a stray light on sights and the messages of the signals were exceptional, correct, rational, internationally fool proof and one could say they were served on a silver platter. After leaving the motel and after Malinda thanked Kyle for limiting his liquor consumption the night prior the duo reached their destination hideout for a time. The duo of Malinda and Kyle found a rental space with one bedroom with the proper fixings for a live in situation and a hide out. The two of them changed their appearances, Kyle got a new hair do and the cold weather would take away his tan. Malinda could not dye her hair for certain reasons having to do with those who were after her. What she did was she changed her lifestyle appearance and her accent was to be dealt with. The duo of Malinda and Kyle waited a while and they did so in good health. One of these days they both planned to possibly separate and disappear into the darkened night light suburbia. The days, nights, weeks and months passed by for Malinda and Kyle, the days at the beginning were easy comparatively speaking in terms of the damnation they had been faced with in being two who were the supporters of a cause they cared for, nevertheless they were the collectors of a payoff although the dough ray me they received only supported their necessities at a time. The nights were silent serenity for the both of them. It was a satisfying feeling for the two of them to finally experience less hectic and normal kind heart nights with each other. They posed as family rather than a couple. This decision of their hiding was a wise one considering people who had seen to much American entertainment primarily meaning movies with violence and false unrealistic propaganda. Before a thought of a fast passing by could take place the days and nights became weeks. About three weeks into their stay Malinda with her wise ways of process and active mode companionship was able to convince Kyle that things were going well. Swell one might say this was but heck or hell of which this was or was not had the turn styles of metropolitan subways spinning with the hurricane saliva spins on wind and only the fathers of tombs torn and sold were able to see freedom inside the gates of the burial places. The burial place is the center of a deploy time plot. The nomad evil people were caught and the time had come in dread naught. Weeks became a month and more weeks added up to several months. With the passing of this time period the periodicals, the obituaries, and the editorials of a Carolina newspaper became the pastime for Kyle. Malinda was another of a different interest type so for her, she would often stay home and read the sports section whenever Kyle had to run errands of his or his and her endeavors. Forever is forever, was, and because. More of the months passed and it would be one year of a peace time for the duo of a passing. At the one year point it was the anniversary of the duo's entrance into their Kill Devil safety home. Kyle did not remember nor had he even acknowledged that this day was to come in formality way. Malinda and Kyle were friends strictly, there was no romantic intimacy between the two of them. So it was on the date of this anniversary in February 1998 with the passing of the four seasons that it was seen by Malinda a possible reason. This reason knew no treason and with these seasons it was a falling in like. It was Lincoln's birthday Malinda had purchased Kyle his paper on the morning of this holiday along with a couple of petty items including one of romance or for safety of a strikeout for her one could say it was simply a gift of appreciation. One of these gifts was a flower for a man the other was a symbol of life. The newspaper was given and Kyle was reading while Malinda in shyness bell curved her nerve and waited with patience as a hoping virtue in virtual fear for nothing so it really was. Kyle tossed the paper aside and it laid with the front page headline in clear view for a read. In early afternoon time after serving Kyle his favorite kind of sandwich, a Ruben from a market deli, Malinda gained the stature she needed, she did so from her social stamina. Malinda approached Kyle after he took his last bite of his Ruben sandwich. He belched lightly and looked over to see an intimidated Malinda. Malinda crossed the small living room where Kyle had just finished eating from his dinner tray. When she got across the room she put an artificial purple rose with glass stem in front of him beside the dinner tray on a night stand next to it. While the rose laid there prepared horizontal and diagonally from him within his reach Malinda grabbed the dinner tray, folded its legs and then she placed it with the proper attire. While Kyle was being distracted from his noontime ending of a movie of his liking he looked to the stem and purple rose. The rose was hand sewn in vial. Malinda was acting like a foreign slave woman with a veil. She was about to reveal something surprising so she got her mind together and she ran her fingers through her hair convincingly enough for an important talk with Kyle. Hair fall like fall fell into placement for a rise and arisen she had done. Kyle grabbed the rose and began to look at it confused, still he was pleasantly amused. "Kyle?" "What?" "It has been a while since we've been here and I um oh god" Malinda paused into a moment of insecurity as she was silent for a short lapse. "What is it Malinda you can tell me" said Kyle. "How long has it been since we've been working together?" "I'd say about four years." Kyle said to Malinda with a question hinted in his meaning. "And how long has it been since we met and joined our cause for the dream?" asked Malinda." "Around six. Why?" "Ah I have been getting some feelings lately, well to be more honest with you I have had these feelings for some time now and I feel courageous." She said with an astute look. "What are you saying Malinda?" "For the past four years we have never been intimate it's like we are related like cousins you know? "We have had to pose as brother and sister of late and I think I'm falling in love with you." Malinda's eyes rose like two black swans of a song, her eyes were glossy and the black holes dominated the colors light and hazel of this brown eyed lady. Kyle sat up in his chair, he grabbed hold of the remote control and he turned off the television. The room's intensity was intensified but for some reason of unspeakable obvious notion there was no tension in the air whatsoever. Kyle looked on a true heroin with no inward notion of a swan song and spoke to the toiled lady of his possible destiny. "Malinda, what the fuck?" Malinda glossy and teary let out a nostril exhalation laugh and smiled happy. She took something out of her pocket. From her small front pants pocket Malinda pulled out a gold band. Malinda held Kyle's hand and she was pleased to see that he had held it out for her taking. Kyle was intrigued by Malinda's uncanny social stamina and poise of a moment. She slipped the band on his left index finger and said while breaking into tears as he did the same "I know we have always been like brother and sister to one another or friends at least but I can't help it after what has happened. "Marry me?" A tear drop from Kyle's left was streaking fast and it went under the left of his chin. They looked into the swans afloat and the female leader of the duo would not be disappointed. Kyle burst a little further and sniffled. He looked straight into her windows and said "I'd love to marry you Malinda." So it was and so it was said they (meaning this Christmas duo) would marry. They did so until death do you part.

32

GREEN GUE OF neon dew grew in luminescence florescent in appearance. It was the wee hours of the morning still. It was approximately 2:46 A.M. in future's 2012 when the unidentified walker once again took notice of hidden motives. Indirectly related to his next find for a motive was something directly related to the commissar case trial of some years back. New star of implosion anti matter corrosive for creation was your basic exhibit A in the commissar and scientist case. The guey substance that had been examined in the vials of a scientific government sector represented the chlorophyll of time eons created in solid mass although it was liquid to solid form like that of burning melted plastic. The vials were broken and the spits of a blood farmer made it to the eyes of storms in hurricane monsoon spins like tornadoes perpetual. Slaved on grids representing symmetric metrics in what seemed like a gasm ploy made the gourds gods and the slaves drooled into the wells of the hiding places. Spasms made the metrics perfectly symmetrical and this defined logic leading to logistic ALGOR, BASIC, algorithm, logic logistics and math. The paths had been taken by a fool and the fool bit his hand loafing in hysterics humored to the hilt. A wizard and lizard became the court guards for the assembly, they were in a human form and they were judge and jury. The section was not perfect, the objections were rejected, the subject was not the fool and the assembly was not crooked. The green made a smell like soiled dirt feces with ecoli, the fertilization bacteria cured by no word miraculous. The green substance was put away with government T.H.C. and lysergic acid dythilamide into vials. The vials were placed securely. Unidentified walker overheard a peculiar conversation at just past quarter until 3. Another ringing and she answered the phone again. "I!" . . . . "Oh okay?" . . . . "What!" . . . . "No!" . . . .? The woman hung up the phone and immediately dialed a number. "Yes" . . . . "Give me the Jesus Christ Church of Ladder Day Saints representative at your shelter facility, okay I'll wait . . . . "Do you think I was born yesterday?" . . . ."I am not a religious person but I was guided to call you and tell you that I saw what he told me." . . . . "Yes, spotted in the subway there's a blackout jackass." . . . . "Yes I know no trespassing." Unidentified walker heard his signal cue and at exactly 3 A.M. he slipped back out of the shelter back door, this time he would need his night vision binoculars for sure. The walker and non alias moon reflected, projected, the learners of the morbid past were to be cured and protected. Unidentified walker went south to one of the presently darkened city streets. He turned into a subway entrance on more than a hunch. A flash flashed up high in the sky that changed to a 1 second bluish sky with stars. This no name man with his tactics of expertise sneaked past some police, a turn style, and an escalator doorway. Binoculars for night light lightning were fastened. He was in for a déjà vu surprise, a reprisal, and a possible alternate ending. He made an affront to an accused convict. The convicts were hiding in this cavernous below. Rats scampered below in this underground hellish swell dwelling and the squeaking of the rat vocals spoke the non word for a house of a rising starry night. Outbound trains just sat there sleeping in darkness awaking. The fakes frothing formed the lies above and beyond. The goals of the new space age set unidentified walker as receiver one way; walking and talking. Possessed in torment's toils blood boils and so the blood flesh coils wound up dead from beneath wings afire. Organics on a degraded peasant mistreated a violent minority. The minority plot opposed was upstanding assumed major. Security sold souls German of old time west or east. It was commissar material. The unidentified walker walked the steps to the still escalator with his vision binoculars guiding his way with sufficient prelude. Writing on the walls of this metro subway was small scale. As a matter of fact it was so small scale that the writing was usually not noticed. On the wall was a graffiti piece of art modern era it resembled a car something like a space age convertible corvette with characters counting to three of them. Aboard this spray painted art emblematic the faces of the three held elements surprised. Two of them sat in the front and one sat in the back. All three had facial expressions dramatic. Universe sets of former static heeded way in tradition of an omen. Above the spray painted graffiti car was the symbol star formation. Over the art on the wall was the sand grain on this wall for which this emblem was. The grains of sand protruded in centimeter fractions downward along the emblem car. This was the symbol of a number trying. Of three symbol people in this car featured was a driver who was a blue eyed blonde woman typical in sight and likely in fashion of a stereotype in society's eye. This was a woman with no apt promises for ability or insight. In the passenger seat to her right was another, a man who had eyes colored strange, possessing and seemingly deceitful. His enamel shined in gleam vicious one might assume with evil's smile and a face persona style of a free man formerly condemned. In the back seat was lady ava le Maria so it had appeared, she was pulling off a robbery with a gun pointed at the two in front from behind without them knowing anything. Unidentified walker noticed this graffiti work of art. He stepped to it with his night vision switch turned on for his sighted in insights. From his back pocket he pulled out a matchbox and he flicked a wooden match on the flint to examine the significance he had detected for reasons he presently was unable to fathom. He allowed a one minute flicker flame moving the flame out and about for a peering at this something symbolic and spiritually justified. Unidentified walker looked over each face. While examining the first face he felt that he was the devil himself with a spawn life purpose of human flesh and blood outward spanning universal and versed in versus. The face of the blonde woman seemed to look back at him in questioning attempted adaptations. Her face was like milk and her garments appeared to be made from a silk worm. He felt a feeling when he moved his match to the left a little. This feeling was like that of a fearing adrenaline jolt possessive of candid thoughts. This was the face of a man. The man's face stared back immediately thus the increment totality of this jolted feeling. The man's face stayed still, no shadow illusions for optical brain hallucinations but unidentified walker stared ever so intently looking for phenomenon. A sound of whistling wind came in the form of a cold breath from the corpses of death megaton. The wind came like a New England overnight frost immediate but it was indisposed. Wind from a New England ghost ship sail and the flicker flame blew out. Unidentified walker stood in a present pitch black sight of no sights whatsoever. He had turned off his switch. A fast flint flick and a sound from a match flint came from Sister Sarah's thumb and index finger with a little stick in between. She was holding a life lit match flame. She aided unknowingly in assistance back in the 1980 sector sectioned home's sight of blackout one. She lit the spare candle at the dinner table and the flame replaced the blown out flame of 2012. "Thanks Sarah I was scared to death" Xavier said to his sister after she re lit the dim room. "No problem, just call me commander Mac." Sarah said with unpredictable wittiness. "Another game?" father guardian asked the members of the dark sector session in season. "Why don't we talk about the upcoming school year?" mother said dubiously. "I'm going to a new school this year" responded Xavier. Sarah looked around in young wisdom and when she looked into her brothers eyes she saw souls saved. The hourly times of a locality church chime rang 22 times. Sarah's peering into the windows of the widowed young soul that was her brother was the curse of youthfulness, foolishness, and divorce. It was not to be denied. Xavier was once married to an inner soul inside that had met demise with the loss of his grandmother. Another flint flick and a flickering quick allowed the 2012 unidentified walker to examine the third face on the graffiti wall with only one design presently. He moved the newly lit match to the face of the lady Ava le Maria and a sudden tremble could be heard above. The loud tremble grew into a rumbling sound with deep bass. Unidentified walker was about to place his night vision binoculars back on his head but before he raised them half way to his forehead a flashing of light in intervals of three seconds apart came from down the long metro subway corridor. Unidentified walker became curious immediately. He forgot all about the graffiti emblem and he started to walk towards the flashing that was lighting this corridor from around a corner about 40 yards away. Unidentified walker became the light man stalker and so he continued walking. The walking became a fast intensified in shape pace jog, a jog, and a sprint ending with a bolt. At the end of his bolting he slowed to a stop at the corridor opening where he could see the three second interval flashing start to lessen in fragments of its intervals of blackness. The flashing went from three seconds to two to one and even less to quarter second flashing strobe light like. In front of him around this corridor corner of a strobe flash was the light flash of Salem lightning and he saw flesh in the form of a figure of the commissar in black shadow that seemed to shine in the strobe color of the flashing. The rumbling ended fast and abrupt. It was a stopping to any feelings of confusion. The matter of the third motive of the 2012 blackout was being determined. The flash became one continued lightning bolt lit still yet mobile energy. The stopping of the strobe effect gave unidentified walker a clear view of the commissar. The commissar was in his spitting image of black shadow shining. Xavier felt a calm but curious phase shift of cat kill curiosity. The commissar was no monstrosity and the secret of the sauce green came in a dripping from the commissar owned black shadow figure's open right hand. From the right hand of a shadow shadows black dripped and when the gue hit the floor it changed in a color hazed to florescent off green, a sort of nameless unidentifiable color defying ohm and prism law. The figure of the commissar held up his right hand like a wave gestured and from the underlay of just above the wrist a blood red dripped and changed to blue as it drip dropped and spurted to the ground. All of a sudden there was darkness complete, the strobe light stopped its continuance. Another rumbling and a thunderclap and somehow the corridor was lit up. Where the commissar was standing was a reprimand commandment. This symbol real was wood and leaf in the flesh of which it is. A sexual spore poured a water drop on top and over from atop was a light of the shine light spinning. At the spot of the commissar's arrival and disappearance stood a lit up tree with seven branches and leaves of beautiful chlorophyll green stuck out from them like stems stained. Unidentified walker had found the significance of seven again, he had subtracted lust, greed, envy, gluttony, sloth, wrath, and pride. The deadly sins were then questioned by unidentified walker with "What is a sin? A sin of a wrong or a committed act consequence to one self?" unidentified walker pulled a hood over his head and became a dream character caught on sand reflection in metro.

33

A RE-LIT FROM SUDDEN darkness flame flickered again in dim light from a minute ago and mother makes a subject attempt "Sarah, how's that teacher of yours? You know, the guy who agreed we could hire you a tutor?" Mother asked Sister Sarah the annoying question in the manner of guidance parental. "He's mental mom, I mean all year all I've wanted is some space in class so that I can compete with the high honor students." "You're full of it." Father unwittingly interjected with stress on mind and a caressing hand on his daughters back side. Mother laughed, Xavier committed to matchbox car larceny in grand times and Sarah thought up another lie, maybe a plan for a sick faking and some hooky on a nicer day, a long weekend did not sound bad to her but longer the weekend might had been if the power outage was not solved soon enough. The lights that were out were rumored in the neighborhood to possibly go back on some time on this blackout lightning strike night. It was likely in the opinion of father guardian the last hour of the 1980 blackout. He had heard earlier that day that the city power department with some help from the highway department was to fix the outage situation in full at the neighborhood power station. Avoiding electrocution was a must do obviously so it had postponed the curing of this weekend situation. 1980-2012 and for the next 32 years the fears in open fire dens were to be healed like a constant Christmas morning lifetime. Done duo disguised out did where they were posted in the upcoming time frame but the term they received lame brought six together from the claims shamed. Family of four duo dawning is two married and the lawn was to be mowed for the summer, it was to be the beginning of the factions in action for oneness and a six numeral takes the chess square spot in the back yard. It was game on or backgammon tries for a triangular try angle angelic triple double try. A mouse, a mole, a rabbit hide and the plan falling was born in a countdown from 32 down to one and to a level playing field. Sister Sarah was fair lady she bent wills and healed the swill of mother from the pains of a lifetime. She had felt the alcohol in a sneaking and the boy hidden weaved a wedding web in defense of the movers. The movers moved to the power station and the sun dropped from the sky slow and normal. Only the perception of simplistic brilliancy was able to see the sights of the third world universe and the six separate saw the ins and outs of the house of the rising sin. The sin was a sun, the sun was deadly and the six with addition addiction arts of one made seven and to heaven went the one from hell. All the way to the gates they fight back against the forces of absolution. FIGHTING FROTHING MORBID TIME BLUR IN TOTALITY/ TOTAL TARE TOTALITARIAN COMMUNISM SEIZE/NO APPEASE GET ON YOUR KNEES AND BLOW A MIND AWAY/WORDS IN SAID A BLACKLIST NO SIGHT SIMPLISTIC READ/A REDDENED OCEANIC SCENE/FORNICATION MASTURBATION A CLAIM IN NEW WORD PRO/SATAN SEOUL ATLANTIC BOWL/MESSIAH PIECED ON KNEES/MUSIC WRITING HERES SOME FIGHTNG A FUCKING DAY FRENZY/WAKES ON FUNERALS IN CATHEDERALS THE DROOL IS ON YOUR MOM/DING DONG DOORS DEFEND THE WHORES TEMPTATION NO MORE WRONGS/SANG IN SONG AN HOUR LONG/ THE HOSE IN PAIRS ATE PAIRS/FROM APPLES BITTEN A BELL IS SMITTEN/SMUT DEIS GUARD AND LIKE/IN THESE DAYS YOUTH HAD LEARNED TO FUCK NOT RIDE A BIKE/VICTIM CHILDREN BURNING MOTHERS AND FATHERS LEFT FOR LOANS/ MAKE CONCERN AND HOLES FROM WORMS A JESUS CASTING STONES/JUMPING BONES INFANT MOANS A SICKENED MOTHER DYKE/GET YOUR BIKE OR FLY A KITE RIGHT IS MAKING MIGHT/ MESSIAH DEVIL NO ITS YOU THAT YOU INSIDE MUST SEEK/ A COOL A NERD A FOOLISH WORD I HOPE MY SON'S A GEEK/FACE OF DEATH IS FACE OF LOVE THE UNDERTAKER THRILL/KILLS WITH PILLS A SHOT SYRINGE I TOUGHED OUT ANOTHER BINGE/ GROSS A QUOTE THE ENGLISH MOAT FROM FRANCE YOU GET A KISS/A JAP A SWISS A CANDID MISS YOUR FRANK GOT IN MY YEN/BACK IN THE PENN A LETTER SEND AND NO TOMMOROW STOPS/SUICIDE DROWNED IN FATE FROM HATE IS BORN A LOVE/ PENTAGRAM WITCH STAR MAN NO FALLING FOR A LIAR/A NEW DAY SCAG I AM A FAG SO LIGHT MY PANTS ON FIRE/FROM DESIRES PUTRID SIERS THE HAMMERING DOG JUDGE/GODS OF

FIVE OR MAYBE FOUR A FIVE SLAP AND SOME JIVE/1 ALIVE AND BILLIONS MORE ONE DAY IS ALL OF WE/ THE ARMS OF FAITH HAD BEEN UNLOCKED THE ROSE IS CORKED AND COCKED/ AN OUTDONE GUN A LIFE OF FUN A LEARN DETERMINES MAN/A WOMAN GROW FAIR LADY KNOW AND MARRIAGE WILL COME BACK!

34

JONAX CONVERSATION HAD its positive aspects to the spy game of which was still set to the oven's fan on a stove back burner. The grids grew in their grinding, the conversation involved might be considered to be dominated but it was truly denominational. Sensational outlook was the quote plot and ploy in defended. Pretended for the way of which it was is no just cause to Judas, Jonah, Jonax or Jedidiah of John for a matter. The metric meadow meter metrics meeting on the space grids equalized the semi symmetrical imperfect tear spheres that were the starry beings of star dusted suns counting to a million. They were the eyes of soul life and the heart was for Renessa of her Jonah. Jonax tributes the problems in this phase and the method of wicked witchery way was the set of these voices that her Jonah or Xavier (if one prefers that named entitlement) ever so blatantly and bravely set the cosmos of the singular pagan unit being of beings into motion's emotion. Genocide was not the plan in the case of blackout but more so this was an organized plot of martial law opposed by the defense play for a ploy. The laws of martial in the case in fact concerning the voices heard by young Xavier back in 1980 were just example matters. Slow death from a plot, a ploy defended the melting pots, and the bandits of time were not caught in the days of mournful youth. A booth for communication among the law monger was strong in its structure for theory but the theory was not doable for acknowledged. Decision predecessors possessed for Solomon kings, the young boy of a finding and unwinding change shift of the times was a gonad. Nomads had made the testicular stimuli universal have our out bound universe take such a chap shape for multiplicity of all meanings. Mathematical, sexual, spiritual, sensual, sabbatical, tempest with witchery and techno-wizardry, mystery, truth, and weather faces lined in front of chapels. The stuff of life was part of a trinity scientific of spirit spit mixture. The hurricane passed into an eye of a bigger storm perpetuating. The universe was part communication and so it was that Xavier her Jonah was of edifice humans and the manias timed took lunacy songs to the word spoken past written writes. The lunatic soothes himself with chaos becoming the mania maniac himself but herself soothed in sunlight bright mending souls in vanity times. In wants of a name in vein all involved in blackout felt the cell crippling genocides inside thus we have the torn. Thorn head, puss bled and bred the child of no wrath, math, paths of makings on might rights Midas Carl Jung and vision sights of a side. A wide open poem holds inside pride for the Christmas duo making the true a person but who and who else was truly only is. Deicide was the word problem indefinitely. Slow as was death itself the suffix cide was taking sides. Young as we are the movers in the blackout story have taken a side. All of them within the varied versions of the story line's multiplicity hidden is forthwith formed by the births from the new comer. A butterfly flew freely to the duo when they were down but it was a vulture that was to save our souls for the case cause. The vulture had sought Lady Ava Le Maria of the camp in her youth so it was said but in past life reincarnation. Death and life, life and death, death was a lie and life is a breath in first and last inhales, exhales and premature ejaculations. Stretched out above were the clouds stimulated. The cumulus of which they were had made foreskin the forsaken. The Jonax communication as was is in the now forever in it shall be. The words spoken by her Jonah alias Xavier in the role of Jonax most particularly went downstream into the crystallized meadows and shadows befell. Jonax was a Russian as a former Soviet of fictional characterization and she watched from above as another. The other played role not of a fair maiden mother lover but more so she was the heal plot ploy for the guidance of the new Maria. Conveniences inconvenient babied Xavier her Jonah so bad that he in his liking for Maria in soul's life had laid her to rest in the times of the commons era. Sent back in time the lady of Lady Ava Le Maria did see life and from the towns and the cities onward was the lands of no play, plot, or ploy for a genocide, deicide, infanticide of savior magnitude or homicides common every day city violence. Infanticide was option for the singularity pagan unit and from it were asinine damnation. The infant kill of Maria was prevented in full in the non time of fall in the seasonal time reddened by star winds wound down the hands of the clocks of towers. Towering in a shower of this sun time of a daze was the origin unit. This unit being was the representation in full of all beings and was not the follower or leader of a language. The being could not kill or be killed it was all who was and is and this will always be. Freedom tormented the toiled minds and manifest destined souls sold. The souls were saved from a bottled message, it was from her Jonah and the prey pity pirates held it together, they were the vagabonds. One was all all was one and win was the name of the game for the avenue lady of Mary. This lady of the street saw time fold and fall and with a calling and so Maria moves forward. She wanted to stray from the term word of her being which was the being offer of worldly words defined, two words of entirety "the destroyer." Refugee camp parental of Santiago Chile was birth bleeding barren land in times of the 19th century of which this phenomenon wrath child was born. She had bled the torn eye cuts and healed from the bandage of the same word set in syllables of trying. Sighing fathers sighted made dawns of the year of 1871 A.D. seem normal nevertheless normalcy was hard to come by due to comparisons to other lady Maria existences in both the 2oth and 21st centuries. The pretenders of the times of a foundation for this refugee camp parental cried in shadow reflections on dirt ponds for the pawns they were set to be. Alliances in camp on the other side knew of genocide sufferings and some would have mothered from the pushes of the camp births onward and so it was that this other came destined kingdom on the other side bred a sight sided with the cides suffixed for pained ones. The water rise grew a rising rose for a pushing and the well water was low. The low took octagon clay and the town became a dump and the dump became a populous of granite sculptured city with the walkers on waters and the escapists of slaughters. Earth orbit order thermosphere magneto-receptive proprioception senses all five and a sixth with significant seven as one is exceptional contained youths. They came fast it was the able bodied campers with clay for the knowing town. Two offer omen or victory for justices true were in caverns in 1879 and 1979. The girl named Maria sighted farms, the boy of the X spot drank the well water and so he on the last day of October 1992 read the sign untrue for the last time. An attempt was taken on this night and it had come from the times he escaped the knife rods in between the chambers of gasses. Harassment caresses of killers and a willing thrill were absent of the guards. The bishop was beaten by the anti guru predecessor. The proper pro light expansion set sights on bloody ink and the black drips of red became sadistic and then malicious. "The grapes were delicious!" October 31st 1992, are you ready for a caption? Rapture times a crime brain branding surgery and horses of the gods involved made laminated envelopes on poles with night lights. The poles were magnetic, the rapture not yet, the blood became an anesthetic and the happiness calmed to undone pathetic. Exhales succeed the suffocation escapists arrive at the sign of the sun and salute the talking lady of America who holds the welcome slab. The new clay is daytime the night absolute and the callings of the leaders let the liters drain for the celebration time of a new time new city town celebration day. Numerals haven heaven countdown again.

35

IT WAS NOW a warm South American February in Santiago and Maria had learned some of the valuable lessening lessons from her mending of a hem. Maria in mild mannered state of mind for the troubled young girl who she was inside had built her inner foundation with old time style like a modern extrovert. She had appeared to her friends as a refusal refugee unit being. There was a liking for sure but still her lingering mind, body, and soul made her the talkative dreamer among them. She was derelict material and her foolishness claimed by others had been tormented by downs. Her dreams, needs, and basic wants stressed her mind but the easy put downs put out by her fellow peers and her guardians defeated her whenever she looked up into the starlit nights of the Santiago Chile sky. On a cool for Santiago February night nearing the decade of the 19th century 80's she was peering into the night sky and she could not help but wonder what was out there and why it was that when she was sleeping she would dream in Spanish communication of a new star, a birthright to a race dementia demented and peaceful from common, an interesting outlook this is when pondering on the definitions of any high standing society with snobbery and above the weak outlooks. The twinkles of the stars were young to even a little girl who was to turn 9 years old the next month, these twinkles gave information to her inner being of the brown dwarf she was herself. The information was from a universe abound but the new information came from sources on her being, the dwarfs and gnomes of inside astronomy, planets, stars, and galaxy hurricane swirls churned twilight inside of the hairs of her brow. The forest forces nearby gave off its stench as she noticed a Galileo discovery upward of centuries back. It was a non twinkling star and the former home of a broken mirror mirage tusk ram. A band of refugees who downplayed the dwarf star dream saw her as another tool for their garden of average but the one day aged Maria was to reach the short lifetime expectancy of her potential and so it was that she was the hoe of a star garden and the wormholes in her skin pores brewed strong storms making her awareness of a falling short of a dream absent. Obsession was to come in due time for Maria but some distractions from land pirates of Argentine descent were to descend. Maria was to aid the life light of the angelic refugees refused. Orphans sinned and made sound like sires. Maria became tired as the Santiago night hours passed by and so it was that her nightly tradition of star gazing had to cease. Maria wandered gloomily in her common feeling of this nightly regretful disappointment. She had an appointment with the sandmen. She wandered into her tent and made sure her daily mending materials were put back in their proper placements. Onto her night hassock of this large tent for refugee parental she rested. Maria did not fall asleep for hours. As she lay lying she thought about other refugee types and she dreamed hoping cause for her planning. Her ears heard a scamper predator pest nearby and she fell asleep in fear. She dreamed of becoming an ambassador of an embassy but her Spanish communication limited her understandings. The sad said truth was true that the persons of this camp were unable to ponder on ambassadorship or messiahs for that matter related, the fellows of her like, dislike, jealousy, envy and middle of the road of this camp simply had no means for such academic governmental knowledge. The dreamed Maria dreamed was of a second coming unfathomable to herself, it took place 113 plus years later. The morning rising sun came up and the living truth told tellers were to deal a hand. From the west came some witnesses to this old time of an era's evils. A band of refugees heard some ruckus over yonder by some brush, it was a band of rebels from a foreign cause they were armed to the hilt and when Maria had woke her up she was . . . . not to eat her first bowl of nourishment right away nor was she to go to the water place for a filling of her cup but instead she heard sounds of terror. Voices stern and possessive of apparent evil boldness were cold and the armed band was now passing through, they were threatening for sure and the guardians of their children wanted to be sure that the camp remained . The band of Argentinians abound were members of a non uniformed unorganized force of your common perception of what South American piracy might be. They were seeking the coastline for a meeting. The leader of this pirate clan was a determined man. The leader and his clan struck fear into the pitted souls of the members of this refugee camp parental. A questioning ensued immediately, fears of kidnapping, adult abduction, pillage of the villagers, and a loss of supplies seemed to appear imminent. Maria hid by her hemming station just feet from her set up hassock. Some of the Argentinians searched nearby. One of them made foreign linguistic in slang vulgar small talk to their troop leader, he asked him what they needed and who he was to take away if need be, he also asked the leader if any food rations would be gathered for their travels to the Chile coastline. The troop leader had left tracks in dirt on the natural flooring of the tent interior of Maria's home, he was thoroughly searching the tent of Maria and some of the other tents occupied by other refugee families were being searched through as well. Other tents were to be searched as well afterwards, the children of the camp had been stone faced but the fears of instant death from a shooting of one of their guns or a stab from a bayonet might be a doom that was to be avoided by some serious compliance. The foot tracks of the flat foot boots of troop leader made a trail in Maria's tent from its small crevice opening to the other opening whereas the canvas overhang became non tent like and hung horizontal by the hassock tie to a tree branch solid, the canvas was now like that of a poorly hung awning. Maria still was hiding and her breaths trembled fear fragments thus had weakened causing diminishing admonished and from this relinquished her dreams of a new star were distinguished the foils of the death blackbird destroyers red firewater was extinguished and the star still hellish was Spanish in plain English. The chill thrill from Chile blew solar sonar wind at stars and Maria was sainted knighted demon girl in horizon galactic vision swirls. Chile was decent descendant plow land agricultural from a heating logistic at the point of Maria's victory hiding and she was the new dark horse rising. The troop leader said his foreign slang vulgarity in a breath breathed cough and he spat on the earth of the mid sand and dirt. A global job and a leaving of prints on grounds inside the Maria tent spilled slave water phlegm. Spaniard former Maria of a future past life was half life still life and she a wisher from the genie lamp made numeric requisition. She held position and the fear trembling had left her. Outside the tent by the opening where the awning appearance was hanging canvas the band of rebels met for their plan. Girls hid by the small ration station gulping rice grains and downing mineral fluids that remained there from the night before whereas the preparer of the rations beforehand guarded the boys and girls with their compliance and their handing over of any supplies needed for the troop that was disturbing the camp members. Distribution was not to be overly devastating nevertheless the camp was definitely affected. Maria then made sure of anothers' safety, it was a younger girl aged four. The four year old girl was the savior of angelic she was to be aided by Maria and in return an awakening might happen for the paths of righteous. Maria and her four year old friend spoke some whispered words and the two of them remained hidden beyond the hassock tie after they had cleverly and sneakily tiptoed over behind the back of the tree of its tying knots.

Rations of some rice and some vegetables grown afar were packaged more thoroughly accurate with a wrapping and tying than would commonly be. The giver of this supply was not one to panic and so it was that the troop leaders packaged this efficient enough for the troop an amount of food with some other items gathered in an ordering, a flare from the cooking area, a couple of packages of acquired liquors from other passers by, this would be some boxed packaged bottles of wine with some vinegar, the troop also made way with two pocket knives that were used by the ration preparers for the rare fish cleanings that they were sometimes privileged to do when they were delivered some fish from the Chile coastline. Beyond there was nothing but some sand and an Argentina back and behind them. The troop packaged these items in their carry sacks and lucky for the refugee camp people they had decided not to abduct or kill in merciless way. The troop left and the demonic star dreamer named Maria wiped a dirt tear that looked like mascara from the face of her fellow post infancy friend find. Inspiration had come, tragedy was to strengthen them and the campers had survived and dodged the bullet.

36

SANTIAGO CHILE REFUGEE parental had met harder times in the fairly recent past but this statement is not true. The relations between Maria and her four year old friend who was named Carmen at birth had been learning new ways. She had now seen her first shocking experience. It was uncommon for the camp to see such a friendship that was to now develop. Nevertheless and regardless a deal was on in this new time of some food loss and Maria was sure that the camp was to recover from a fear rattling and a near death threat to its people. As for the losing of some food the hand outs were going to have to be lessened for the week until delivery was made by those of unheard of incorporated. Corporate elite light up and out in downs of the 19th century and a mystery incorporated existed before and after. Half rations were served for the first daily meal of two but the kids in sympathy for the experience were given breads and the elders would make this sacrifice sparing no personal expense. Expended normalcy enhanced the Maria mind and she was given permission from Carmen's caretakers to look over Carmen, Maria did so with an attitude adjustment. This would cause her to share deep thoughts fathomable to the four year old Carmen regarding common matters. Maria did so in evening dusk light times and the conversation led into hours late and intimate whereas Maria would be all by her lonesome doing her common night practices of star gazed dreaming like light of the day. The night sleeping dreams unconscious interactions of the mind of Maria were animated in upheaval of the ultimate ultimatum universal and perpetual. Poured stains of chemicals from Maria's food consumption gathered the antimatter of her heart felt relationship anew. Maria's brain chemistry drip dropped in timing of common bonds around her. She felt a feeling anew, she envisioned starry nights, she doubled her visions as a two eyed Cyclops, and Maria once again brewed in Chile. She was to dream in suspended animation. The following morning after suspension dreams and another star gazer night beforehand and prior was the Carmen request in directions directed derogatory to the vision of a parting and it was prominent prerogative for the stay at the permanent camp ground. Carmen made questions of a quest regardless of initiatives that supported her willed destiny unknown to herself and to Maria. Maria guarded light and lifelines and the infinite of the minds beheld in infinitesimal scatterings mattering. A smaller feeding than the day before with half the breading of yesterdays handouts and the two of Maria and Carmen walked into the tent of Maria and Maria began to give a sewing lesson. In the language of her ethnicity Maria began to speak to Carmen in manners good and courtesy better and uncommon, the well wish sent the fish loaves and the needles of this sewing healed a moment with nonsense and demented reality owing. "See you take it like this and then you push this through like this so the thread in that little hole on the back of the needle fixes your garment." Maria showed off to an amazed four year old wanting. "How do ya get da needuwl trew de howul in de back" Carmen asks Maria curiously while she thought of the words of her young peers. "Very carefully I guess?" Maria responded while she shrugged shoulders up with manners for her friend in common Carmen. "Now you see you have to be careful when you thread. The distance between threads should be timed and measured naturally." "Measured?" Carmen asked a one word question. "Yes my little Carmen measuring time and distance is important for any threading of a hemline. I noticed your little doll is ripped at the seams. That's bad timing. No four year old girlfriend of mine is going to have a doll with a tare in its gown. Would you like for me to sew it for you? I can sew it for you sometime soon but I first have to finish mending this cloth design I'm making for my mother Consuela she has been my caretaker for three years since the epidemic time." When Maria finished this questioned offering she motioned with an eyeing gesture that was friend like towards Carmen's little girl persona personal and the offer was more than medicinal it was actually downright hospitable. Carmen liked hearing this offer from Maria and although there was no social means of stupidity American style back in 1880 Santiago it was truth that Carmen felt Maria's warmth and she thought that she was cool too. Carmen pointed to some thread weave spinners in a small pile they were empty on the ground. She was reminded of days ago. There was still half of a footprint left from the war boot from the troop leader who was likely somewhere down the coast by now. Carmen just kept listening to Maria give her sewing lesson like a likable know it all but Carmen was inattentive for the most part. Carmen wiped away the small pile of empty thread spinners to the side. Of the empty spinner thread holders there were maybe seven of them that just lay there scattered about. The boot print was half existent, it was the print of the heel and a half portion of the flat foot section from the print from the stepping man feared, gone, and strayed from the camp. The print that Carmen was looking at represented a fossil print from a searching abduction failed becoming a minor stealing crime. When comparing such an incidental crime to the problems posed on the South American coast back in this era of late 19th century times examination reveals that petty shoplifting for purposes of parenting were commonplace in certain areas but there was the realities of the times of the land piracy existing. The problems in the cases of the refugee manors existent were pursuing other matters of crime level concern. There was this present problem of abandonment of course it was, is, and likely will be for a long time but such crimes as this may have led directly or at least indirectly to other neglecting factors caused. This was obviously a result of over concerning distractions that will more often than not lead any of the various eras depending on location into common confusion lands with learning disabilities. Rape leading to refugee children, malice leads to temptation factors, the stealing of money or clothing supplies had lead to lessening in fragments compared to a money problem therefore value is diminished in land worth and also values are then diminished by devouring certain human intellect and so in the hot heat humid blaze of the Santiago Chile sun that beats the bands on sides right, wrong, or indifferent it leads to the lives of two simple girls. Maria sewed and taught and Carmen examined a fossil boot print. "See that? My threading is measured near perfect. See how the sides are lined up like this?" Maria showed off to little Carmen an undeniable mending of her present garment project while Carmen looked for a moment and then she ran a finger across the fossil print in the dirt of the awning and tent floor of dirty desert like hard soil sand. The print flashed an outward gleam somehow. Maria stopped speaking before she started to speak again and she noticed a bewildered faced Carmen moving her hand around in sunlight shadow mix and she was looking at the shadow of her index and pinky while some sort of gleam enhanced a shadow after effect from the moon that was nearly full in daytime and the big orange blaze fire heater sun that moved in the Santiago sky. "Look I ken make dis light change." Maria became astounded and wide eyed. She noticed from the form of Carmen's right hand that Carmen held in light gleam with her index and pinky outward was somehow causing some release of relinquishing of the energy of synergy. The explanation that was just explained was instant thoughts wordless and fast. "How is dis happenin? Said Carmen the girl who questioned in requests found by fated undeniable improvised intentions. Maria started talking "I don't understand this but it looks like a woven hemming from you doll or something." Maria was slightly dumbfounded, she kept examining the illusion. The sun then moved it was hidden immediately above a fairly thick cloud patch at the side causing the interior underneath of the tent top and awning like canvas to darken inside leading to the over effect of a darkened room apparent. The print fossil started to change and the section darkened further where Maria sat with a needle and thread and Carmen kneels over. Now the boot print was anew and was becoming. A symbolism transparent became existent, vivid, and shadow like. It was transforming light. Laws of science and logic were starting to be defied. The print started shining with anno dime shines dominatrix materials of an element similar to silica like quartz appearance peering upward. The two of them examined the hand and the print closely. The units went into a singular mode and the sights from the visions of the two little girls were one and they unified unison sights of a finding. The shadow reacted to gleam glow. Carmen in child's play of the serious continued to play shadow puppet. Carmen's right hand made devil horns with index and pinky. The print then glowed in the dark. It took on an appearance of a beast with a face in the shadow. Carmen changed her right hand formation three times by first making her index point downward at the transforming shadow and print on the ground. Next Carmen stretched out her hand with four fingers and her thumb was inward towards her palm. Finally Carmen made a two fingered peace sign. In her eyes you could see them change with intensity during all four of these shadow puppet hand gestures. The four finger point with an inward thumb made the boot print shadow appear as a pair of rodents feeding off of eggs from the nest of a large bird, the one finger downward index pointing gave of the act of a bird pecking at a mystery object, the third and final one was Carmen making a shadow puppet peace sign that caused the two rodents to appear to combine as one giving off from the three dimensional boot print detailed the shadow of a rabbit with long bunny ears. The sun became unhidden from the clouds. Maria looked puzzled but confident. Maria looked to Carmen and she did her best to explain her perception of what this real illusion was. Maria wondered before speaking to Carmen what the significance of the transforming symbol just was. Carmen looked at Maria in sun and Maria commenced to speak to her. "Destiny do you know what it is Carmen?" "No, what is dat?" Destiny is what mother Consuela told me about for years on our bread rice grain mornings. She told me to eat well in order to fulfill it." "But what is it?" said Carmen. "Not sure myself or if any one is really sure what that is Carmen but destiny might be telling us something with what we just saw." "Can destiny get me in troubul wit ma ma." Carmen said like a cute filthy refugee pained for such a happening situation. "Destiny might not necessarily get you or myself in trouble Carmen my little girlfriend but I think I have seen the future in my dreams." Maria stated sentiment seemingly useless but it was more useful than she could possibly imagine on this heartfelt strange life day of their lifetimes. "Wut did yu dream of?" asked Carmen. Maria felt a darkness leave her as all of a sudden with no moment noticed of a pausing of any life lines, guards of lives made the day's destiny. Maybe it was even simultaneously impossible or beforehand but nevertheless the clouds were obscured and clearing. The hanging sun of a calling for a Mother Mary vision falling came back out from above them and rising is the virtual virtues in valiance's vitality. Light intensified with half life dark half incarnation it then reincarnated immediately and shined back into the awning canvas tent of this refugee parental campground and the two faces of Carmen and Maria shined in sun. The shining faces of Carmen and Maria symbolized pairs of fire spheres of an above linger finger figure 9 analog creative in natural superior. These symbols of two were dawn light from the fingertips of intention and symmetry indeed was by these fingers of the young Carmen. Two stars in settings. 9,5,7,2 and 6 the numerals of inside found hidden places called a nest hive. Never before were they out of order until the symmetry of spherical fires blazed trinity sights in eyes seeing and sought the axis of the earth in Post Meridian dusk. Maria neglected to answer Carmen's last question.

37

THE MINT MAN washed his hands of it. What is was, what was, is is and what is always was, what it is never was, never is the never ending word and nervy but not nervous was the mint man. The United States Mint sent green welcome outbound and from the sounds of those who had policed them the water surrounded the skills. The police of a metric longitude latitude astronomic ocean became motion. Notes tender were play money monopoly pieces in checkers chess but the mint played 45's. Minced meat was the threat for breathers and so it was that in forms of non words for better or worse the caretakers moved in timed families of a natural flocking. To the docks the undertow pulled them with the waves of an old coral reef sandbar. Scarred destiny willed and so is became was but was was and a miracle of time made is. Is it all is it a being? A be? A queen bee with bees or a whaler police car is? Stars fly down for the good crown and the devil himself sent the saint into hell for instinct smell in the bred born body of an Englishmen. Mass one kilogram, Virgin land and Gin, hemp damned in shears, Main street mass, western Virgo version Carolinas, Rhodes phantom of no can do for Providence, Nuke corks screwed in place for nude storks delivering the babies, Mary's land Amsterdam, The strict of Columbia, and the popes of the Vatican minus mattered ties anno doom. Moon beam glow for the brothers brew Maria way down south two centuries away but in the original 13 colonies at the half way plus mark of 19th century Lowell Massachusetts well water gathered for a feasting for the angelic. God have mercy? Devil boys with toys made noise to battleaxe the music they could not face. The faces of pained whether in weathering mind storms whereas basics of lotus bore the doom and in moods of the risen hopes frolicked from walking prey the leaves on the trees fell in the England of new for news! The paper scriptures sent out by the male boy of mailings miles away was in the city the entire timid time. He read the times and in the roads of education he perfected the sighting he waited in patience way. Xavier became poet prophet, he was opposed as president philanthropy by profiteers and the filled screw holes of holistic becoming nudes majestic for empathy and sympathy thus grew for the rights of the words written. Change plots mixed with Xavier ploy boy who grew into man and on the planet of plans for the gifts given off from from hell claiming came with a pearly lay of oysters. Boasted in a toast the fires blazed and Xavier saw singular sides on frames. He photon mega bled in seeds planted and had witnessed the savings of souls. Xavier although inbound outbound knew the mint was a curse but the light dust universal and beyond perpetual did not dent and so it is the Xavier was known to one as her Jonah. Demonized energized prologue prolific specifics made Atlantic romantics but specific Pacific contained truth and contributed to terrific. Awesome outcomes not to be undone grew some soil for a mid Atlantic boil Pangea denied this and Francisco sand dawn it made rice for a trolley captain on a San Fran trolley of same life the boil mixed in surreal it defeated the continuance of stretching infants for a selfish feed and nonsense bleeding. The veal feel should be thrown in the garbage. The mix of time from ohms law made the mid Atlantic boil transfer with Pangea time alternate tectonic. The grail held tonic and the art of handmaid human good defied inside of our selfish human physical weakness and at the end of seven days Hilo or somewhere close by erupted thus balancing earth in a shift. Jesus freaks terminology defy technology in grand time new age space age former golden age Scientology, please forgive me? Satan has mercy? Mercy fates, rates, ingrates, export crates, straights Massachusetts crooked claim, Californians, competitive New Yorkers and the Masses crashed into her Jonahs wall. Xavier Xevon Tareynton megaton tone in typicality reality put down by the easy it was so easy! A breeze came sonar style and two digits digital re lit the fire flame for a feeding the waves were denied and a beauty Korean girl made a stand for no reprimand time. The wine was for drinking and the wheat was not for metabolism. The bread of life was of their flesh and with a mesh of air stitching Salem brewed and the camp was set for a liking Viking like Gi King of Japanese 25th century folklore. The faces Nippon gave were in black and white vision scope and the little child of post infancy watched. He gives of a grimace and the day after Christmas the Core of awe was on an awning spawning her Jonah was yawning in dawn and the wand knew time was for an is always was. The Korean girl and the English man be-wed! Ireland argued for a credit point and the other half of the duo of a christening sang in harmony on that day. The French gave a present to the able bodied in the name for and from the deeds of one Franklin Delano Roosevelt. Deal one deal two or veal in pukes you? It is time for prioritization mode lords houses of the mackerel. Get straight human race and in grace pace a sighted face was on the planet of a past war is was and the water will flow from a European effort. Affront cunt bunt in stunts made runts, the runts grew minds in surprising element for merit Merrick in debt mending and the mint worked with president philanthropy and it was groovy. The people of tomorrow borrowed the times for yesteryear. The strict district sent confirmation justice from a mailing out in times of the stars. Columbia brew in night oils boiled the gaseous passions of sin non-deadly and friendly made a pass. The lasses of harassment laid in the tents for evidence and even the troop leader who left his foot print behind in the form of an etching fossil knew at least deep in the subconscious that intentions for the goals of the true could heal the lights of the dark half and so it was that the crustaceans that resided in the North Atlantic were devoured and a shower strong battled directions long and hard with attitude and Maria was born nude in Chile. The nets for the loaves of the little fish saved them but the rising sun over Atlantic horizons spreading bought should down in towns the homes off of an island made an Asian part from prayer she became prey and grew into the ways of a lover. As mother she saw the doves turn to the butterflies they sighted the vultures and aided the inspired sculpture that had hurt the scalpers. The pigeons of New England, New York, New Hampshire and New Jersey saw two go down for the secrets of top prioritized, the dogs of wars were messed memoirs but the cats of the spring alley sought dinner from the garbage dumpsters and found the rats of a parlor parallel owed in grams and the madams sighted within nanoseconds and they grew wings. The rats were ferrets and the wars made the existence of a black shadow dog. Xavier was mad so when he became her Jonah the becoming days of a falling grew into fall and walked down halls like the defenders of the sides of fate where the new born pigeons for the eastern lightened cites that would be fed in manners of old men and ladies missing the days of parenthood. Xavier takes away an ex and become a veer, Avier was vile a while and in style of this trend Avier went one down to veer or vier fire if you choose it, away with a V shape and Vier sounds like sire but it was Ier like an eye and an ear of a hawk, Ier took I and became the E.R. ear. The E of a find was taken away and became R became "are" but the E ended at the end and a ray was shot for moon beam May. The months had started and it was not the mints years of fiscal but untypical as this might sound physical became sound and around and round the merry go round went. We end the lesson of a common learn with day one. This my friends is not to be the beginning of the end or the end of a beginning but to the rather was is it and this was is and was is the star's start of a winning season and the race learns the true meaning of reasons. The story of blackout is plain as black and white.

38

MODE OF MODEM motive for the frolic strayed was in time and motive four was mode modular motives for. A drop poured but the drop of steam from the pipes made the temporary shelter morning seem like the shelters of permeated. Drips dropped while the patrons who showered early drew the fears out from the sterile waters of the heated pipes of the metropolitan winter. It was approximately 5:04 A.M. the generators powered what they could and candles had to make due and do. Unidentified walker had returned to the blackout shelter. Unidentified walker had realized in full that the three motives he had dealt with on this strange night of the 2012 metropolitan blackout were covered in motion plan and sufficiently compensated for. The shelter was forum for him and the blackout was likely to be over during the course of the daytime happenings. Unidentified walker was very phased by the phenomenon of which he had experienced inside and out in full ever so blatantly on this hell or heaven phenomenon night. It was not yet light of day nevertheless the confession he received from the confessor meaning the message man who is the commissar had done something that might had been considered holy or biblical but to the phenomenon age called the space age this was nothing more than typical scientific phenomenon combined with the sciences of hidden story historical keeping of the past. Unidentified walker had obtained a locker at this establishment for the day's remainder. He placed his night vision binoculars in his locker along with any items that he needed to be put away on his person. Unidentified walker locked his locker and he in knowing that the sun was to rise in about an hour or so had decided that although he might need to get some sleep that he would instead attend a morning coffee breakfast gathering in the upstairs of this temporary blackout shelter venue. He stepped his way into a band of people common for your metropolitan madness. Unidentified walker waited in line filled a cup and took a seat. The unidentified walker was still close enough to the main desk which was conveniently located just yards from where he sat with his morning cup of coffee to hear some interesting conversation on the phone line that sounded like small talk but that was in all scopes of a true and real reality a conversation of providence that was to lead him to an unexpected motive four. The phone rings and the night lady for the blackout shelter answered it and began to speak in mild mannered conversation. "Hello?" the lady said saddened in night toils while feeling the feelings of a tired night shift metropolitan shelter worker. She remained silent while unidentified walker just listened to the small talk not inherent of a hint of suspicion or a suspecting of any more excitement after such a crazy night. A few moments of some loud enough bickering for unidentified walker to overhear it with others from the person on the other line and the night shift shelter worker stopped after a hand to the forehead stressing tired of tiresome gesture and then she responded to this phone call with any effort at all that she could muster for a tired woman, lady, girl, or maybe at this point just a bitch who wanted 7 A.M. to arrive so as she might say "go the fuck home." She speaks back into the land line phone of the sheltering. "You what?" . . . . "But!" . . . . "Now wait one second you!" . . . . "I don't care if the computer is hacked by some 2 bit megabyte wanna be finga lickin freak!" . . . . "Well than I guess." . . . . "Huh?" . . . . "I was saying before I was rudely interrupted that I guess you might as well just tell these people that taking over a computer and causing a fatal error is not fair play. I have a mind to . . . . uh yes?" . . . . "Yeah I know that!" with the anger submitted by this last knowing acknowledged quotation from the woman lady bitch becoming had not noticed that the unidentified walker raised a brow in secret unnoticed himself to his surroundings! He began to listen intently and his curiosity became intense. The woman lady bitch was livid but nevertheless she was a tired one for definite. The bitch became a wise wizard lady of the good witches if they did ever exist and unidentified walker stalked the desk from aside it after a nice swallowing gulp of his coffee beverage. The bitch made a determined face for such a scarce stated state of the tired being that she was and she talked further. "Okay I'll check them but I don't remember how to do this that good, maybe we'll luck out and lunch will still be served" . . . . "I know that." . . . . "Okay what are they?" The woman lady and bitch combination took pad with paper and wrote down some numerals in a jotting. Unidentified walker began plotting for the ploy anti to a plot and great Scott the lady wrote some numbers down in a quick transfer audio of a jot. "Yes" yes" yes" yes" and yes, and what's the entry code to that?" . . . . "Yes." she stuck the paper in a slot beside the computer modem to the shelter and the unidentified walker watched and thought. Lady woman madam left her desk and her jot scribble of what was possibly insignificant nonsense. The jot scribbling was more likely nothing of such subject matter involved involvements in motive four possibilities. A minute or so passed by whereas the madam had entered the cafeteria for a fixing for herself and a stock check for her lunchtime cancellation concern. Unidentified walker walked unsuspectingly overtly and slyly to the desk side where the computer modem with key board lay. As the unidentified walker had suspected in his spy glimpse examination in fiend finding for fondness his fondness for what he saw peeked his curiosity. Curiosity might have killed the cat and as the other saying goes "look what the cat dragged in" the unidentified walker in his spy stalk had self will thus become a trade spy jack, a jack mind you that had climbed the beanstalk. The cat or feline slang was literal slang because the dog wars were dragging and dogmatic lies were a drag. The nosed dogs of a vicious scent scented senses seven t-minus two thus equaling five in a down counting! Curiosity made dog mat welcome dogma and the lying to madam misery of a night sent the unidentified walker to a situation quick line jotting himself. Unidentified walker quickly grabbed an extra paper from a pad. He did so without a problem seeing that staff was short at the post 5 A.M. hour and not to mention the potential onlookers who were standing around in the rest of the room. Onlookers if there were any were not suspicious in the least. A quick jab grab unsuspected of her pencil and he jotted down the following numbers that she had obviously gotten over the phone with words to go along with them. At the end of the jotting was a four digit code that the madam bitch in prime had jotted for a reference. The unidentified walker jots down the following. 9 Celsius, 5 Kelvin, 7 fear heights, 2 dwell, 6 add, and entrance code referral 1980. The unidentified walker quickly and easily without needing to look around just shoved his jotting down into his back pocket. He was aware that the bitch's shift was to end at 7 A.M. The unidentified walker then overheard a quote he had heard sometime back during the night in between the occurrences of motives two and three. From distant stance he heard the following "Clever knife fight between that that monster who just left those two in a living hell. Such a shame for a Sunday to have such a tragic ending huh?" this quote from an anonymous man of the same identification as the man talking on this matter at an earlier hour had in result of his speaking given the unidentified walker a fierce non farce undying undeniable feeling of déjà vu and deathly and literal worded deadly danger of a staged strange world night. At the time of hearing this quote one could not say that the unidentified walker thought nothing of it but from the loins of stomached gut wrenches taken in fearing days were pages of hearings in sky world's files out of common orbit ohm life. The unidentified walker with the jotted note in his back pocket then had realized in full that motive four at the early morning time of what was now approximately 5:37 A.M. was objective and that he had to execute an attack plan and thus he would make a game of it. Downstairs in a stairway skip trampling unidentified walker with no regard for keeping any silence in sly spy style reached the bottom stairway stairwell hall. He fast paced in a near run to the locker area dodging all passer bys with ease except for a street hood who made a tough face at him with a remark that the unidentified walker just ignored in an essential and most vital retaliatory and saving move. The lights were to be in full bright later on and generator power was still inefficient. Light from a new risen sun was barely anything but the walker was able to key his locker with a feel. Unidentified walker managed to pry open the locker with a pulling underneath the night vision binoculars he had made use of on this night. He lifted his bag case and zipped down a side pocket where he found his hidden large screen smart phone module touch screen with Bluetooth component of rarity like that of governmental possession. Obscure and silently the unidentified walker stepped into the men rest room and then into a stall. Unidentified walker took a seat in the darkness near fall to some who had no choice but to shower in shaded areas with only distant stick up battery powered light bulbs to light the way. Unidentified walker sat on a toilet seat, his favorite hiding spot in times of twilight nights, he sat in a taking a shit style and spat on a screen, he did not chat on line of his cellular but instead he took affect after he line chat, spat, and shat. The modular mode went as follows. 957261980; 9 Celsius-5 Kelvin-7 fear height-2 dwell-6 add reference #-1980. 9 Celsius; Sunny slay sea say see saw was thaw Sunni Shiite sight non compliant and unrelated lesser. Modem mode code one and done 5 Kelvin; knifed in I.V. evil makes a leak Keller in vein there is a name not to do that with! 7 fear height; the tall man who was monstrosity attacking made mode code action for a Crispus Attucks attack and another version of a Boston Massacre. 2 dwell; the Christmas married duo warns hell awaits! 6 add; 666 1980 . . . . flash . . . . .2012-match! A click of a button was pushed. It was a send button on smart screen in a Bluetooth mode. Modular made makes come on strong in the making and so it was that the 2012 flashback to 1980 was deemed possible. A flash of light it was as well for the natural course of the time unaltered from the 32 year era and generator generation from of 1980-2012 A.D. The man known as the unidentified walker moved forward in paces of a thought process and he went from formulated forums of gluten gluttons to the forms of man kind. Unidentified walker was obsolete of pain although bereft of such feelings. He sat in twilight and had deep dreamy thoughts of a falling man pig.

39

1980 FLICKERING CANDLELIGHT beckons and the family sector made a reckoning. Sister Sarah and company would have to make due for what father guardian had said and had found out from some reliable anonymous sources that the 1980 blackout would likely come to an end within the next two hours. Sector sectioned secret secretary girl of a stated mind state altered in the common way and did so in good health. Sister Sarah would not mention the swill but still mother was no pig and father saw glutton people as victims. The conversation of this night was past the point of a game and twenty questions in the opinion of Sister Sarah and Brother Xavier might have been aged at seven but not feeble minded was this Xavier boy. Due to his hearing of the voices of the beyond pawn pond was the thriller motive in daytime. Wherein whereas bare ass Sister Sarah who had sometimes played the role of brother baby sitter when the parents would leave on certain days was no fool and in the eyes of mother pained from the piggish swilling of the drink was whole nevertheless. Father guardian whom was to guard the red light in defense for the people with the hopes of the blue light flashing in the future he meaning father in a name had known his downed role as victimized of no choice. One day he might have had his regrets fully on his strained mind but in placements of a betting the bedding for the three and father himself who had made four members of the five jibe when included was always there and the food was on the table for mother of the guard. Xavier was for the one for all and all for one sector sectional and mother was the chief chef. Disrespected was Xavier oftentimes in his kid travels he first wanted to be a baseball player but Xavier never could get to the park on time for sign ups. Father wanted him to play so bad but his work was not play and Xavier would have to settle for games of baseball with his friends on the fields of the local baseball and softball parks during spare time away from the needed study times of this youngster's young lifetime. Sister Sarah wanted to play the guitar and she was A Lennon fanatic, she was hacking away at a late age 14 to be precise but she had learned her first song by this point and Xavier was jealous. Xavier wanted to be a basketball player next once he had seen a man who played at the forward position for Boston. This Star college player was drafted from a north central state college in this era of time. Xavier was inspired by the Garden place in Boston and the square block floor that was mantled and dismantled again so that the hockey team could frequent games at this magic Garden as well. Flags hung as pride banners and the team in Boston to Xavier's liking of the game that he wanted to be a part of had no manners. Spanned banners across a ceiling gave him a feeling not to fray from his first real dream. At the time 13 of them banners hung from the rafters he wanted to see badly one day at the garden place and he would finally see them including two more making fifteen by the time he was twelve years old, another at 13 years old when he would see a game five world champion win the following year but the Boston team who were known as the beast from the east lost to the best from the west and the Los Angeles team had deservedly taken a sentence away from the world "The Lakers have never defeated the Celtics in a world champion series title." Xavier was to fight like a tiger and at age eleven he had finally managed to sign up for baseball. Clinging to a dream was keyword for any written words of rights written in the constitution. When a deal concerning the five jibe sector section guides were set to the post modern times to come in the future whereas moderate would be a term word that was to lead to bipartisan compromise. Improvisation sensationalist extremity personas of the willing way counted to six and accessed the parties of green, laws natural, liberty singular derivation to be restricted at the will of the buyer, liberal original tearing from totalitarian, conservatives public republics of can, democracy words written and said for radicals origin inspiration created, paired confined people of the communes in community, and so in combination the sector sectioned is was, was and is, and thus the outlook of non sectioned independence people are most becoming. The sector sends a wavelength of bond strength in the names of the deceased of the square of the Ivy League's section creation in the city near Revere. Off subject was this offering straying from the youngster dreams of one Xavier Xevon Tareynton in socialite days. It is truth regardless however that the meanings of life's life long errands of a day and long term endeavors related bond our creativity and give willing guidance to oneself thereby originating non brainwashed personal thinkers who can obtain or basically retain remaining bravery and speak the common words of the collective subconscious mind which just may be the unified personal and original personal mind of each and every last individual without pain, fault, or seven sins or seven virtues leading to temptation. Father guardian drew a breath inward gasp from an interesting think back flashback of his sentimental childhood, mother thought up a scheme to take a ride for a rare fun occasion with Sarah and to avoid any accidents, Sarah thought hard on how to rock the nation, and Xavier wanted a popsicle but would settle for a watery grape freeze pop unfrozen. "Sarah after the power goes back on what do you say we take a ride and get our hair done?" "Sure mom but I can't make any guarantees that you will look as good as me." Mother laughed silly and assured Sarah that safety was no joking matter and that a hair do might be imminent disaster but at least they could be twins for a day. Xavier finished a freeze pop he had mistaken for a popsicle but it was actually pretty good almost as good as a kindergarten Twinkee! Father asked Xavier a weird question. "Hey buster have you learned your times tables for math class like I told you to do?" "No dad but I am reading enough and I haven't had any papers to be signed for the entire school year so far." Father guardian looked over at Xavier and thought for a moment, he spoke a few words in consideration "Never mind their lies Xavier when we get you signed up for baseball you're going to knock one clear out of the park!" the four sat in a moment of silence and the anthems of America remembered the colors of the Union Jack. Another mystery gust of wind from nowhere and the candle blew out again red white and blue with sister too sat in fable time darkness.

40

INDECENT EXPOSURE AND expletives derogatory may have indemnified a frolic glitch for the people residing on the hard sands that lay over the refugee camp parental where Maria and her young friend Carmen had their bonding revelation but nevertheless a setting was just. The overseers of refugee camp parental were not to put at risk any of their young. Therefore the organization lacking at the camp that was in question that had dealt with this seemingly deathly threatening danger was only made obsolete in part that is by the chosen mercy of the troop band that had made this threat. The sweeping and taking of some of the campers possessions was unfortunately inevitable. Possession was not as rare as might be expected at refugee camp parental in this time frame. In fact at the start of the eighth decade of the nineteenth century this time frame posed your common obstacles. The country of Chile and its population was of course not able to access modern communications 20th or 21st century style so it had to be accepted that the spreading and aiding for such concerns was to be rendered lesser than hoped for. A fast spreading news story of old time such as the shot heard around the world of old time revolutionary wartime Concord Massachusetts the first fired shot spot of the American Revolution could not be expected in means comparative even though the shot heard around the world was fired from an old revolution cork rifle well over one century prior. The land of Chile had its sufficiency of government, military, and this land was limited enough despite the peoples wanting for justice. Dignified intent this was a feeling in, at and of the camp people themselves as well as those of the land of Chile and the

Santiago city. The Chile people who were now involuntarily a component and an ingredient in a master plan that spans in times past and well into the distant future of this 19th century era it had become part of the sky world's master plan. Maria sat down on a large boulder in starlight. Carmen was with Consuela back at the canvas awning area. The moon of one second past shined presently to Maria's mind in timed eyes. The moon shined crescent like the symbol in an African nations flag. Maria gazed up but she did not see the theory spectrum as it was laid out for those of futures vision. She did not bare witness to chemistry light life totality but the reality of her lacking language mind of a potentially innocent girl caused her to acknowledge herself in being the theory theoretical component that was in phenomenon cosmos reality her envisioning herself as a human being inherent with an undeniable tendency for natural evil. Maria continues to gaze upward and from her victimization experienced she wished upon stars not to be the ship vessel destroyer in prime but rather this young Maria of only eight wanted to be a caretaker. Her inhumane human existence made her the heroin to evil woman, the gift plot to evil man nevertheless her age defied her as forces of good whom in such a case of reality cosmos astronomical could be viewed as evil. In all reality life was to be balanced by symbols of Asia, sighted in reflection by African hopes on two sides, and an Englishman of a supposed draft was sought out in a firing ages in the future by imbalance leading to liberty and justice but unfortunately liberty and justice although truth be told was and still is just an outlook based on situations of history. Maria thought of Carmen with Consuela and she wondered "new decision old decision, what's the difference?" Maria panted for a moment and she became of the tears of shining eyes in gloom. As a victim girl Maria thought with whatever knowledge, wisdom, or language that she had obtained that could ever exist from her limited resources for her mind. She felt that her body was stronger in willed reality than any false souls of either her own imagery or the spit images of her fellows acknowledged. Looking up she faced the skies of multitude stars, she gleamed upward and continued her proceeds. Zodian Zion Zodiac the signs constellations were bare and she was unable to identify them. Saga Sagittarius repertoire obscure was a glance of inefficient macroscopic and the stars were amoeba paramecium light life paradox but the paradox was unorthodox and Maria saw a pot and a pan and she had thoughts of fable dreams and an unable to be known to her Peter Pan. Pandemonium pan with a handle was small pre-decided anthem moths who drew modes on night light sights and the big pan handle reflected a pinprick on a peninsula and up north from where she was so far away the gulf of California on the land that was Mexico felt waves from a moon push and the minnows mellowed pains of this girl who would be a minor. Microscopic topics tropical were toned topics they one day became telescopic for a prophet and holy mackerel the girl named Maria was at a focal point. Focused Maria was on the unforgettable dark dog night of which this was. Scenery around her was normal but outbound she saw a tally of pinprick atomized infant infinity finite. Dog night dark light the sights of cosmic chaos were tamed for the girl who had brewed in Santiago of Chile the 19th century gold coast to this process universal perpetuated and parallel. Undone outcomes, in dome outcome the light of a second passed had struck a bolt of lightning into the space station of humane energy, it was the heart of Maria that was stricken and sickened as her physical being was from the Santiago Chile intense humid heat ablaze from an old sun her thoughts were for the guidance of her true being of the destroyer. Lawyer Tom Sawyer and shark fin heckles jives of a vibe whaling sent sailing the ghost ship carrier for destroyer opposition. This heroin was to face the dawn of man.

41

THOU THING ART is art manifesto fragments flamed on presto not to be confused with majestic. Liars prolific have taken the soul life of the lovers not be heard and never willing to confront bad or downright evil intentions. Old English scripture in uses by users and the dogma abusers have not out wit the thief who was the clerical literary hoist. Hosts will tell you to mellow the fallen and follow but hearts are not hollow henceforth from the asinine snobbery a robbery offering temptation to the original intentions of our common human understandings have not been done by devils but by pebbles converging in empty spaces universal. Filled holes, broken souls, finality cosmic multiplicity in singular sides to the other sides widens the expander. The expander is us all a collective sand melt not asleep anymore and so forthwith in force is a will to the newer and more correct moral paths of darkness prime. The light is a cult laceration scheme the dark is the dark side of a systematic beacon and the dark is the beware of dogmatic sign for in true this dark half has a shelf life and in midterms of the watts that measure was pleasure in your rooms. Smooth soothes groove in motion and the craft is taken by a thief made into clerical and thou art thing is now this thing thinking and whether plain or advanced the being of beings intended to the goals prime shall not wallow in nations or worlds pitied. The liar laid down arisen and turned to stone from a seducer this grew the produce from the soil. A boil on the leg of the expander perplexed and bore the fractions of fragments causing cases. Mazes undid tomorrow but our today is yet still another breath of the kiss that caused a timed earthquake. The shaken foundation called lost was renamed in the south east United States a country anew made a match with expansion and a crane built a crib from a rib for the old Pangea continental jigsaw puzzle that has been re put together by human possibilities and guiders to the expander. Reprimand Misunderstood reprimand taken by the expander as well and all was well for the two dynamic and paired by the Reds of countries of colorful. Wonderful evil morbid good misunderstood and the tempted will not fire on a stem of this arisen. The arisen was a rose and from the bowels of a brain insanity hated and evil was simply us to be fed by the other side the other side is the good half of nature. Feed the planet and set the wills into motion but give heeded warning to the born. "Thy" is a word for "the" and "the" is thy will. Then is a matter to be concerned with. "The" is formula beginning and winning is a message for deceivers. The receiver has been taken by obsessed and the leaders messed with. Professors have not opened up the tombs alive and the vials they drink from cannot poison the others who lay the laws of the old homeland. Time altered, faltering, slayings of men women and children defined by the word identified with "atrocity" and this word would be "genocide" a word not understood but a process of fair play freewill sending still lives into motions around the circle of life. The books of life were opened the seals have not all been read and the intrepid interpretations have told us that the end is coming but we the people have not received a will. Above it all and beyond stars or anything that can be understood by language, the infinity of the elements, metrics and periodical modern and old school is the outside universal existence non existence persisting presence present, it is not in the past altogether but its moves into the present which is the future again. It is true in entirety that within the mysteries involved in blackout the various methods of which have varied the linguistics involved in the story of these blackouts involved show that there is a lesson to be learned. The lesson in such a case as the blackout story is concerned is not taught by the teacher and this story is also not taught by what one would conclude as a student or an apprentice to the vast measured mystery involved. The blackout scenario in case of its dynamics of sound mind has been taught to all of its characters whether they be of evil or moral intent that there truly is no battle to be fought, no sides opposed for unnecessary wars, nor is it a put down to those who must compete in the political, social, military or international realm, nor is the story of blackout intended to be degrading. The spirit of competition has been over played there are no purple heart heroics or upheavals of our inner needing for the falsehoods that seemingly deceives life. From this misguided individuals move into life's mistakes, misfortunes or the conflicts of our experiences that a people of a planet cannot bare witness to any longer. Bare witness might be an off statement so to state this more clearly it is simply matters of sadness and war torn lunacy that can do without. May the story of blackout through the teachings of the duo bond and the interrogation examples of those who were eliminated in this story set a path of freedom true and maybe as a unified race among nations togetherness something can teach the learning need of the difference. This difference is not as hard as would be assumed it is the common bond of originality a truth of selves only realized through the process of learning through our human life times of the earth's tragedies. The tangent of this motion has not ended the blackout scenario and so it is that now the story of blackout shall take a turn into a new time process of origin destiny and not of origin intention. Redemption of days timed is inevitable to those involved in the adventures and the misadventures of some involved either directly or indirectly in our story. A marriage to symbolize the love of the Christmas duo did well however some were left dead, two of them by flesh wounds from the hit man to be interrogated in New Jersey had such a fate. Maria is the stargazer destroyer who we wonder as she does of her truth in ways and her meaning of origin intention. The dwarf star of her dream world in its bracket numeric as a 9 numeral mends her insanity to sanity leading her to care for a friendship that came to be due to one of the tragedies exemplified in an example just like those tragic examples in reality that have in cases rare yet true led to victories for the moral pioneers of all times. The man of the night who we call the unidentified walker has as the Christmas duo has, as the hit man and the two deceased has, as Renessa and Xavier her Jonah and he of Jonax and the multiple personalities of intention has, as the other members of the section sector five jibe has there is an action reaction making the spark lit flame to a wick of a universal being candle the lighting of intro inertia universal contact millennium.

42

THE FLAME WAS lit by sister for the last time of the 1980 blackout. Family five jibe of the sector sectioned begins to play. "Mom?" "Yes Sarah what is it?" "Do you remember the legend tale you used to tell me about? I think it was something that had to do with the new race of people or something." "Oh I know what you are talking about Sarah, you're talking about that fable I used to recite to you it was something that had to do with a mystery people misunderstood and hurt by those in abuse of power." "Yes mom but you said that the people were victims of some kind of a mistake from us or some kind of instigation causing them to crumble within and victimize their own." Father guardian interrupted momentarily, he needed to say something that was of Xavier's interest, "Xavier do hear these two I told you about this with your mother and you stared at the globe for hours it is a sad case Xavier people say it shouldn't be bothered with. Needless to say Xavier the legend tale these two birds are speaking of is not alike the freedom we have in our United States. Never mind this nonsense. There is enough light from this candle for the two of us to stroll over to the fridge and have a couple of sodas it would certainly be a better delicacy than another one of those stupid freeze pops you're sucking on half of the god given day." "Okay Dad why don't we have a drink and let these two solve this fable feeble misery mystery." "Yes Xavier and don't worry so much about papers to be signed you're going to do so good in history and geography when you are of age I'm sure." Father with Xavier went over to the fridge and they had their fix and father guardian was very proud of Xavier's ability to snap out of his apparent immaturity sometimes and this was true even for a seven year old who could speak like an adult of moderate to good intelligence. Mother and Sarah continued talking over the times of a commencement of the legend fable. "Are the victims able bodied?" "They are well versed in construction for who they are they also have dealt with quite difficult situations of a law declared from what is considered less than a state of emergency because they are put down by a government that is supposed to tell its people the truth." "Is there going to be a nuclear war?" "I don't believe in that there is the weapon but that is not as far fetched as this local tragedy." "This isn't a tragedy mom this is just a small time emergency for the neighborhood I am more concerned with Xavier's paranoia at times. Why didn't you ever tell Xavier the fable? "Xavier is different he is part of a family that does not know where it is at yet. I know he likes his basketball but someday he is going to make a difference his mind is unique and his father is making him read all of the time, if his school work gets better and we avoid any family tragic distractions he might do much better." "I'll keep an eye on him mom and I keep a diary and he likes to write from time to time, that feeble fable might make able and in due time I will sing and play and the nights of such dark times will heal the wills of the legend fable isle and Xavier will meet a bride." Mother with Sister Sarah suddenly, sanely and serenely interrupted by two of a father and son pair returning to the table with beverages. Father Guardian spoke while Xavier watched over having heard words wise. "Impossible dream Xavier huh? Do you ladies think our Sox can do good this year?" Sister Sarah was a ball fan so she expressed her more than fair-weather opinion. "Dad we've heard the let down stories of 75 and 78 I like our team but I am not jumping on the bandwagon like my little brother here. "Father asked Xavier one question "What do you think Xavier do we have a shot?" Xavier answered with a glimpse into a hopeful future "No dad not likely this year but we might get one this decade if they play their cards right." "How many sectors in our unit?" "One!" "How many units in a sector?" "The same." "How many runs to win a game?" "One." "What are they gonna do the next time they get to that pennant?" "Win!"

43

THE INSIDE OF the temporary sheltering was darkness in steams sweltering amid the poured drops of black blood on the metro bloods who had been curdling in the cellar with their cell lights of blue. The blue lights they had were flashing passion mesh strobe scenes to the commissar who had become a part of the whole big picture in the frame of this night painted. These brothers in blood of lacerate blinding had become the Americans original sinful in exposure but the cripples they had fought against sailed on the oceans of the minds for the flash line of lit ways meaning. The minds that met in darkness allowed surviving unidentified walker to escape and the leader sent a smile from the veil of a mobile in the combine of sacrificial sacred disguises. The unidentified walker made escapism art in simplicity from a flame thrown. The extinguisher was the sight for god and the red of it held in compaction the cellular interior to the stone called the seventh. The stone was of the inside and the strong storm that had surrounded it let in an alternate ending and so it . . . . as the end of a beginning. The phase to be sent out was produce, the mazes on the rails of a telegram made languages into song. The undone hero who scored the highest at zero revealed the number of which the way had been given in the point of real totals. Totaled from the tides the unidentified walker walked into the rising sun and in wondering about his night of four motives he had determined it to be true to himself that the motive in totality of the human mind was the tidal wave of a notion that was to heal the fire waters and turn existence into the dirt grain. The grain of dirt was to feel the feel of the greenhouse effect in positive from the trickery of good evil and the pavilions of millions of stars sent the form of the zero numeral into perfection symmetrical hypothetically. Oval eyes watched in hopes for the new race that only made sense from a process, critters they were. Maria in unrelated in directive motive to the motivation unidentified walker was the stalker and her talk held her back and so the destroyer of Maria in Saints of eyes had drifted into the meaning of the carrier ship. From the ship the jets of the blinding wars would take off and so it was in writing that the sights of the flames from their mach 3 seeds speeding of a sending would not be destroyers but would land the maiden in defense of the innocent tom fools. Unidentified walker walked on throughout the outside Metro of the neighborhood block whereas the nearly complete story of the 2012 and 1980 blackouts had halves. From afar where the meadows once flowed the wizard witch waters from a dell flowed the dandy lion flowers in showering of empowerment fence digitized old time modes of reflective deflection melts on water making the screens of futures communications accept the words of the mystery communicators of a system out there beyond universal understanding standing. Beyond the universe the information had come and the walker identified was the walker of his claiming. The unidentified walker was assistant apprentice to the travelers on the outside lines. The travelers on the ropes of the nooses that had been frayed in disarray had dissected the plot and the ploy boy who was on an occasion multiplicity. Jonax let Jedidiah know that he was to visit the father one more time in this place of ill forgotten business. Unidentified walker heard the noon time church bell and on the eighth ring of the chime. Something in a match of time flamed sent a whizzing wizardry above down in the form of a spell and the crystal ball of this sighting was clear as the crystal it was made from. The drops from the sun shower hit waters in multiple drippings splashing tiny bubbles around in shapes of a natural form. The water started to pour down after the sight of the 2012 blackout had heard the eighth ring of the chime. The drops of time ago fell into the dell not far away or that long ago. Unidentified walker heard some ranting and raving while drops of this falling rain started to moisten his head and hair. Unidentified walker reached into his bag where his night goggles and other items were. He grabbed a cup that tributes in a symbol the arts of the handmaids, so as the sweat of the braves braids cooled from the water falling in the past the hand of the unidentified walker reached out and the art cup began to fill for the walker to take a sip. The unidentified walker wanted to make a toast with himself because from the ranting and raving he heard he had realized by the time the rings had faded that the 2012 blackout had been solved. Over at a local convenient store across a way by another school venue was the light in a doorway turned on and activated and through the windows of this place were screens lit in blue lights and he read a message on his grail. Incidentally in 1980 a simultaneous hurrah was to happen at the same time speaking in theory that is as was in picture frame with the exact moment of alternate time at the sounding of the eighth chime ring. Sister Sarah, Xavier, father guardian, and mother had heard it. From outside in darkness came a sound of a dreamed emotion. The cling clang ring of vibrant motion back and forth sprung from springs, a street alley of a cat fight escaping for two, and also from the night springs up high sprung an autumn falling and the rain fell at the moment of this sound. With the sound of this first Hurrah the 1980 lights had gone back on for the neighborhood and for them a celebration cheer of a minute fragment long enough to remember came with the arms of four of the jibe up in air in full bright. Meanwhile in the past related; back in Kill devil of the Carolinas Melinda with another in the name of the two dead from the shots fired of from the hit man there was change and now is known the true meaning of the new day witnesses. From a science of gravity related was a willed way of this Duo's unified thinking. Remnant parts from the computer van were imitated and obtained from outside information was the impostors of a lessened numeral defying. Misunderstood complications were solved by a green solvent and a pulling of mother board wires by the unidentified walker and company. The pulling was a scratch on the skin of the newly wedded Christmas duo. With the pulling of the past time and a maneuver made with Kyle's assistance a touch on a screen sent a signal wavelength to the mechanism replacement and thus the light went back on 32 years later and 32 years ago. The hit man who swung from doors had been subject to interrogation he was questioned in full and in his guilt of a found conscience from fearing was over. Veering members had learned of his possible demise they believed that this New Jersey hit man who was in New York for a time had met certain death either or this hit man was jailed or he was subject to disguising and used by other evil forces. The hit mans brother was a member of his foreign legion which was the reality in trueness. The brother with others felt sad from learning of his losing situation. The two members who cared for the hit man learned by way of a loss and a gaining of vision was possible. The computer wan was long gone from the blazing fire that had burned it back at a Jersey gas station. At a secret combine disguised a learner some knew this to be true so by way of special task force permitted by an authority figure figuring was the satellite message for the golden boys. Another message in numeric form was sent for the fallen. It was a driver of another van in charge in special times. He watched the screen in the more modern computer van. The screen played the rerun of a ball game ending and the number eleven was half life existence for the multiplicity dimensions in numerical. Two structures stood in sun one tributes at night for no more hurt. As the mystery man escaped again in his van in the future after he had seen the sign on the structure of edifice defined he thought again of a city that was built in a day. The van in the future was driven away and the driver who knew the win was won stopped at the very same mart of the Jersey slaying for mercy's example. The new driver in charge with authority got out of the van and walked inside the mart store. He grabbed a cup for a fill, he filled it. He then grabbed a copy of a paper and purchased his items. Outside the figure of this authority unfolded his paper after a swig from his cup and he read the headline that said in bold print BELEVABLE!

44

10 TO 1 odds for a comeback from 3 games to 1 down–Angels Red Sox Pennant 1986; the eighth grade was not even half over for Luzzin, Zimmerman the man, and Xavier of identities. Pretending not to be noticed had been the main motive objective and no subject matter of school work was going to stray Luzzin and Xavier from the fun they had had on their most recent day of playing hooky. It was a becoming Late September a few more days had passed by for the parochial eighth grade in question. Meredith mistresses of written writes were not in the wrong and from stones cast the cast of 13 of them had been writing insights in poetry in their diaries read, their homework assignments assigned, their words they read learned them subject matter of humored sex education. Manual friendships quested the tests until none mattered except for the finals of the true questions pending. The year of 1986 was special and most pivotal to the history of this secret world blackout story. From it was the inspired hope of oneness for the thirteen members of the eighth grade graduates to be parochial in this city place in 1986. It is no lie for any of them to tell you including the fourteenth member and the others who would teach and learn for the remainder of this school year for in 1987 the dream was only begun as they would graduate and start the first day of the rest of their lives. Luzzin was at his home of last week's hooky headquarters, Zimmerman the man was a wild eyed Sox fan frenzied from a three run home run that had appeared to seal the pennant three game comeback sweep for the red hot 1986 red sox, this three run shot was cracked old school right hand hitting style into the smack dab center of the Fenway Park's green monster left

field wall old time netting and when this shot landed in the net out over the left field wall the camera of the national station channel filming this game 7 set a beauty over the left field side wall in over by the chalk line. The camera shot showed arms flying and flailing of a thousand fit frenzy sox fans while 35,000 standing room only red sox hopefuls could be heard across a nation. Xavier was watching as well of course. He was with father guardian on the couch watching on the edge of it while ten others from parochial and more watched this game seven completing comeback sweep with intensity and anticipation for a healing of the 1967 impossible dream. Metro was in the cards dealt. Innings past on from the fifth inning outing whereas the sox fans had made a lightning strike and from the fifth it went into the sixth, seventh, and eighth inning. In the bottom of the eighth inning the red sox were eliminated with a third out and they were out of luck for some insurance in this eighth outing of an inning winning anyway and so it was that the 1986 American league pennant went into the top of the ninth inning. A message on construction in a form of a number and word was to be a message in inning outing nine. The final pitch made out number three for the Angels of California and as the red sox pitcher stood on the hill 90 plus feet away the entire Fenway crowd, the baseball fans of Boston and the commonwealth with New Englanders abroad, 10 students of future graduation not to mention the trio of Luzzin, Zimmerman, and Xavier himself threw hands and arms in air celebrating a winning season. So it was just as the four of the five jibe members threw their hands in air back in 1980 when the lights came back on it was certainty for some of a secret that a word wrongly taught is not worthy of scrutiny. Father asked the question of runs for a win and the son answered it. Regardless as the proud red sox people stood in a crowd or sat home and watched on screens of lands on a night of believable impossible the message of healing hope came in half form. The red sox pitcher looked up as the others of Boston did on this memorable night in 1986. The famous Prudential building of Boston showed a numeral number in bold form written from lit windows. The sign of light in Boston was read it was a large light number and the number was a symbol . . . . 1.